Bard VI

Sunspear

Books by Keith Taylor

BARD *series*
Bard I: Bard
Bard II: The Return of Felimid Mac Fal!
Bard III: The Wild Sea
Bard IV: Ravens' Gathering
Bard V: Felimid's Homecoming
Bard VI: Sunspear

THE DANANS *series*
The Sorcerers' Sacred Isle
The Cauldron of Plenty
Search for the Starblade

**For more information
visit:** SpeakingVolumes.us

Bard VI

Sunspear

Keith Taylor

SPEAKING VOLUMES, LLC
NAPLES, FLORIDA
2025

Sunspear

Copyright © 2025 by Keith Taylor

All rights reserved. No part of this book may be reproduced or transmitted in any form or by any means without written permission.

ISBN 979-8-89022-256-5

To Anna,
my wife, soul mate,
and best friend

The epigraph to the prologue is from the *Annals of Ulster*. The chapter epigraphs are taken from *Cuchulain of Muirthemne*, Lady Augusta Gregory's retelling of the Red Branch legends. It was based on previous oral and written versions, and set down in the Kiltartan dialect.

Prologue

Calends of January, 516: The battle of Druim Derg against Failge. Fiachu was victor. Thereafter the Plain of Meath was taken away from the Laigin. —Annals of Ulster

Mist mingled with a fine drizzle of rain made a grey mantle over the battlefield. It muffled and rendered directionless the sounds of iron crashing on shields, the grunts and gasps of men straining to deal death, the triumphant yells of some and the dying shrieks of others. Because the fighters could not see far, this battle was even more chaotic than most, turning into small groups of warriors who could recognize each other by little except their roars of "Fiachu!" and "Failge!"

There was one combatant that even the mist and insubstantial rain scarcely hid. Tall, strong and fair, he moved with confidence through the turmoil, making for any spot where weapons clashed the loudest and the bellows of "Failge!" were fiercest. A conical bronze helmet with gilded cheek-pieces guarded his head, and blood flecked it, as it flecked the thick moustaches that flowed to his collar-bones. Blood flew from his ever-moving sword and oozed over the wrought bronze spirals on his shield. It vibrated, that shield, as the tall man glared about him from hot blue eyes; he felt it quiver on his arm and heard a low moaning sound accompany the throb.

That reverberation meant danger. The tall man barked, "'Ware foes!" to his half-dozen comrades, and the words were scarcely off his tongue when a group of warriors, ten or more, came upon them out of the thin grey percolation. They too were bloody and some had wounds. For a little space, they paused at the sight of the septet. Then they raised a hoarse cry—since by this time their throats were raw—of "Failge! *Failge Berraide!*"

Instead of shouting the name of Failge's rival, Fiachu, the warrior with the golden moustaches roared out, "*Sunspear!*" Then he charged.

A lean fellow with lank pale hair raced to the attack at his left, another on his right, this one helmed and swinging an axe with both hands, his movements swift but abrupt and impulsive. His comrade, the lean one, plied his sword with skill and care, the intent, mechanical semblance of a smile on his face.

The other four bounded to the fight naked aside from leather kilts. All had curiously variegated hair, streaked and tufted different shades of red from auburn to sandy. They appeared to be kindred, and one was a woman. Shieldless, hands clenched on a spear with a great barbed head, she voiced ear-splitting war-shrieks of "*Sunspear!*"

The supporters of Failge outnumbered them, but the advantage might as well have been the other way, and doubled. The tall leader caught a spear-thrust on his shield and struck straight across in front of him, brow-high. His edge slashed through nose and eyes into a startled brain, and his adversary died blinded without knowing he was either blind or mortally struck. The long sword slanted left and its edge came down on a second Meathman's knee. Bone cracked. The Meathman staggered.

Before he could recover, the pale-haired warrior drove a short wide-bladed sword into his side, twisting it. He was known, if not as the strongest of fighters, as quick and adroit, crafty to seek the best of it and take advantage. He gasped a quick laugh as the Meathman went down.

He of the sharp abrupt movements (Tachdan the Sudden was his by-name) fought fiercely, but the unarmoured redheads raged in frenzy, the woman not least. She ran her barbed spearhead into the belly of one big fighting man, and though he struck at her with his club in return, she dodged the blow. Twisting his entrails around her spearhead like thread around a distaff, she dragged it back with blood welling around it, then kicked savagely at the wound. The man struggled to raise his club again, but feebly, as though it weighed like a boulder. She struck him down with her spear-butt and then stamped his temple to shards with her bare heel.

Guts hung like streamers from her spear as she returned to the fray.

Her kinsmen fought as much like demons as she. Their strength and vitality, like hers, seemed unnatural. Nevertheless, the tall man with the long sword led, and they followed, killing until none of the Meathmen were left.

They comprised only a small group of fighters. There were many such diverse ones on the battlefield now, the main forces having divided chaotically into many lesser brawls. The big golden-haired warrior raised his arms to the mist-obscured sky and cried in challenge, "Where is this Failge? Where is Failge Berraide? Let him face us!"

He yearned to meet the opposing leader, for his own glory and to have a decisive effect on the fray. Instead they found themselves on the outskirts of the battle, due to the worsening visibility and the vagaries of the fighting. Except perhaps for the pale-haired one, it was not where they desired to be.

Now they returned, guided by their ears and luck, to the thickest combat. A hot red reek of blood emanated through the mist. With Tachdan on one side of him and the lean, pale-haired fellow on the other, the tall leader shouted "Sunspear!" again and plunged wildly into the fighting. Around him, the men of the north, the Uí Néill followers, the men on his side, called out the name of Fiachu as their battle-cry, but he of the yellow moustaches bayed his own epithet, Sunspear, and his war-band echoed him. His long blade shuttled around and over the edge of his shield, finding unguarded throats or sides with precision. Both swift and strong, he seemed to have eyes in the back of his head. Those who attacked him found him practiced as well, a man of fatal skill. Those who tried to take him by surprise had always one—at least—of his two near companions to deal with, and even the shifty, pale-haired one never failed him, though he liked best to take foemen unawares. As for the red-haired fighters, near-naked and constant in their fury, they raged and struck like wildcats. Two of the men plied axes, one a heavy short chopping sword with a single edge. Its cutting side split to the vitals, while the thick straight back of the blade shattered bone at each blow. The woman leaped and whirled like a maniac, her barbed spear ripping flesh, her shrieks of battle-joy rising higher with each foe she sent into the shadows.

"*Failge Berraide!*" the golden warrior yelled, mockingly even though his breath came short and harsh with effort. "Show me your face! Are you a laggard, do you fear?"

"I am Failge Berraide!" came the answer, out of a close-packed mass of fighting men that suddenly confronted the seven. It issued from the throat of a brawny giant splashed with gore. "Who is this howling fool who calls for me?"

"Ruarc mac Amalgaid! Ruarc Sunspear, lord of Airgi-alla!" The younger man controlled his panting breath and made his voice resound. It carried far through the muffling mist. "I call for you! Ruarc Sunspear!"

Failge laughed harshly and raised his arm to gesture for a charge that would make short work of the seven, since he had vastly more than that behind him—maybe a hundred. Opportunely for Ruarc Sunspear, the self-proclaimed lord of Airgialla, dozens of his own adherents came out of the drizzle to back him, having heard him announce his name and come running in response. Some belonged to the strange red-haired clan that fought with such strength and fury. One warrior, not of their number but strong as a young bull, with the stubborn forehead of one too, whooped gleefully.

"We cannot let you have all the sport, Ruarc!"

"Just kill two apiece and leave me the rest," his leader told him. He smiled with ferocious serenity at Failge, who held a long sword similar to him own, and whose shield was hacked into uselessness. Like Sunspear, he carried red wounds and ignored them. "Or shall we settle it between us like heroes, one to one, strong Failge?"

"We know what will ensue if you kill me," Failge said. "How if *I* kill *you*? Will you agree, and consent, and order, that your war-band take no further part in the battle?"

That was likely to decide the battle. Sunspear knew it. He did not hesitate.

"I agree. My oath by the sun and moon and stars on it! Most of my war-band is here, now, and the rest, that I seem to have mislaid for now, shall know as soon as my friends can tell them." His tone became indulgent. "But the chance that you might kill me—is not one I'd raise high hopes on if I were you."

Failge shrugged, an act which lifted a goodly weight of muscle in his shoulders. The stiff bull's hide epaulettes protecting them creaked. He reached for a new shield, and two were thrust at him instantly. He accepted one made of linden wood and rimmed with hard leather. Its cover bore a pattern of interlocking red and yellow spirals.

"Let us not blow more wind at each other. Let us fight."

They trod close, each with his shield raised. Sunspear's, of finely worked bronze with an intricate scalloped border, and green and red enamelling, might have been some ancient king's. He claimed it was.

Surely it carried the image of a green-haired sea queen and moaned softly when danger threatened.

Each man's long blade slanted back over his shoulder. They were much of a height, Failge Berraide the more massive, and older, seasoned in battles, though not so much older that time was weakening him. But although Sunspear was less bulky, those who knew both men knew they were about equal in strength, and Sunspear moved swiftly.

Knees bent a little to allow for sudden movement, the younger man wore an easy, gracious smile. A curious gleam appeared to hang about him, as though whatever sunlight filtered through the mist was preferentially drawn to his person. Above the smiling mouth, his eyes were intent.

Failge tried a quick, shearing cut at his neck. The target was small between the lower edge of Sunspear's helmet and his shield-rim, but Failge's hand was precise. It *might* have worked and brought the fight to an end at once. It did not. The younger man raised his shield just enough. Failge's edge scraped its bronze surface and Sunspear, moving in, shortened his grip on his sword-hilt and smashed at Failge's face with the pommel. Failge moved his big shaggy head aside. With a ramming thrust of his shield he made Sunspear lurch back.

"Good!" the golden warrior laughed. "I do think, now, that you had real power in that thick body, Failge Berraide—*once*!"

Despite the gibe, he was impressed. He assumed a back guard stance, sword held behind him, slanted now towards the ground. For crowded combat it was a bad position, but in a single combat with plenty of room, it had advantages. The sword could sweep through a greater arc, gathering force, whether sideways or overhead. Sunspear attacked, shield and shield leg leading, striking down at Failge's shin with the lower rim. Failge got his own shield's edge behind Sunspear's and heaved it aside. A savage cut of his sword almost crippled Sunspear's upper arm, but he escaped by springing quickly back. He retaliated with a quick, sure-footed rush and a stroke that took a slice from the side of Failge's shield.

The spectators raised a cry at seeing that. They had quickly grown restless just to stand and watch, though one and all they respected single combat. Picking old foes or fighters of repute on the other side, they called taunts and challenges which drew instant response.

A dozen other combats soon began, circling about the opponents Failge and Sunspear like planets around a central sun. The main groups scowled, threatened, and might have fallen upon each other en masse, but other voices cried out to wait, to see who fell, Sunspear or Failge. They prevailed, though hardly.

Each of the two had learned something of his opponent's fighting style. Sunspear moved with fluent grace, big though he was, shifting with ease from one position to another, while the heavier Failge fought chiefly on the defensive and waited for the chance he knew from experience *always* came. Once, he thought he had it. He raised his shield like a roof to guard his head against a high overhand cut, while slashing at Sunspear's thigh. The younger man bent his other leg, straightened the endangered limb hard, and shifted sideways. He took a shallow gash on the outer thigh but nothing worse. Red blood flowed down Sunspear's calf. His eyes glinted with ire.

He was somewhat swifter, his coordination smoother, but Failge was nine years more experienced in battles, affrays and single combats. Often enough, that bone-deep knowledge told him what Sunspear was about to do, but he could never be certain. Sunspear had a fire-swift imagination and his strokes burst with little or no preceding swing to give him away. For his part, he was often frustrated by Failge's habit of having his shield or sword always in the right position to parry Sunspear's efforts. The Meathman was basically a little stronger, withal.

Each had gathered a notion of the other's quirks or soft spots, too, the ways in which he might be taken. Failge reckoned the younger man too confident, and though he had shown control so far, he could lose patience, for his nature was hot; he might be lured into an ill-considered rush. Sunspear appreciated the older man's massive strength, the timing of his blows, and especially his infuriating way of having his shield ever in the right place. A narrow segment of it was gone now, though. And Sunspear judged Failge to be the least bit weak-kneed, not in the way of lacking resolve, but in a literal way, perhaps due to old wounds. His footwork, the crucial footwork, seemed a little slow, a fraction clumsy.

Failge attacked then, taking the initiative, hoping Sunspear would think his strength was failing and he had grown desperate. It was not true. Sunspear, cocksure and lacking deep reserves of patience, might believe it, though.

Sunspear

Their swords rang together; rang again. Failge's blade flew aloft. His opponent's flashed, and bit into Failge's shield where he had hewn a slice from it before. The edge caught in the tough wood. With a grunt of triumph, eyes alight, Failge drew his sword back and high for a great swing that would split Sunspear's casque and head together.

Sunspear yapped a short breathless laugh. He wrenched his sword from Failge's shield in an instant, a feat of astonishing strength, and caused Failge to stumble a little. His great stroke lost impetus. It rang loudly on Sunspear's long bronze shield, and Sunspear struck back with a hard drawing slash to the side of Failge's neck, just above the epaulette of triple-layered bull's hide.

Blood sprayed out. Failge Berraide staggered. Sunspear pulled his blade in an arc through the air, red drops following it, and cut backhand from the other side. His weapon bit into Failge's great neck again, through the muscle, through the spine, out into the air, and the head sprang from the big bunched shoulders.

Failge's legs made two shambling steps before the big body fell prone. They kicked and lay quiet. The red-headed fighting woman grabbed the head and raised it high.

"A goodly crop of Macha's hazel-nuts, and here is the fattest!" she shrilled. "Pluck more! The day is our own!"

"*Failge Berraide is slain*!" sounded the cry. The forces of the Uí Néill, of Fiachu, yelled it loudly, eager to believe it. Those of the opposing side who did not believe, and did not wish to, had little choice when they saw Sunspear come against them, the woman beside him, lifting Failge's head with one hand and plying her spear with the other. She took half a dozen wounds, ignored them all, and killed without fail.

"I see—Sirega—your appetite is keen as ever!" Sunspear panted.

The tide of the fighting turned. Meathmen and their Leinster allies fled, or owned themselves beaten. Before long they stood with stubborn eyes and high heads—but empty hands—before the leader of the Uí Néill on this day, Fiachu mac Anroth. A grandson of mighty Niall, he sought power; all that he could get for himself, but more for his clan, which would still be there when Fiachu mac Anroth was gone. Grey-bearded and nearing sixty, but strong, he had fought hard, and he knew he might have lost this day without Sunspear and his war-band. He eyed them with appreciation, but some mistrust. This tall golden youngster hungered for power too. He had achieved much already.

Fiachu sat on a makeshift throne of cut turf, with cowhides thrown over it. He held a fine sword, notched in the fighting, across his knees. The woman Sirega, standing beside Sunspear, still carried Failge Berraide's head, washed clean of blood and recognizable now. She herself was not. Nor were any of her kindred. The gore glistening on their limbs obscured their tattoos. Fiachu thought with distaste that he would not care to lead those savages, or have them in his following.

"That is indeed Failge," he nodded. "You slew him, Sunspear?"

"I myself, lord."

"That was well done. A man of his hands was Failge. Now send we for the chiefs of the little tribes who hold this territory, the land from Uisnech down to Birr, and ratify that they are clients of the Uí Néill now, and we their overlords—not King Illann of Leinster!"

"And for my support, lord?" Sunspear's voice was mellow. "Shall the Uí Néill recognize my rule of the nine tuatha and shall we pledge friendship?"

"A matter for the lords of my clan to decide, when we return to the north," Fiachu reminded him. Sunspear saw well enough that Fiachu doubted the wisdom of that, but had no intention of seeming ungrateful in this hour. "I shall urge it with all my power and by the red hand, I can see no other outcome! It has been well earned."

This committed Fiachu to nothing, and even less did it commit the powerful Uí Néill. Sunspear knew it. Upon that return to the north to which Fiachu referred, he would have to be persuasive.

Lugh of the Long Hand! he swore silently. *If some other outcome does ensue, there'll be satires of cursing, and bloodshed to make this day seem tender!*

Some hours afterwards, he relaxed beside a stone-lined cooking pit in which a young pig was roasting. The warmth from it pleased him. His wounds had been salved and bandaged, and though they stung it was not for the first time. Close beside him were the four young fellow bards who had been his comrades and followers for years; Tachdan mac Lugo of the quick temper and hot brown eyes, Mathgadro, with his lean face and pale hair, the bull of strength Dub Dothar mac Gai, and Niall, swiftest and most skilled rider in a quintet of excellent riders.

The rest of Ruarc Sunspear's war-band had gathered closely around them. The red-headed clan hunkered together in a tight group, and even the other warriors of Sunspear's entourage stayed somewhat apart from them. Their leader understood that, but he paid the redheads high respect because of their fierce valour and their ancestry. They on their part, despite their wild ways, followed Sunspear because he had been their father's favoured protégé.

Mathgadro, as usual, spoke without moving his lips much. He opened his mouth freely only when making poetry, especially his corrosive satires. He spoke now, also typically, with mistrust.

Sunspear

"It's to be depended upon," he said softly, "that the Uí Néill will try to dodge their obligation to be supporting you for the rule of Airgialla."

Sunspear was unperturbed. "I got sureties of them beforehand. To renege after today's fighting would disgrace them, and there are factions among them to be exploited, so. They are aware they will need our fighting support again. I suppose they will try to reduce my power in the future, when they see they have let it grow too much—but in the future, Bluetongue, and we'll let it concern us then."

"Would you think there is a concern that *we* have let lapse too long?" Tachdan growled. "Three years too long? That traitor bard Felimid?"

"He slew our great mentor!" Niall said with rage.

"And he humbled your pride, Tachdan, and he rode a horse to victory that had thrown you, Niall. But that other thing—be mighty sure, it's unforgotten. Dealing with him had to wait, as we began to establish the Red Branch anew, and now his grandsire and grandmother are in the earth, and he, from what I hear, has been idle to an ill-advised extent. His error, his fatal error."

"*How soon?*" Tachdan demanded, avidity in his voice and eyes.

"Once we secure our position in the north a little; not long. Then we shall go looking for this Felimid, whose hour is past due, and we shall destroy his life and make a desert of it—and I tell you all, you cannot be more hungry for that consummation than I. Now let's enjoy this day, and be content."

He inspected the meat cooking in the heated pit and pronounced it done.

Chapter One

"O Naoise, look at the cloud I see above us in the air; I see a cloud over green Macha, cold and deep red like blood. I am startled by the cloud that I see here in the air; a thin, dreadful cloud that is like a clot of blood. I give a right advice to the beautiful sons of Usnach not to go to Emain tonight, because of the danger that is over them." —The Fate of the Sons of Usnach

"It was a red day and a day of blood, aye. Fiachu won it."

The speaker, a monk named Brandon mac Finnlug, had just brought a shipload of hides, shorn fleeces and linen to the White Isle, a place blessed by sailors. Brandon had the weathered look of a sailor himself, though young, and he was one, his hands toughened by oars, ropes and hauling on nets. He wore a Celtic monk's distinctive tonsure and—against the rule of some monasteries—a beard.

Abbess Caithlenn listened with both ears, for this concerned her son, and therefore her. Brandon had just come from the north, from beyond Connacht, from the big bay hard by the lands of the northern Uí Néill. His news was recent and should be accurate.

"He won the plain from Uisnech down to Birr, then?"

"Truth. The Fir Bile, the Fir Tulach and the Fir Cell are all client tribes to the Uí Néill now, not the King of

Leinster. A red terrible day on which that was brought about."

"With the help of Ruarc Sunspear and his war-band, we are told," the abbess's son murmured. "I've always time for news of that one."

"Be careful how you handle the truth, my dear," Caithlenn cautioned. "That has not been the case these three years. You have been glad enough to forget about him. And you have not decided whether to move your rook."

"No. Well." Felimid the bard replaced the piece on the chessboard. Its squares, like the pieces, were cut from white birch and red yew. "Shall we finish the game later, mother mine? My concentration is gone. Let me say that I have always time for news of Ruarc *now*. Three years ago it seemed to me that I'd be hearing nothing about him ever again."

"They talk of mighty little else in the north!" Brandon exclaimed. "He has a large name and he hates the cross." He nodded energetically, his forceful speech exposing big uneven teeth, his soulful brown eyes flashing. "When his mentor Dicuil the Fiery died—and Dicuil's father was a demon, it's said—"

"Not merely *said*," Felimid interjected. "Cairbre and Ogma! I attest that it is so."

"I'll agree, then. And Sunspear fared north with his companion bards and those fearful children and grandchildren of Dicuil's. He entered Uí Néill service as a client. The sons of Niall gave him lordship of a tuath, one tuath, and almost before they knew it he had a second, then three. Now it is nine, and not just any nine."

"No. The nine from which Niall took a royal hostage each, and so gained his by-name." Abbess Caithlenn's voice, mellow and fluent, was also troubled. "The kingdom of Airgialla. That is power, and Ruarc hates the cross indeed, worthy Brandon. How did he gain such power so soon? He began with almost nothing."

It was in Felimid's mind that he ought to have paid more attention. He had dismissed the early rumours of his enemy's rise. After five years in exile, five years in which he often carried his life in his sword hand, he had wanted peace and ease with his kindred and, he supposed, let it become indolence. He had not even sought tidings from the spirits of the air. He had taken it for granted that Ruarc Sunspear's ambitions—which indeed were far from realistic—would fail, and be the finish of him.

Evidently not.

And why not?

That was Caithlenn's question, on all counts a baffling one.

Younger, she had been called Caithlenn the Beautiful, and like other famous beauties her loveliness had caused trouble; her youth had been turbulent. Even now, her hair streaked with grey, evidence of the years to be seen in her throat and hands, mature men, confident men, swallowed hard and grew abashed in her presence. She behaved with grace, but those who sought to seduce her, or treat her more roughly, even pirates, got no success. Many a pirate band held the White Isle sacrosanct, indeed, since its monks and nuns gave aid that seemed miraculous in time of storm and shipwreck.

Abbess Caithlenn wore a robe of fine oatmeal-hued linen, worked at the sleeves and hem with coloured thread. The rule of the White Isle was not harsh. The sea imposed harshness enough, and Caithlenn's apartments were no austere cell, but a suite pleasant with panels, screens and hangings, one depicting Deborah giving judgement beneath a palm tree. (Felimid had noticed before that the Deborah in that tapestry bore a resemblance to his father's mother Umai, poetess and seeress.) New rushes and sweet herbs of spring covered the floor. On the outside it was neatly set stone, almost a yard thick against the gales.

"Almost nothing," Felimid repeated. The green eyes so like his mother's gleamed with thought. "Yes and truly, for while he does have the powers of a bard, and the fiery magic he learned from Dicuil, and four companions who are bards, masters of satire, that is not so much, against the great power of the Uí Néill in the north, and they are not a breed that gives tender welcome to rivals. Fergus my grandsire said it. If Sunspear was intending to remake and rule the old kingdom of Ulster, in *their* teeth, before he kept his threats against us, his task would be impossible and old age a thing he would not attain. We might forget him."

"Wise Fergus was wrong for once," Caithlenn murmured. "We should have remembered him."

"Rule Ulster Sunspear does not," Brandon said, "but he has gained the rule of Airgialla, and three years ago that looked no more likely. Maybe magic aided him. He did begin with something more than you said, though, young sir." Felimid gave Brandon a fleering look. The monk was hardly his senior by that much. A *young sir* from him was out of place. Brandon did not miss the look, but he kept his countenance. "The men and women descended from Dicuil pledged to follow him, support him against all Erin if required, and they are a terrible crew. Their name for having demon blood is surely more than talk."

"I met two of his sons," Felimid said. "No amiable meeting that was. Tell me more of the Fir Dicuil. That they are red-headed and intransigent I know. Not much else."

"There are lies told about them, no doubt," Brandon conceded. "Nevertheless the talk is consistent. The Fir Dicuil were the greatest pest in the north until Sunspear took control of them, and reckoned scarcely human, with their fierceness and theft and plunder and robbery and murder. Their women conceive at a look, almost, and carry their babes to term in a mere five months, often bearing twins, or even three babes at one birth, and they grow swiftly. Despite their violence they heal swiftly, too. They lie in bed a nine-night from wounds that would kill most; then they are back on their feet."

Felimid, whose trade was telling stories, as a rule heard stories like that while hiding a smile, but this time he was disposed to believe. He had encountered Dicuil the Fiery, and been the subject of murder attempts from that direction. A demon, or something that might well be considered one, had been the agent. Dicuil himself, Felimid had reason to know, was but partly human. The same, it followed, was true of his many offspring, and if they were preternaturally fecund and vital, it was no cause for surprise.

Felimid remembered, with a shiver even though the dreadful *ollamh* was dead, his first sight of Dicuil. Ruarc Sunspear had presented him to the man (if he was one) in King Illann's pavilion in Leinster, at the Carman gathering. They had hoped to make him one of their company—then.

Dicuil's fair ruddy skin was tattooed from brow to chin with writhing, leaping patterns of flame in some lurid crimson dye. Small, dense and furious around his lips as though bursting from his mouth, they exploded up his cheeks and into his hairline, while his hair—a great thick spreading mane to the waist—was variegated in three hues, saffron, ginger and black. He wore a crimson robe. A ceremonial knife, with a glowing red gem in the hilt, hung about his neck on a chain.

He was something out of an elder world of naked, implacable elements and the sacrifice of firstborn children.

He had been all of that, and he had planned to bring such a world back. *He's dead*, Felimid reminded himself. *He wasn't wholly human and now he's dead.* Ruarc Sunspear still lived, but he was human, no older than Felimid, and no more powerful in bardic magic. It seemed, though, that he had contrived to become a king. How? In just three years? When it was not in the interests of the mighty Uí Néill, and he was not even *righ-domna*, eligible for kingship, how had he done what he'd done?

"The tale I heard in the north is that they held the heathen bull feast," Brandon offered. "They sacrificed a white bull as the *Tarb-Fheis* requires, and the poet Eochu drank the bull's broth and wrapped himself in the hide.

Then four druids, who were made druids by Dicuil in his life and are part of Sunspear's household, cast sleep upon him and he dreamed who should be king of Airgialla. When he awoke it was Ruarc Sunspear that he named."

"Convenient is that!" Caithlenn said.

Felimid smiled in a way that matched his mother's tone. His imagination painted him a picture in bright pigments of the poet emerging from his trance with the whole red-headed breed of the Fir Dicuil around him, eyes fierce and murderous hands ready. The penalty for a false utterance was death in any case, and there was no choice but the choice of Ruarc Sunspear that his followers would accept as true.

Maybe, even, Sunspear in fact was *righ-domna*. He had claimed—Felimid remembered now—to be descended from Conchubor mac Nessa, and thus a candidate for kingship in Ulster. Likely a boast, for Ruarc made extravagant claims, but if enough folk believed it, and it suited the powerful Uí Néill to accept it . . .

"Having the rule of Airgialla, what is this fine enterprising man doing with it, would you know?" Felimid asked.

"I know," Brandon assured him. "The whole of the north knows, and word goes like fire with monks as with bards! He is building anew the palace of Conchubor mac Nessa, the Red Branch House, bit by bit, on its old site in all its magnificence, and gathering heroes there."

"His notion of heroes," interjected Caithlenn.

"His notion," the sailor-monk agreed. "Already he has raised a new hall, much as the tales say it was, with walls of yew and bronze, well crafted. And a man I think trustworthy told me the pillars are inlaid with gold."

"He was not so rich three years ago, or rich at all," Caithlenn said. "His dire master Dicuil was the one with the great retinue and the wealth he extorted from many."

"Maybe he bequeathed it to his protégé," Brandon suggested. "His sons and daughters seem to have all attached themselves to Sunspear without question."

"Maybe," Felimid agreed. "I remember well that great magnificent barge in which he came to Lacth's dun. It was worth a cattle-herd in itself, with a chieftain's hall thrown in."

"Besides the gold, he'd need many craftsmen and artificers, and to pay them, and much common labour," Felimid said. "There has been nothing at the hill of Emain Macha since the palace was burned in the face of its conquerors, long since."

Brandon contributed, "My friend told me that carpenters and metal workers and others worked for nothing, to establish again the Red Branch glories."

"Cairbre and Ogma!" Felimid choked back a laugh that could have seemed scornful. "Our Ruarc Sunspear has been mighty persuasive and enjoyed, so he has, an inordinate amount of success!"

In the stories, the Red Branch Hall had a ceiling of silver. Felimid was sure Ruarc Sunspear had not copied it that far. Even the silver hoard Felimid had once found in Britain would not be enough.

"I have heard," Brandon said soberly, "that Sunspear made a promise to be avenged upon you, over Dicuil's bier, and said he would destroy the White Isle also."

Caithlenn smiled with disdain. "That he did. He said more. He announced an intent to destroy the faith and drive all the Cross-worshippers from Erin. Since that was more than Nero and Julian the Apostate together could do, and since there are churches and crosses all over the world, I am not shaken."

Brandon, who lacked aristocratic birth, showed less contempt than Caithlenn but equal confidence. "His big brag, which he has made to many, would be more impressive if his close neighbours were not who they are."

"And who are they, now?" Felimid asked.

"The church and monastery of Armagh, no less, that was founded by holy Padraigh with a bishop presiding, and which is so close to Emain Macha that any brisk old man can walk the distance in half an hour—with a bundle on his back! Armagh is by no means destroyed and its monks are by no means driven out. That must infuriate Sunspear, I am thinking, each time he hears its bells and hymns gainsay his boasts."

"Yet he forbids the monks to approach his outer rath within a spear's cast, I am told, and had the first ones who came with conversion on their minds to be fiercely beaten and thrown out. Also he promised that the next to annoy him and his heathen rout would have their heads set on poles. None has been so eager for martyrdom as to test him, and his bards, especially the one called Bluetongue, make virulent satires against the monks day and night.

Despite their faith, some fall ill and a couple have died. He—I mean Sunspear—says they will suffer worse in the end if they do not leave his kingdom. Thus far it stands at that impasse, and the Uí Néill lords intervene on neither side."

Felimid's mobile mouth curled into a snarl of sudden anger. He seldom showed such feeling. "The bold Ruarc promised to set my head on a pole too. It is sure as the sun sets that he remembers it. Nor is that all he is wanting, and he made threats against you and your house, mother mine, which he now has leisure to pursue. Unless I go to him, he will come proud and aggressive to me! It is better, and gives me more initiative, if I go to him."

"No!" Caithlenn cried, rigid. "You cannot, Felimid! You your own self said it. He would remove your head even swifter than he would a monk's, wickedly as he hates them. Go to his Red Branch House and you will die there. For nothing!"

"Never be afraid of that! I'll not go to his gate and announce myself, for I do know what would happen. I'll not go in disguise, either, for they know me, and I suppose he has magicians who would be quick to see through pretence or glamour. I'll present to the lords of the Uí Néill, who must give a bard welcome, and when I am their guest, protect me."

The horrified tension left Caithlenn's body, not at once, but it departed. She leaned back in her chair with a sigh.

"Yes. That will be better, my son, and it would be unwise to sit and wait, I suppose. Take your father's ship *Osprey*. She's swift, and still seaworthy after all these years."

Felimid shook his brown head. "You need *Osprey* here, and it's better I go unobtrusively. That vessel is distinctive even if I repaint her and put shabby sails on her mast."

"Let me take you in my ship," Brandon offered. "My brother monks and I are skilled sailors. From Skellig Michael to the Giant's Causeway I have sailed, once to Dalriada, once to Falga, and once even to Lyonesse."

"A gentle offer. I take it gratefully."

Brandon held out his rough sailor's hand and Felimid gripped it in his sinewy harper's fingers. Caithlenn smiled, though concern still wrung her heart. She doubted there were many better men with whom her only son could make a voyage than Brandon.

She was troubled about other things, though, and kept her lips shut concerning them until she had a chance to speak with Felimid where she could be certain none would hear. She walked with him on a high cliff over the sea. The booming waves made it unlikely that anyone would hear them at twenty paces, and Caithlenn made sure none was even that close.

"You know that perhaps it will come about, if you travel north, that you may have to enter Sunspear's dun. You cannot say no if he should invite you there."

"My birth *geas*. I know."

Those with bardic powers and magic in their marrow had liabilities too. Felimid was obliged, compelled, from the hour of his birth, if he became a bard—and he had never wished for anything else—to enter the house as a guest of any person who asked him, harping and singing there upon request—king or bondman, friend or enemy, man or woman, wealthy or poverty-stricken, human or otherwise. There were no exceptions. And if circumstances forced a man to break his *geas*, his fate was imminent.

"Your birth *geas*. Yes, my dear."

"Sunspear does not know about it. Now that Fergus and Umai are both gone beyond the sunset, none knows, none at all, except me, and Suibni the *fili* and you, my mother, and Lacth my foster mother. You and Lacth and Suibni are three I would trust with my life. Would and do."

"Do not be foolish! It's not necessary that Sunspear should know. If he bids you be his guest in Emain Macha, the centre of his power, and make genealogies and herosongs for him, then whether he knows your *geas* or not, you will have to accept! And he might do so. He might offer to forget his vengeance if you join his cause. And while he might not behave treacherously to a guest himself, a number of his folk are capable of it."

"*That* is the one thing you need not fear," he assured her. "Mother mine, mother mine! Never will he abandon the idea of avenging Dicuil, nor ever will he invite me under his rooftree as a guest. I'm sure of that."

Caithlenn looked over the grey thundering sea.

"I'll not be at heart's ease till you come back from the north. You are my only son. And so fine a son."

"I'll take care and be watchful, I give my word. I survived in the wide world where the lives of bards are not sacrosanct. Anyhow, I have only one *geas* to trouble me, not nine like Conaire the Great, each of them more improbable than the last." Caithlenn looked no happier. "Do not fret so! Remember that Dicuil the Fiery could not finish me and steal Golden Singer, and it's sure as the Sun rises and sets that he tried hard enough, with all his wizard's power. If he could not, Sunspear will not."

Chapter Two

After that, he stayed for another while with Scathach, until he had learned all the arts of war and all the feats of a champion; and then a message came to him to come back to his own country, and he bade her farewell. And Scathach told him what would happen to him in the time to come, for she had the Druid gift; and she told him there were great dangers before him . . . —The Courting of Emer

Lacth of the Booming Shield, Felimid's foster mother, and a very different woman to his birth mother, yet loved him as much as did Caithlenn. Big, brash and indelicate, Lacth had been a notable fighter in her time, and defended her dun against enemies as a leader, after her man's death in ambush. She had held it. She still held it and still led, though her hair was all grey, not merely streaked with it like Caithlenn's, and she walked with a lurching limp from her old injuries. Rumour said that once a man had derided her, under her own roof, because of that halting gait of hers, and since he was under her roof she had done nothing about it at the time, but afterwards she had paid him a visit to rebuke his bad manners, and he was not heard of again.

She had instructed a number of promising youths in weapon-use, Felimid among them, and none ever complained that her training was inadequate. Her children were Felimid's foster-sibs. Her grandchildren romped and played through the dun, those old enough to walk, in fear of nothing because of Lacth's protection.

She glared at Felimid.

"You come here now for your ancestor's sword?" she said scathingly. "This three years you left Kincaid on the wall! You never practiced with him but in the most desultory way when you came to visit. No other blade either, that I heard about. My honour and my name for hospitality, Felimid! Did you think you would never need to fight again?"

At that he had to laugh.

"Once I returned to Erin? No, foster mother, I did not reckon that! I'd barely set foot on Erin's soil but I had to fight a fellow poet, and a little later found two monasteries of the new faith about to make war each on the other! But I'd bardic studies to pursue and I was years behind. I'll be needing magic as well as a blade. Against Ruarc Sunspear especially."

"Trust the blade," Lacth advised him succinctly. "Sunspear is truly as skillful as he thinks he is."

"We cannot be doing everything at once. Suibni is Chief Bard now that Grandfather has gone beyond the sunset, and Suibni tells me that war and kingship have gone to Ruarc's golden head. Maybe he's well practiced with sword and spear, but he's let slide his bardic studies while I've pursued 'em, and that may bring him detriment."

"May!" Lacth echoed. "Failge Berraide was formidable, my darling. He met Sunspear in single combat, and now he's headless. That is just something of a detriment, too."

"I shall avoid meeting Sunspear in single combat," Felimid said gravely.

"Forgive me, but from what I'm told, his four companions have not let their bardic training lapse," Brandon interposed. "Bluetongue in particular makes satires that are killing."

"There!" Lacth said.

Felimid shrugged. "They were none of them trained by Fergus and Suibni. Thus they do not discompose me. But I deny I left Kincaid there on the wall. I know that I took him down three times, and so you must recall."

"Three times," repeated Lacth with scorn. "Three times, and the longest of them a bare couple of months. Quibble with me and I will clout you backwards! You are woefully out of practice with a sword, and with spear and axe too, I suppose."

"Somewhat. Admitted. Well, I never expected I'd have to deal with the tall Ruarc again, and I was mistaken. Nevertheless I have been through all that with Caithlenn on the White Isle and tedious it would be to repeat it."

"Just so that you own you still have to deal with Ruarc Sunspear, since he was not so obliging as to fail and die. Begin weapon practice now and sustain it daily. And before you leave, by the Morrigu herself, by the dread war queen, you will show me how much skill, if any, you retain. Seang!" she said briskly to her serving-woman. "Go find me Eichra the Eel and ask him to come to me, bringing with him the Creditor."

The Creditor was Eichra's sword. He had bestowed the name because, Eichra said, it always got what was owed it. As for himself, he was known as the Eel because he was supple and hard to grasp. No-one called him slippery in the matter of keeping faith, however. Lacth, straightforward and blunt, reckoned him a trusty henchman.

"Yes, Eichra the Eel," Felimid agreed. "I've had him in mind. I'll be telling you why presently."

He reached for the sword Kincaid, hanging on the wall among other weapons—all serviceable, but made by the ordinary skills of the current age. He drew the blade from the plain leather scabbard in which he had carried it through Britain and the Baltic—and on the isle of Sarnia. Never would Felimid forget cliff-girt Sarnia or its pirate chief, Gudrun. Despite himself, a thrill ran through him as he touched Kincaid's staghorn grips and gazed on the silver pommel shaped like a grinning cat's head. The excitement was there no matter how he assured himself he was a bard from a hundred generations of bards, that poetry and the harp were his vocations, not edged metal. But he descended from Ogma the Danann champion as well as Cairbre the bard, and his father had been Fal, who rebelled against tradition and turned reiver on the wild sea. That too ran in his blood.

Felimid drew the sword. Kincaid was the first weapon ever forged from iron in Erin, long ago by the first blacksmith, Goibniu of the Tuatha De Danann, the people of the goddess. The iron came from a fallen star recovered from the bottom of a lake. Learning how to adequately work it had called for a descent into the subterranean realm of shadowy, enigmatic Mider. The time spent there as Mider's apprentice had been a mere three days in the sunlit natural world, but nine years for him, and the sword Kincaid was Goibniu's finest work.

Thirty inches from pommel to point, the sword was slender, finely balanced, with a smooth channel down the centre and inlaid Ogham symbols in silver on both sides. As Felimid closed his fingers upon the hilt, the weapon seemed alive in his hand, almost ready to leap and lunge by itself—but that, of course, he wouldn't do. Kincaid would kill shapeshifters, monsters, even demons, many a creature that no common metal could harm. His wielder, though, must have courage and skill to send the blade into them, at the same risk faced by a man bearing any ordinary weapon.

"Long enough you've been about taking hold of him again," said a voice with a mocking note in it.

Eichra the Eel moved as fluently as his name implied. He swam like one as well. Properly, he was Eichra mac Ronan, but he had been on bad terms with his father before Ronan died in battle, and Eichra the Eel pleased him well enough. His features were odd; not so much ugly or deformed as a little mismatched. Narrow blue eyes sat above plump, rotund cheeks and never seemed to be looking directly at you, though he missed little, and his jaw, by contrast again, was pointed. His mouth looked as though there was scarcely room for it between his chaps. The physical incongruities ended below his neck, however; in body he was lean, tough and pliant. Those who supposed his narrow shoulders lacked strength were mistaken.

He had fetched his sword the Creditor as Lacth bade him.

"Long enough, Eichra," the bard agreed equably. "My needed studies, and settling home after being long away. But she of the booming shield takes a like view, and there is no argument I can find to refute her. Practice is called for."

"It is! By the gods it is! If you intend to stand by Lacth when that upstart who now claims he's a king comes against her. He said he would. We were both here and heard him. It's in my mind that one day he will."

"Hmm, yes. I don't think I shall wait for that day. I think I shall just travel north."

Eichra raised his eyebrows almost into his hair. "Interesting. I like the plan. But some of that practice first?"

Felimid acceded. Each young man took a round leather-covered targe from the wall. Lacth, saying nothing, watched closely. Although her broad face did not betray the worry, she was asking herself how either of them would fare against Ruarc, who by substantial report had taken the head off Failge Berraide in single fight. That had been a feat.

Felimid and Eichra confronted each other, the bard left-handed, his opponent the opposite, a situation the bard faced in almost every combat, exercise or earnest. Other members of Lacth's household came to see, her sons among them and her daughter. Brandon and some of the monks looked on agog, besides, though violence was not supposed to be their dish.

It was normal for two fighting men's shields to be diagonally opposed, and their swords also. But Felimid was left-handed to a marked degree. His sword-hand and Eichra's fronted each other straight-on; their little round shields faced each other directly as well. Thus, they had often to parry blade against blade, and use their shields as offensive weapons, ramming at the other man's body or striking at the opposing targe, surface against surface. Locking shield-rim behind rim could be more effective, either to lever the other man's defence aside, or shove him off balance altogether if he could be caught with his feet ill planted.

The swords clashed and shrieked. Edge scraped along edge. Felimid soon saw that Eichra was indeed more in recent training than he. He saw also—not to his astonishment—that Eichra had never fought as desperately for life as the bard, against such a varied and lethal set of enemies. Probably he had not fought arrogant lordlings like Justin of Calleva or Avraig the hunter, as swift with their blades as they were deficient in manners, and surely never a *werwulf*, as the Saxons called them, like Tosti Fenrir's—get, a savage berserk even in human form. With utter certainty, he had never encountered the like of Koschei the Deathless. Felimid still dreamed of Koschei sometimes, and awakened sweating. Even a more meagre pair like the treacherous Frank Hugibert, and the foxy merchant captain Pascent, might be outside Eichra's experience. And so Felimid, even while he owned himself rusty, and Eichra as being skillful—not to mention eager to prove that skill against Felimid—reckoned he was still the master.

The two shifted light-footed about the hall, sunbeams jumping from their blades and flashing across the thatch and rafters above. Even as he parried Eichra's quick strokes and sought a way past his guard, Felimid noted some of his mistakes and struggled not to laugh.

Eichra was a proud one; he would have taken offence.

Sunspear

From the beginning Eichra took the initiative. Now, thinking to fool his adversary, he stepped *out* of the attack, backward on his left foot, holding his shield high. The fighting distance altered, he made a fast overhand cut, twisting his hips to add force and leaning into the stroke. His target was Felimid's sword arm, the upper arm, though he pulled the stroke at the last instant; this was practice and he had no wish to cripple.

Eichra failed to pull it enough. Enthusiasm, and a bit of jealousy, kept vinegar in his blow. He knew it himself, a fraction too late, and knew also that his move was not easy to counter. Eichra's back leg had been taken out of striking range for Felimid with that initial step. The bard did not try for it. He slanted his shield across his body, high, and Eichra's edge met the surface with a hollow bang. Felimid thrust. His blade slid diagonally between them, the point passing through the air a hand-span to the side of Eichra's neck.

It could as easily have gone *through* his neck, had the thrust been meant and the battle real. They both knew it. Felimid grinned, hiding the twist his stomach gave at the thought—*what, still soft after these five years past?*—and Eichra grinned back.

"Stop," Lacth commanded. "Your blood's too hot. Eichra, that was good, but it's a ploy Felimid knows well. And you, Felimid! Were you well in training, you'd have brought your shield over twice as swiftly, with your feet better positioned too. A disgrace, so it was. I am telling you, practice daily, if you think there is any chance you may come sword to sword with Golden Ruarc, as some are calling him. I urge it. No, I command it, foster son, and if I find you haven't, I'll disown you! Eichra, Brother Brandon, bring me reports of him when this is over."

"You taught me arms and behaviour, Lacth of the Booming Shield, and on my word I'll observe your advice. Daily."

"It's well. Booming Shield, eh? That reminds me." Lacth gazed earnestly upon him. "I've heard that in Emain Macha our lad Sunspear found, and now bears, the shield of Conchubor mac Nessa—Ochaine, the One that Moans. It vibrates and wails when the one who carries it is in danger. Maybe it is true, maybe not. Just bethink you of it if you're ever planning a stealthy approach to that one."

"I shall. Thanks. I'm scarcely desirous of a great bloody combat with him like Cuchulain's with Ferdiad. That won't solve much. Breaking his power is what seems to be needed, and for that I need to learn how he ever obtained it to begin."

"The Uí Néill may know," Brandon said. "They are his neighbours, and he fought on their side at Druim Derg. Still they may be uneasy about him. I would be, in their place."

"Yes, go to the northern Uí Néill," Lacth advised. "That's a not-inconsiderable journey in itself, over dangerous waters, but Brandon and his fellows know them as a henwife knows her own yard and all its clucking birds. They will get you there."

"If it's the will of God," Brandon agreed.

That left no room for debate.

Chapter Three

He did not waste any more time talking, but set out on the journey. —The Wedding of Maine Morgor

Mighty flooding had come to the estuary of Sinann in the winter, as it usually did, and along the shore it was evidenced by broad mud flats and salt marshes. Curlews and oystercatchers hunted their food in the mire, competing with flocks of shelducks, the drakes gaudy for breeding. Others wheeled overhead in flocks. Out from shore, gulls and gannets shrieked, eyeing the grey-green water. Dolphins raced merry through the waves, keeping pace with a curragh running down the estuary before a breeze that felt sharp on wet flesh.

Sleek as the dolphins themselves, the curragh flexed to the waves like a live thing. Felimid sat towards the stern, holding his harp in her worn leather case, a chest of the magnificent clothes that Pendor the wizard had conjured for him, and certain other needs, stowed under a thwart. The sword forged out of a fallen star, not so mundane, was there beside the bag, out of deference to the monks. So were Eichra's weapons and those of the bard's foster brother Tuathal, amidships. Lacth's three sons had insisted that one of them go on the voyage, at least, and

Tuathal had won the gamble, which pleased him greatly. His attempt at winning a bride in Connacht had gone amiss and he was restless.

His weapons included a bow of thick elm, short but powerful at close range, with which he was skilled enough to have gained the by-name *an Saighdeoir*, the archer. That was an accomplishment he had gained while Felimid was away. It was not a common one in Erin. The bard thought of the long Danish yew bow with which Gudrun Blackhair had been so expert, and concealed the pang he felt.

"Where did you learn that art, brother?" he asked.

"Leinster," came the answer. "You know there are many foreigners coming and going there. This was a mercenary from Demetia.* Many a feud and raid is carried on in thick woods there, many an attack by robbers, he said, and it's excellently useful to shoot shafts fast from a bow that does not catch over-much in thickets. It does not carry a far distance, but in such an attack you don't need to shoot over the skyline. Well, that's oft the case in Erin too. I have been thinking I may have to use this bow against Sunspear and the Fir Dicuil."

This was a lengthy speech for Tuathal. Not gifted with eloquence, he was nevertheless pensive, and known to be

---

*a kingdom of south-west Wales

trusty. In most situations his views were useful; more so than Eichra's, which often were tainted with contentiousness and acerbity.

The Eel was resourceful, though, and a difficult man to frighten. He could be relied on in danger. Felimid was glad to have him.

The eight other souls in the curragh were monks, robes drawn up about their trousered thighs and beards wet with spray. Oengus, the oldest, short, broad and strong, sat in the stern near Felimid and worked the big steering paddle. With the wind behind the curragh, as it was now, he scarcely had to haul the bar to make the craft respond. It bucked and skipped. Brandon stood far forward, scanning the sea and the island a few miles to the north—which they were passing at the furthest remove possible, a distance, to those in the curragh, still not sufficient.

The island's name was Cathaig.

"My hope and wish, the monster is keeping to the land this day," Felimid murmured.

Oengus agreed, spitting to leeward. "A very holy person might have the power to banish him. I know of two monks who tried and were not seen again. A warning against too much sinful confidence in your own holiness."

"Oh, true for you. I grew up beside these waters and I never saw the monster or desired to. By report he's huge, solitary and does not meddle with folk as a rule—or like intruders. Not that he is troubled by many. It's said that once a hero went ashore on Cathaig to kill him, and another time a whole war-band, but they failed to return and there is a dearth of fellows ready to follow their example now."

"Doesn't he destroy sometimes?" Oengus asked. "When anger is upon him, perhaps? I have heard he is known to smash ships."

"There are stories of it. There are always stories. It's said he has one terrible eye and great thick clawed legs, but when he takes to the sea the legs become flukes and his huge tail flattens out like a paddle, and the purpose for which he takes to the sea is to eat, the provender he prefers being whales. Maybe that is why he attacks ships on occasion. Maybe he mistakes them for whales. When I was little there was a poor omadhaun they said had survived from such a ship, the only one, shambling and muttering and rarely saying a thing sane folk could comprehend. He could not go near the shore or endure the sound of the waves. Never came he to Lacth's dun without getting a meal or a warm place to sleep."

"Aye, that's the way of Lacth of the Booming Shield."

They left the island behind and fled down the estuary towards the open sea. Brandon came aft, moving like a sailor born. Indeed, he moved and worked in the curragh better than the bard, despite Felimid's time with Gudrun Blackhair and her rovers. The bard commented upon it.

"Thanks," Brandon said, pleased. He knew that Felimid had sailed, and with whom. "I was born within sound of the sea, and for that matter one of the men who taught me, before my beard grew, was Nasach, your own father's captain once. Nasach the Sombre he was known as then. Married, with children and grandchildren, when I knew him, and more mellow than once, I suppose."

"I suppose," Felimid echoed, not over-encouragingly. He had never seen his father, who died at four-and-twenty in the way pirates generally do die, and that he met his end fighting to cover the escape of Caithlenn and her infant son from their would-be murderers was not, to Felimid, immense consolation. And even carrying that knowledge, he, like his mother, had fallen wildly in love with a proud headstrong reiver and sailed with her until fate overtook her.

"I am sorry," Brandon told him. "That was carelessly said. I know your father's story, to be sure."

"Yes, and my mother's, too. Maybe you have heard about Gudrun Blackhair." Spindrift hissed past Felimid's face. He shifted his buttocks on the hard thwart. "I knew Nasach too. I know members of Fal's old crew. I've heard much about him, and I'd far rather have known him. Sa, well. That tide has long since gone out."

"I am sorry," Brandon said again. "We are few of us wise in youth, as I do know, for I am young yet. Abbess Caithlenn is known now for her devout faith, and for good works in storm and shipwreck. You, too, have made the White Isle more effective thus. The selchies have become her friends and even the Chief of the Seals himself. Your commendation did it, I know."

Felimid smiled, a little derisively. "I made their acquaintance on Skellig Michael. The monks there told the selchies they have no souls, and they took it amiss. I am no authority on souls, brother, but I gave my opinion that those austere monks likely did not know what they were taking about and the selchies would be received more politely at the White Isle. And killing of seals there is a cursed and forbidden thing now."

"A thing I regard as forbidden to me also. The grey seals have saved more than one man from the waves."

"So they have."

The wind held and Felimid was glad. The curragh, which had no keel, raced over the water with the breeze astern, and the strong, heavy-set monk at the steering-paddle worked diligently to keep her so, while his brothers handling the sail laboured to the same set purpose. Broadside to wind or wave, a curragh was endangered.

They left Cathaig behind and flew down the estuary towards the open sea. With dusk they came to the broad mouth of Sinann and the long headland on the north side. Dragging the craft ashore in a sandy cove, they ate hard bread and cheese and drank water. Felimid did not mind the simple fare. He had subsisted on worse while exiled.

"A few hours' rest here, and maybe the sky will clear," Brandon hoped. "Then we can sail due north by the stars, and fetch the isles. The more miles out to sea as we pass the cliffs of Moher, the better. Have you sailed past the cliffs, son of Fal?"

"I have not."

"It's ill to be caught on the water with the wind blowing towards the cliffs, so. A gale worst of all. You may stand atop the cliffs then, and throw a pebble out over the sea with all your force, and the wind will blow it back so that you must duck as it whistles over your head."

"A dark spirit haunts the cliffs, they say," Eichra remarked, but scornfully. "A witch-hag responsible for turning many a sailor to white bones on the sea-floor."

"Or just the sea and the rocks," Brandon countered, giving the Eel a look. "I have been past the cliffs many a time. If the hag has existence, she is helpless before faith and prayer—and good sailors. We'll get safely past."

"If there are no monkish objections, my harp may get us some favour from the spirits of the wind, should we be needing it," Felimid said. "They are not demons, worthy brothers, but being powers of the air they can be swayed by music and words, which are airy. Though I also would put my trust in seamanship first."

"Glad I will be of your harp and your powers," Brandon told him earnestly. "And I know you can row."

"No misgivings?"

"In the Aran islands we have a college of *banfilidh* for our neighbours, who know the moods of the sea as few others, and prophesy from wind and wave. Your father's mother Umai founded it before a monastery there was even thought of, except by God. We have never quarreled with them, though we have not converted them either. They have given us warning of storms to come, and we've learned to listen and stay ashore; they have not been mistaken yet, to my knowledge."

"I'll visit them," Felimid said. "The last time was in my fifteenth year, before I went away. Befind, the sharp-beaked and sharp-tongued," (Brandon grinned) "was the college head then, and still is, so Umai was telling me before she passed beyond the sunset."

"And that's the truth."

"Maybe they can venture a foretelling of how it will go the rest of the voyage north."

The sky remained grey and low, so Brandon's decision to rest a few hours on the point remained the same. Felimid drew the ancient harp of Cairbre, Golden Singer, out of her leather case and ran hands over her shining strings. They were true gold. Only the Danann artisans of old had the skill of working gold to the tensile strength required of harpstrings. Yet even they broke or wore in the end. There were just three spare strings left. Time passed, and all things passed with it.

Pure shadowing tree of true music, Felimid thought, and began to play, a quiet murmur that granted the monks easy rest on their sheepskins. Felimid thought of the monastery in the Aran Islands, the first, he believed, that Brandon had founded, and of the *banfilidh*'s college nearby, a sisterhood of magic and prophecy. Some cross-worshippers execrated them as evil witches, some, like Brandon, gave them goodwill and received it in return. Elsewhere, such juxtapositions were fierce fires waiting to burn, like the proximity of Ruarc Sunspear's kingly hall—*how had he done that?*—to Padraigh's see of Armagh.

The new and the old. New things had to come. Fergus, although very old, had seen that clearly. *Rest well, grandsire.* Ruarc Sunspear, though young, did not see it at all, and held Felimid a traitor to Erin's entire past. Something of a joke, since Felimid's soul was steeped in all the vivid colours of those tales and magic, and he had ample misgivings as to Padraigh's new faith.

Tuathal approached him and sat nearby. "You ought to sleep," he said. "The next part of the journey may be mighty strenuous."

"Difficult to dispute, that. But I'm troubled by thought."

Felimid tried to calm those fretful thoughts with Golden Singer. His nails moved on the harp-strings, plucking them skilfully and with heart, making soothing melodies. As he played, he began to assemble a poem.

Sunspear

"New faith has come from a distance untold
To this land of all lands enchanted,
And grey stone crosses stand carven and scrolled
Upon lands by proud kings granted -
Alternate with ogham pillars of old
Fir Nemed and Danann once planted.
But Morrigu, Macha and Badb rule war
And Manannan the surging seas,
Though church bells chime from shore to shore
And the crosses may sprout like trees.
The live old trees in the groves of oak,
Too holy for fire or the axe-man's stroke,
Remember the moon and the Druid's cloak,
And the snow-white bull with its gilded yoke
Across which the grey rain slanted.
The harp still rings and the drum still booms,
The pipe cries dirges and prophesies dooms,
While the Crooked Beasts from the earth's dark wombs
May rise when the gods are scanted."

Felimid pondered the lines, considering inner rhymes and more perfect scansion in places. It was not complete, either—it needed more—but he could add more another time. Now would be a good time to sleep for a couple of hours. Tuathal had fallen asleep already, but Felimid's mind still would not rest, and against his will it turned to other things than poetry. All he knew about politics in the north had come from travelling bards who stopped at Suibni's college, and it was his own fault that he had scarcely troubled to listen, sure as he was that Ruarc Sunspear would have no success.

A mistake he would have to correct now.

Chapter Four

Then he fought with the waves three days and three nights . . .
—The Only Son of Aoife

Three days afterwards, they made the Aran Islands.

It had been a strenuous small voyage, even as Tuathal of the few words had predicted, though it began well, with a clear sky in the early morning and the wind ceasing to blow as strongly from the west. With the sail full and no need for oars, they had swept merrily north for about an hour. Then the weather turned cantankerous, with rain and squalls, and after midday a chill steady blow took them further out to sea than they desired. There was little choice but to run before it, bailing out the rain water and battling a wet, weighty sail. The monks prayed, while they had the breath, while the pagans Tuathal and Eichra found more relief in cursing.

Felimid, with his bardic senses, looked to the sky and saw great boisterous air spirits, their shapes always changing but most often seeming like vast birds with grey wings beating as they wheeled over the sea. Despite his advance to the fourth degree he could not command them—no bard and few magicians could command the elemental forces—though in exchange for Golden Singer's music they might oblige him. He decided to save that for another time. He and his companions were being inconvenienced, put to trouble, but not faced with the direst danger.

Of course, should the curragh suddenly capsize, his last thought as he sank would be that he had left Golden Singer's intercession late . . .

They were blown further out to sea, but as Brandon said, it was not all bad as long they could keep slugging north. They wanted to stay well clear of the fearsome cliffs of Moher anyhow. At worst, if they missed the Aran Islands altogether, they would hardly miss the Connacht coast. They could land there and make their way back.

Then, as always unpredictable by any but a Druid, the wind eased, and then shifted about to raven from the west. It also blew slightly towards the south. The curragh was impelled straight towards the towering cliffs its crew most desired to avoid. Shivering, soaked and cold, the monks and the other three sprang anew to work that warmed them somewhat—but not enough. Fingers chilled and stiff, Felimid thought his hands on an oar would do them more good than on the harp-strings, and he had experience rowing. He bent his back with Brandon's monks, who were, as he found, as expert in this activity as in praying, and rowed in deft unison. The narrow-bladed ash oars, though, did not bite the water as strongly as he would have liked, and the seething foam at the cliffs' dark base was like hungry slaver.

They barely won past.

Beyond the cliffs of Moher lay the islands, edged with rugged bluffs and limestone screes, the shores thick with samphire. Little patches of pasture lay above, between great fissured slabs of the local limestone. Felimid sighed with relief as they approached, though the smallest of the islands, which they passed at speed, water hissing under their craft's ox-hide skin, had a great ominous rock off the south-eastern side, too near for comfort.

"Known for wrecking ships," Brandon said. He did not seem worried at all. The sang-froid of a sailor and the faith of a Cross-worshipper combined.

They sailed past the midmost isle of the three, and the second in size, like the first with screes slanting down to the sea and wide paves above, split by great cracks in which good fertile soil had accumulated over the ages. There were dolmens and stone forts of those lost ages among the flowers, too. Felimid would have been interested, but for severe, growing pain in his left arm and side. He supposed he had rowed too hard when, unlike the monks, he had become unused to that kind of labour. Nevertheless, a strained back was better than lying in the sea at the bottom of Moher's cliffs.

Formidable cliffs edged the largest island, also—Ara Mór, where Brandon had established his first monastery—cliffs as high as Moher's or higher. They passed a strait and came to a cove of brilliant blue water. Above the sea stood the common monks' cells, a small church, a little graveyard with inscribed stones, and tall carven ring-crosses, all surrounded by neatly built dry-stone walls. The bard stepped ashore with a sense of relief, and walked up a steep path to the guest-house with his harp on his back, but his sword—and the weapons of Tuathal and Eichra—wrapped in an unobtrusive bundle from respect for the monks' peaceful ways. They were not like all monks in that. Felimid had met others who were ready enough to raise weapons, and even war on each other over a question of who should be abbot, but Brandon was not among them.

"How is it with your bardic power?" Tuathal asked him, walking at his side. "It fades in churches and monasteries, I know."

"Not all. The grim ones, yes, the death-sites. On Skellig Michael it did. Wherever are the ruins of Rome, those harsh straight lines and ordered shapes, bardic magic fades too. Rome's way was to magic what sowing land with salt is to crops. But I kept my bardic power in Kildare, the shrine of triumphant Brigit. She's more goddess than saint, anyhow, the goddess of fire and poetry. And it appears I am keeping my powers here."

"Aye, Brandon is not above a prayer to his Christ *and* an invocation to Manannan when the sea rages wild."

"That madman Sulghein would have raging fits to hear it," Felimid muttered, remembering the wild monk of

Lansulcan with disaste.* "Dewi in Britain would take it badly also."

"Would you retain your magic in—Armagh, say? Are you knowing?"

"A fine question. I doubt it. Armagh is Padraigh's foundation. My grandfather knew Padraigh and did not find him agreeable. I'll not be setting foot in Armagh if I can avoid it—but I may be constrained to."

He set his teeth as he continued the climb between grey rocks, spring grass and flowers. The pain was growing worse. He did not think anything was too much amiss, but plainly he had strained the muscles in his left side. Tuathal noticed. He suggested the monks, those of them who knew the craft of healing, look at the bard. It wouldn't be well to have cracked ribs go untended.

"I've no cracked ribs," Felimid assured him. "It wasn't I the sail fell upon! Torn muscles, maybe, but I doubt even that. I reckon they are only pulled and strained."

"You can't be sure. During that squall you fell down somewhat hard. You need some rest. With what you are undertaking you do not wish your sword-arm or harp-hand impaired for use, so."

---

*BARD III: THE WILD SEA

"I do not. But Ruarc and his redhead henchmen will never pause to ask me if I'm rested, or my sword-arm working, if I meet them. Better I practice—with my right hand, but elsewhere on the island than here, or the monks will be offended."

"And then the stars will fall down," Eichra said with a lip-curl. "They share this island with a college of sea-witches. That doesn't trouble them."

"*Banfilidh*, not witches," Felimid corrected him. "Belike the monks have nothing against them because they give good advice to men setting forth to sea—the monks included—and do not redden weapons either. I've a use for their prophecies myself. It's my hope they can give one."

His grandmother Umai's prophesies had been trustworthy. A poetess of rank, she had been a noted prophet too, and founded the college here on Ara Mór before Brandon was conceived. Its chief *banfili*, Befind, had been taught by Umai from the cradle, and she also had a considerable name. Whether or not she told him anything helpful, it would be churlish to pass this isle without a visit.

Later. For now, Felimid wished to lie down in the monastery's small guest-house and get, if he could, a rubbing with some efficacious liniment. There would be no complaints from him such as he had voiced at Rochusa three years before, either, and which had provoked poor

Saraidh to yell that he was finicking and shiftless. At least no imminent war hung over this place.

He had worse injury, then, than pulled muscles. He must have gone soft in three years of ease—well, physical ease. Suibni the *ollamh* had put him through demanding paces of spirit and mind to attain the fourth bardic rank. He'd even gained some of the knowledge and power that went with the fifth, but if his head came off to a murderer's blade, as Ruarc desired, that wisdom would go with it.

Brother Oengus, the steersman, came into the guesthouse, ducking his head below the stone lintel, necessarily, although he was not tall. His meagre bundle of possessions dangled from a big gnarled hand. With Eichra and Tuathal he filled the guest house to capacity.

Tossing his bundle beside the last empty pallet, he shook his bearded head and spoke gravely.

"My gratitude to God, but it's a blessing we arrived! The stepping of the mast would have worn and ceased to hold, with any more contrary winds. I reckon it was imminent and close. The curragh needs a new block for the mast and some other work, before it dares the waters again. The angels were kind."

Felimid whistled. The bottom of the sea had no appeal for him, but of course they had risked that destination once they left land; men always did, setting sail. He was inclined to thank luck or the old gods for survival, himself, but he was a guest and he deferred to Oengus's belief.

Eichra twisted a derisive lip but made no comment. Tuathal *an Saighdeoir* continued to inspect his short elm bowstave.

"Your brothers' faith and prayers preserved us indeed. Will repairs take long?"

"Cannot be saying. I don't know if a big enough block of seasoned oak is ready to hand on this island. We may have to fetch one from the main shore."

So, then. Felimid could expect time for his arm and back to recover. He should have time to visit the *banfilidh* as well. After that, maybe Brandon would be willing to sail into the north, all around Connacht. He had sailed further.

"Have you been much in the north, Brother Oengus, among the Uí Néill?"

"A few times, bard. A few times. So has my good superior Brandon. Like most chiefs, they are pagan yet, though they make no objection to the faith being taught and even grant land to monasteries. There are two great clans of the Uí Néill, and of course they are rivals, though they do join against common foes. Sunspear's kingdom, Airgialla, stands to the south-east of them, and across in the east is the remnant of the Ulaid, cherishing dreams of former power and nursing rancour against the sons of Niall, considering them upstarts."

Sunspear

Felimid had forgotten the Ulaid, but Oengus was right. Ruarc Sunspear would be aware of their potential as allies or foes, and Felimid wondered what he was doing at present. Surely not allowing grass to grow under his feet.

Chapter Five

"It is looking into the future for you I am," she said, "to see what will be your chances and your fortunes..."
—The War for the Bull of Cuailgne

Felimid and Eichra made their way up a typically uneven slope, the gaps between the rocks flowering with cranesbill and vetch. They practiced with weapons as they went. Felimid carried only his sword Kincaid, and wielded it in his right hand, while the other man bore sword and spear, assailing the bard with both. He had a considerable advantage, and used it to the full, knowing Felimid would hardly thank him for soft treatment.

Felimid called on his own advantages in turn. He used every trick he had learned among Gudrun's pirates. Surer-footed than Eichra, he made use of the uneven, rocky ground, moving quickly and well, but his left hand, the skillful one, still unfit for use, stayed tucked in his belt. Eichra had bested him twice on this walk, and for his pride's sake Felimid wished to avoid making it three times.

A chance came. Eichra the Eel missed his footing a little. Felimid struck his spear aside with the flat of Kincaid, the impact making a sharp crisp sound, and then cut at Eichra's hip. He would have pulled the stroke, but

Eichra parried with his own sword and there was no need; his spear spun over and was suddenly levelled at Felimid's neck. Had he thrust hard, the point would have gone *through* his neck.

Best to Eichra, three out of three, after all.

The Eel acknowledged that it meant little. "With that blade in your other hand and a shield on your arm—different tale." He said it unwillingly, yet he said it.

"Maybe, but I cannot be holding a shield yet. If I meet one of Dicuil's grandsons and I'm injured or at some other disadvantage, he will not make polite tryst for a future day and let me pass."

"I am interested," Eichra said, "to meet one of them and see if he's as much as the chatter avers."

"Oh, if we encounter one, I'm sure we will find out."

Felimid walked a few paces and retrieved Golden Singer from the rocky depression where he had left her. He set her on his back with a slight wince. The pulled muscles were better after days of rest at the monks' community, but they were not fully recovered yet. Even moderate weapon-practice was maybe not well advised. Yet if Felimid met Ruarc's companions Dub Dothar or Tachdan the Sudden, or any of Dicuil's progeny, he would need all the practice he could cram into this journey.

The slope they had climbed was gentle enough, if the ground was uneven, but at the top it fell sharply to a cove of tawny sand, a high bluff at one end and a limestone sea-cliff at the other. Two boathouses stood by the shore, and further back the college of the *banfilidh*, called sea-witches by the ignorant. The buildings, unlike the cells and church of the monks, were constructed of timber and wicker fetched from the mainland. From the mainland also came the turf which burned inside, and sent its smoke rising through hooded holes. The *banfilidh* did not make a virtue of discomfort, an attitude Felimid liked.

"What is *that*?" Eichra asked, pointing.

He meant a curious structure unlike the others, built close to the sea on a great wave-worn slab of rock. Around it were stretches of gritty sand, other rocks, and between them swathes of bright green seaweed left by the tide. It hardly seemed practical, that structure, but it had been shaped with meticulous, loving care and obvious effort. Dry-stone work, it had the form of a round spiral shell, about six paces across. Patterns of darker rock in the limestone added to the impression of a huge seashell. Its single opening faced the sea. Presumably, a spiral passage led inside, growing narrower towards the centre, where there would be a small round chamber.

"The Seashell is what they call it. The *banfilidh* go to the middle—having, I'm told, to crawl the last part of the way—and curl up there entranced. The sounds of wind and wave come in through the opening, the sea's voice. They focus and strengthen on their way in. The *banfilidh* can understand it and prophesy from it."

Sunspear

He was not one of the *banfilidh*. Still his bardic sight discerned patterns in the waves that rolled onshore, patterns with meaning. Tall figures with beards like seaweed paced briefly on the small beach before fading into the restless sea again. Not the Children of Lir, who were flesh and blood, but rather the elementals of the waves.

One sight he did not see. As a boy he had occasionally witnessed sleek magical ships of the Children of Lir sailing swifter than any ships of men, elusive on the horizon. The last of them—probably—had departed Erin's world for another now, led by green-haired Niamh and her captains. A little more of the ancient magic had departed with them. Felimid sighed.

He and Eichra descended to the cove, seen and marked by the *banfilidh* and their servants. Their coming, he was sure, surprised no-one. Wind whistled over the hall and outbuildings, fingering the oat-thatched roofs, the straw and the craftsmen having been fetched from the mainland, like the timber. Tough criss-crossing ropes covered the thatch from the ridges down, anchored with dangling rocks along the roofs' edges against the frequent gales.

Eichra carried their weapons, all in one bundle, wrapped and secured. Taking swords and spears into this college, without leave, was hardly better manners than taking them into Brandon's monastery would be. The harp on Felimid's back, here as everywhere in Erin, made them safer, more welcome, than any weapons could.

Anywhere, Felimid thought, *but in Sunspear's hall.*

There was no palisade or rampart around the college. It too had better guarantees of safety. Felimid called out, "A bard comes and seeks hospitality! Felimid mac Fal comes, the grandson of Fergus, chief bard, and of Umai who founded this college, honour to her name."

"Honour truly," spoke a woman's thin dry voice, "and you are awaited here, son of Fal. Your mother sent a message."

Befind, chief of the college, thin and dry herself, came towards him from the main shrine with a decisive gait. Her long white tunic carried embroidered strips at neck and hem. The attendant behind her, so much shorter that she had to step swiftly to keep up, wore a yellow tunic worked at neck, sleeves and hem with curling wave-patterns, blue and green. A cowl shadowed her face.

"*Banfili*," Felimid said. "Priestess. It's a good day I give you. I bring my heritage of poetry and the harp. I bring friendship-gifts from the White Isle, with my mother's greetings and love, and desire aid of your wisdom."

Befind halted before him. She was taller than Felimid, and by reason of her gauntness seemed taller yet. Her narrow nose jutted. If the sight of virile, reasonably comely young men moved her, she offered no evidence of it. Her attendant remained silent, but Felimid was aware of an intense regard from within the cowl.

"Be welcome, grandson of Umai, bard," Befind told him. She might have relaxed her formal phrasing at that point. She did not. "You have not visited us since your return, and your negligence only ends now for the cause that, as you say, you crave our help. Courteous."

"I'm at fault," Felimid said smoothly, "and o' course, I was not at the White Isle when you visited my mother."

Befind had not done that in all of *nine* years.

"No," she agreed curtly. "Eichra the Eel, you are welcome with the bard. Muadnait—" She took her cowled attendant's hand. "—you will not know; she has been with us six years only. Come, partake of food. And give greeting to one that you do know."

"Who is that, wise Befind?"

"Do not flatter. He's Odhran the selchie."

Felimid knew him right enough. They had met after the bard's return to Erin. The seal-man rose from a stuffed leather seat in the *banfili*'s quarters, milk-skinned and brown-haired, wearing only a kilt, feet bare, and not quite sure or steady on land. Selchies never were. The sorrow of their fate was that they truly belonged neither on land nor sea.

Odhran's dark eyes shone. "Felimid."

"Odhran! You look fine, and the eye of a friend can tell that best. But how did you come here from the White Isle? It would be a long arduous swim."

"I came part of the way in a fisherman's boat," the selchie answered. "He held I would bring him luck. If you were storm-driven or waylaid by reivers or for any other reason missed this island, I was to follow you and bring you the advice of the *banfilidh*. But now there is no need."

"There is not," Befind affirmed. "You may have it first hand, but after you eat and drink. The monks are not bad but their fare is coarse."

Felimid knew selchies. Odhran might incline to melancholy, his eyes and voice might be gentle in his man's form, but he partook equally of a seal's nature and knew all the harshness of survival in the sea. His white shoulders bore the scars of fighting to establish a harem at mating time—not always successfully.

The quiet attendant Muadnait brought stewed mussels, milk curd, barley bread, butter and sea-kale, with a great roast goose in case the guests were still hungry after that. Odhran tackled the food as enthusiastically as the human men. The platters were scraped clean when they were done.

"Now listen," Befind commanded, as though talking to children. Her glance swept across Odhran, Eichra and Felimid without partiality. "Your mother sent Odhran to me with a plea to foretell, if I can, the safest way for you to approach the Uí Néill, and which faction. I did this for her, for your grandmother Umai, and for the sacred bond between us. Within the House of the Shell, I listened to the sea and it gave guidance."

"I am grateful, lady," Felimid assured her.

"You need not be. This matters greatly to more than your mother and you; it matters to Erin. The terror of Dicuil the Fiery still hangs over the north, where he used to reside and was masterful and overbearing even to kings. None dared cross him. Much of that fear clings to young Sunspear yet. He was Dicuil's chief protégé. He uses that awe."

"He does truly, but his magic and bardic prowess are never like Dicuil's."

"Stories are about, maybe spread by Sunspear, maybe growing from the dread of Dicuil's name, that he is not truly dead and will reappear. That I could not learn from the voice of the sea."

"Lady Befind, he's as dead as a flayed horse," the bard told her bluntly. "I saw and I can say. His angry ghost is all that's left of Dicuil."

"Then that is well." Befind smiled slightly at his young vehemence. "Yes. As for my counsel, here is what the seawind and the waves spoke to me. If you continue by sea, the weather will be fair and you will arrive in the north safely. Advisable it is that you sail with Brandon, to the Lake of Eyes and the great Grianán of Aileach. The omens are best for you at those places. You have not, I think, been to either before."

"No, lady. When I left Erin it was from Leinster to the Giant's Causeway I went, and then across the water to Dalriada."

"Go to the Lake of Eyes by sea. Do not, whatever else you do, travel there by land, or slayers will intercept you. On that the omens were unequivocal for once. The luckiest way by far to proceed is by sea."

"To avoid slayers, is it? And Ruarc Sunspear would send them?"

"No one else at all. For his pride he would rather meet you in single fight, but he has much to do and cannot indulge all his preferences. You would be more vulnerable to spirits of fire on the land, also, and Ruarc can summon those—another good reason for you to travel by sea. Fire spirits fear little, but they dread water."

"I know he can summon fire spirits, wise *banfili*. I have seen him do that, at Rochusa, but there I was able to stop them, with the magic of Golden Singer."

"This about fire spirits," Befind said, looking at him intently, "and you were wise to remember it. They are inconstant, given to whim, hard to compel, and not possible to control at all from much of a distance. Ruarc must be close to you if he would use them to destroy you. I know more of water, but this I comprehend about fire. You as yet, I think, Felimid mac Fal, know only the most refined form, the fire of poetry. Dicuil dealt with the raw tameless fire that devours, and Ruarc Sunspear is his pupil, who learned his magic at Dicuil's knee."

"Dicuil," Felimid murmured, "was not subtle."

"Dicuil," Befind said, "wished to possess that harp you named, Golden Singer, because she is one of the Danann treasures. One of three that are left on the ridge of the earth. Now Sunspear wishes the same, and so long as you keep Golden Singer close about you, he will not try to consume you with fire, because that would burn her too. Keep her close at all times when you reach the north. She's a talisman that protects your life. From fire, at least."

"I'll cherish your advice as if each word was gold itself," the bard promised.

"For your own sake, do." Befind's unsentimental gaze raked his face. "Before they died, Fergus and Umai surely told you about the notables Ruarc—King Ruarc, now—has gathered about him, and in particular, Taladh Teisne."

She did not utter it as a question, but as a fact.

"My master Suibni did also."

"Taladh Teisne is the greatest seer in all of the north. He has no equal there, and maybe none in the south, either."

A little derisively, Felimid said, "His eyes never close and he sees through stone. So common chatter goes. I know that he sees the future, with mighty few errors, which is more significant; I can't think of a use for the power to see through stone. It means he will have foreseen my coming and told Sunspear."

"Clearly!" Befind said. "Something else is known among seers and Druids and *filidh*, which Taladh Teisne will have imparted to Sunspear, and which I don't doubt Suibni the Chief Bard imparted to you. There are conditions upon the manner of Sunspear's death. He cannot die at all but through triple causes—wounding with a weapon, and burning, and a third kind of death about which there are contradictory assertions. Some say drowning, some crushing, some far more improbable kinds of extinction, but all agree on a threefold death or none."

"Yes, respected *banfili*. Suibni did tell me. A hard riddle it is to read." Felimid considered it. "Were I simple, I would say it makes the bold Ruarc immortal!"

"He's simple himself, in his fashion." (Felimid knew that.) "He proclaims himself descended from Lugh. He may be. You have seen how the sun's light appears to love him. Portents and prophetic trances do show a restriction on the way he can die. Keep that in mind! And take care that you keep Golden Singer close. He will go to any lengths to separate you from the harp and possess her."

"I'll keep that in mind always," the bard promised, "and go to any lengths myself to see that he doesn't."

Muadnait, the cowled attendant, spoke for the first time. "If he succeeds, he will have no more reason to refrain from sending you a fiery visitor. I know what they can do. My father was the king of a *tuath*, and when I was tiny, he defied the exactions of Dicuil. Beings of flame descended on his hall, his fort, and everything burned, my father and mother too. I almost did. My brother, my fine elder brother, wrapped me in a drenched shawl and carried me out of the fort, but he died of burns afterwards. My leg was burned, and I limp, but I lived." Her voice seemed to blaze, too. "Not only my leg."

She pushed back her cowl. A puckered burn, plainly years old, disfigured one cheek and that side of her jaw.

The scar tissue pulled down that eye at the corner, not to an extreme degree, but sufficiently to notice. Her forehead and the other side of her face were smooth as new cream. She stared at him with somber, steady grey eyes.

"When I heard that you had slain Dicuil, I danced for very joy, bad leg or none."

Felimid had seen worse things than her face, much worse, and he beheld it with equanimity. "Truth is that I did not precisely slay him; I slew his demon father, in a tower beyond this world, because I would have died else. I never knew it would mean Dicuil's death also. But so it was. He died when his sire did. For your kindred and you, and many others, it seems, that was past due. I am glad I settled your debt with him. Dicuil the Fiery had walked on earth and breathed air for too long, oh Muadnait."

"More truth," she said. She replaced her cowl. Out of nowhere, quite calmly, she said, "I would sail to Aileach with you and the monks."

Eichra, impulsively, laughed. Felimid's own impulse was to refuse, and the refusal was on his tongue, but he withheld it and asked mildly, "Why do you wish that?"

"Because I'll be of use!" she said with hot passion. "I am not the greatest of seers, but I know, always, when fire magic is employed near me. I'll know without fail if Sunspear, Dicuil's own pupil, is near and practising such. The scars on my face and leg tell me. They itch wildly, and at once. Once I am closer, say two days' journey a-horse, I can tell you where Ruarc Sunspear is, whether he abides or whether he travels, for he is the most potent vessel of fiery magic in the north, and to me he will show like a beacon." She amended, "The most potent now that Dicuil is extinct. Are you *sure* that is so?"

"Yes. Sure as sunrise. I stumbled over his corpse the night he died, and I saw him shrouded on his bier. Before I lied to you about that I would take a hot coal on my tongue. Are *you* sure of what you say?"

"It is truth and I attest it," Befind said in her sharp voice. "I advise, also, that Muadnait remain on this isle and not ship with you to Aileach, but that is hers to decide. She's cognizant that Dicuil the Fiery still threatens all who oppose his purposes, even though dead, and will as long as his pupil Sunspear is devoted to those purposes. Nor will Sunspear ever abandon them."

"Which is mere truth, for I never met another man so sure of being right," Felimid agreed. "The chief of your college advises soundly, O Muadnait. I'd stay here. For your sake I say it, though your help would be priceless."

"I have her leave, and I would go even if it meant I was barred from the college, which is my home. I will be of use, and more than use; you will need me. Befind herself has seen that, though she did not tell you."

"And I am displeased that you did," Befind snapped.

"If you refuse me passage in your curragh, I will go to Aileach and meet you there," Muadnait said resolutely.

The bard believed her. "Then I think you had better go with us. For any protection we can give you, and for the warnings and prognostications you can give us, which I do not discount. My oath as a bard, from this day till we part, harm done you is harm done me."

Muadnait knew what that promise meant from the mouth of a bard. Just briefly, within the cowl, Felimid saw her eyes widen and tears glitter. Then she lowered her head in a nod, and the sight was hidden in the cowl so quickly that he might have imagined it.

Chapter Six

In the Royal House were three times fifty rooms, and the walls were made of red yew, with copper rivets. And Conchubor's own room was on the ground, and the walls of it faced with bronze, and silver up above, with gold birds on it, and their heads set with shining carbuncles; and there were nine partitions from the fire to the wall, and thirty feet the height of each partition. And there was a silver rod before Conchubor with three golden apples on it, and when he shook the rod or struck it, all in the house would be silent.

—The Courting of Emer

Ruarc Sunspear smiled a grave, kingly, dignified smile. One of those fortunate men who look imposing and royal even when naked, he was not naked then, but clad in a swan-white tunic with red and gold spirals at the borders, a belt of heavy gold about his waist, each link wrought in the shape of the intricate Dara knot, and a golden torc of antique form around his muscled neck. The twisted, shining strands formed a thick cable ending in a pair of great gold rings, spirals running around them, with the unusual feature of an ornate catch to close the collar. Most such torcs, gold, silver or bronze, were open at the front.

Sunspear went bare-headed. His coiled hair and thick moustaches gleamed bright as his belt and collar. Gold gleamed also on the great seat of judgement where he sat before his house, the restored House of the Red Branch as he proudly called it; gold inlaid in the carved bog-deal of the judgment seat's sides and arms, and hammered gold over the tines of an extinct deer's mighty antlers that spread behind the chair's back. Nine men were needed to carry that chair back and forth—a potent symbol of substance, ancientry and power.

At the right side of his judgement chair stood Taladh Teisne, poet, magician and seer. His grey hair and white-streaked beard both fell thick and long. He upon Sunspear's left was younger, and handsome, with a manner that could make a declaration of war seem amiable—Cuanach mac Rudgal, spokesman and messenger. Some viewed him as a mere court ornament. They were wrong.

The broad grassy space before Ruarc's house held the usual crowd of retainers and guests. Three subordinate kings in the forefront feigned dignified amity and wondered how best to increase their power at the others' expense. Ninedo, the oldest, in control of four tuatha, was also dominant—for the present.

Ruarc's close friends, all young, all poets and arrogant in that status, stood proud before the other poets and learned men. The vicious satirist Mathgadro was probably the most feared. The aggressive hothead Tachdan, Ruarc's cousin, a good man with weapons as with panegyrics, stood beside thick-skulled Dub Dothar mac Gai, whose strength was a byword but whose poems were three times longer in the making than his fellows'. Niall of the clan Uí Dunchada, prolific in poetry like Tachdan, especially in the praise of beautiful women, had a name also as a horseman and leader of swift mounted raids. Like the others, he was arrogant and extortionate; like the others, he was encouraged by Sunspear in this behaviour.

Like the others, he hated Felimid mac Fal.

Jurists in long tunics stood available to give their legal wisdom as Sunspear heard cases and appeals. His bodyguard, the red-headed and redoubtable offspring of Dicuil the Fiery, flanked him and watched the crowd, a full three dozen of them, all ready to slay without hesitation if the king should be threatened. (Or on whim if he were not.) The woman Sirega, she who had fought so bloodily at Druim Derg, stood with feet planted wide apart and held, fondly, her terrible barbed spear. Her hot blue glance dated suspiciously back and forth. She commanded Sunspear's personal guard, which consisted exclusively of her male kindred, and even they were chary of crossing her.

From the solar balcony of the royal house, another woman watched the scene below, reclining contentedly on a silk-covered couch, as indolent as Sirega was energetic, her great blue eyes dreamy rather than fierce and watchful. This was Sunspear's mistress, Aivene, the one who—so far—had lasted the longest. She meant to last longer, though she was too realistic to think she would ever be his queen; for that he was sure to look higher. She was aware, too, that she was hardly his exclusive leman even now. There were other comely women in Emain Macha. Many.

A king of the Ulaid had come to Airgialla that day, also, bringing his daughter and obviously hoping for an alliance sealed by marriage. Aivene had her own thoughts about that. The Ulaid was a truncated remnant of a larger, stronger kingdom of former times, maybe not a sufficiently powerful ally to attract Sunspear, and while Caragh, the daughter, was fair, Aivene outshone her easily. Aivene outshone most. But she did not on that account deceive herself that Ruarc would maintain her forever.

His strong resonant voice came clearly to her ears as he heard several suits and appeals. He ruled, as he usually did, in accordance with the ancient laws, shunning favouritism towards the wealthy and great. Whatever else he might be, he was not narrow. Besides, his devotion to Erin's ancient institutions and laws was a thing he proclaimed too loudly, too often, for any crass breach thereof.

The case before him now involved just that. A high-ranking cattle-chief had expropriated a poorer man, then sent bullies to threaten him when he protested by fasting, close to the chief's dwelling. Protest by fasting had from time immemorial been valid, calling for the one fasted against to give justice or face penalties.

Ruarc wished all cases that came before him were so clear and easy.

Before he could pronounce, he heard mighty yells and a drumbeat of hoofs, approaching fast. A herd of lowing cattle bunched close together appeared, racing across the plain, driven hard by fifteen red-haired riders. Slowing the weary beasts to a halt near the royal enclosure, the leaders dismounted and walked forward, grinning, to salute Ruarc Sunspear with casual respect. Sweating, dusty, and rank with cattle slavers, they still showed the common signs of descent from Dicuil, most marked and visible being their lean strong bodies and their hair, invariably several shades of red on the one head, copper, bronze, saffron, sandy or auburn, in streaks or flecks but always in conspicuous contrast. Not immediately visible, but well known, was their readiness to kill.

"Our pleasure, Sunspear!" cried the foremost, a tall warrior as young as the king. Two severed heads dangled from the saddle of the horse he led. Their eyes were sunken, their bloody jaws clamped in the rigour of death. "Our pleasure and respect! We bring gifts from that munificent king, Illann of Leinster!"

"We are appreciative of his gift," Ruarc said, smiling, "and your hard work in bringing it! Give the beasts to the cowherds to pen, then come and drink."

Bending forward, Cuanach the advisor said with a frown, "Illann could bring war for this, lord."

Ruarc laughed outright. "For a mere cattle raid? I think not. He's welcome to raid us in return if he pleases.

We'll try to give him good sport. And war? We could handle Leinster by ourselves if we had to, but the Uí Néill would support us; they are so obliged. Illann knows it. You fret too much."

Cuanach straightened, his forehead clearing. The king was probably correct, unless Illann, expensively, brought hired warriors from abroad. Whatever happened, Cuanach meant to avoid any fighting in his own person. That unnatural breed, the Fir Dicuil, would rush to it exultantly, and they were welcome.

"Now! A return to business." Ruarc bent a steady, devouring gaze on the cattle-chief before him. "You know the law. You knew it when you set it as nothing. The plaintiff, here, made protest, and notification, and warrant, to you ten days in advance, as the laws require, then sat without food or drink at your door, and his appeal was just, but you refused it. For such unjust refusal, the law of the *feine* is that you shall pay double the amount for which he fasted against you. *Let this be paid.*"

The chief reddened in wrath and opened his mouth.

"Judgement is done!" Ruarc thundered. "Pay! And if attack or beatings befall the plaintiff, it may be that you yourself will have visitors—with parti-coloured red hair. Yes. It is possible."

Comical as the phrase sounded, the cattle-chief did not smile, but paled visibly. A visit from the Fir Dicuil, with the variegated red hair common to their clan, was a visit from death. He muttered acquiescence and withdrew.

"A true judgement!" Tachdan the Sudden said enthusiastically to the faintly smiling—but shut-lipped as usual—Mathgadro. "A noble decision, eh?"

"Oh, noble and true indeed," the satirist answered low. He smirked. "One may question if our golden king would impose the penalties of law on one of *us* who committed the same violation."

"Careful," Tachdan growled. "He's my cousin—and he would never let the matter come to that."

"A public fasting petition? No. I think he would not. Besides, that chief was due for slapping down a little. Ruarc is not reckless and fancy free these days, Tachdan, as he used to be; he's a king, and an over-king, and obliged to behave like it. Which he does well! Do not misapprehend me and burst out in ire! I am just observing that who stands athwart his path to power will find in short time that he's no longer standing, so."

Tachdan bit on a retort. Mathgadro's smooth sneers often failed to be smooth enough for him. Tachdan found them outright flinty.

There was another present who thought Ruarc's verdict worth admiring. The Ulidian king's daughter parted her lips and breathed, "That was just and true. Maybe, maybe, he does descend from Conchubor mac Nessa and rule through the Prince's Truth. Surely he's a fine looking man."

"That he is," her father Tadg said emphatically. "Were he your husband you would do well, my Caragh."

Caragh was young, and her heart beat faster as she looked at the magnificent Ruarc. However, she had a brain too, and she said to herself:

Oh my too-hopeful father, it's known that he seeks powerful allies, and we are not. Equally it's known that he wants a woman of the most beautiful in Erin for his queen, and sure I am fair, but I am not in that company. Maybe I'm fortunate, to judge by the looks she of the ravishing shape on that sun balcony yonder is giving me!

That'll be Aivene. I have heard of that one. I can perceive the poison in her glance from here! If Ruarc Sunspear did favour me, I'd be careful of Aivene.

Maybe neither of us will be his queen in the end. Maybe he will wed a daughter or niece of clan Uí Néill.

It's likely enough he will hold out marriage to himself as a bait to many kingly houses, playing for power, for a couple of years yet.

But he's a fine-looking man. An over-king. And his courage in battle is no mere fabrication of his court poets. He slew Failge Berraide!

A poet himself, too.

Caragh ascribed jealous hatred to Aivene that was not really there, for hate and ambition were foreign to her essentially casual nature. Aivene knew as well as Caragh that

Sunspear played for power, and that she did not hold any keys thereto. Nor did she deceive herself that Sunspear felt passion for her intense enough to outweigh his craving to rule.

Taladh Teisne the Druid had small concern, then, with Ruarc's choice of a consort. He had carried out auguries the night before. If the demanding ritual had not left him exhausted and senseless until dawn, he would have spoken to Sunspear before the legal hearings or any other events of the day had started. Now he made urgent request of him for an audience in the royal apartments, wishing, not for the first time, that kings in Erin were able to follow the practice of Byzantine tyrants and turn their servants into deaf-mutes to ensure secret matters stayed secret.

It was a measure of the value Sunspear placed upon his prophet-magician that he granted the solicitation at once.

The suite lay at the centre of the Red Branch House. It had been constructed as much like the original—or as much in the form the original was touted by legend to have had—as could be. A circle of red yew pillars surrounded the king's great bed, with bronze rivets and collars on each. The domed ceiling could not be pure silver, as it was in legend. Expert carpenters had made it, instead, of ash ribs steamed into curves with bent wicker panels between them, and men cunning in plaster—work had been brought from distant Spain to cover the wattle with finest gypsum, mixed with crushed oyster shells and gleaming white sand. The result did shine rather like silver, particularly at night by lamps. The chamber had carved panels and tapestries below, and patterned mats on the floor in many colours that almost hid the strewn rushes. Sunspear had Taladh Teisne sit and offered him Gaulish wine with his own kingly hand.

"In a few words," he told the aged man.

Taladh Teisne opened the mouth between his gaunt cheeks and spoke through what was still, in his eld, a full set of teeth, though discoloured.

"Felimid mac Fal will come north on the blue sea. Not willingly will he come here, to the House of the Red Branch, but he will go by choice to Aileach, the citadel of the Cenél nEógain. With him will be four companions. I have seen. A foster brother, a henchman, another man who is not human, and a woman of knowledge, are the four. He means to curtail your kingship, and of all folk now breathing in Erin, there is no other, even among her kings, who may be able to achieve it."

"If he lives," Sunspear qualified.

"If he lives."

"Then fortunately there's an answer. It's forbidden for bard to kill bard, but none of the Fir Dicuil are bards! Neither are most of the mighty Uí Néill. Withal, it would look better if he did not perish while my guest here at Emain

Macha, and that suits me, for I'd rather eat dung than invite him!"

"Yea, lord, but by my advice you should invite him. He's under your hand, in your power, here at Emain Macha, and here you can watch what he is doing. He might die in many ways that would not harm your honour. He might even be caught in treachery towards you. There were portents that I could not scan clearly. One prognosticates a triple death. What that may mean I do not know. Perhaps the death of Felimid mac Fal and two of his companions."

Ruarc Sunspear roared with uninhibited laughter. "My fine and wonderfully prudent Taladh, my valued spring of advice! You are knowing as you know your own name that while he walked the ridge of the earth, my master Dicuil foretold that I could not die, descended from the all-competent sun god, but by three means at the same time. You have seen that yourself. Others have seen it. It's scarcely a secret and could not be kept one, not that I would try, for I haven't the patience and by my forebear Lugh's long hand I detest secrets. They always come out."

"This upstart Felimid will have heard of that fate if anybody has," Taladh Teisne said balefully.

"Oh, no doubt," Ruarc agreed. "I've had the prophecy told to me more than once in hopes of reward. Nobody knows how such a triple death can be, and more to the point, nobody has prophesied *when* my death will overtake me. Therefore I'm not troubled. All men die. But indeed, if a triple death is imminent, and must be, I propose to ensure it is that of Felimid and two of his companions, nor am I particular which two! Then that which is foretold may come true with no inconvenience to us."

"I am for that. I saw shadows over the Red Branch House as well. It is cloaked in mist, but there is a way to dispel the mist, a way to gain clearer sight of the future. A sacrifice. The sacrifice of a man."

The king's broad forehead knotted. "I like those not."

"Great Dicuil offered them at times. Our ancestors of old offered them. At Samhain, at gatherings, when a king was inaugurated."

"True."

Once Ruarc would have refused to say it. Once, before he was a king, he had challenged a man and killed him for accusing Dicuil the Fiery of human sacrifice. He had refused to believe it. He knew better now. Taladh Teisne's words were true, that their wild forebears had done so, in Erin and Britain too, and Gaul. Gaius Julius Caesar had told the truth about that, if about little else.

"I'd not sacrifice just anybody for the sake of advantage," Ruarc said, considering, "and some rank criminal would not be worthy the purpose." His mouth formed a smile that was not pleasant. "The bishopric, as they call it, of Armagh is handy; they are our near neighbours and they have annoyed us by their presence too long. By the

Sun! Bishop Ailill is their greatest man. If he vanishes with no trace it ought to dismay them. Two ends met in one."

"A fine notion," the seer agreed. His face was grim, but grim with satisfaction.

Chapter Seven

"Fair is the plain, the plain of the noble yoke," said Cuchulain.

"No one comes to this plain," said she, "who does not go out in safety from Samhain to Oimell, and from Oimell to Beltaine, and again from Beltaine to Bron Trogain."

"Everything you have commanded, so it will be done by me," said Cuchulain.

"And the offer you have made me, it is accepted, it is taken, it is granted," said Emer. —The Courting of Emer

"The *banfili* saw truly. It's said that she usually does."

Tuathal gazed on the shores of the Lake of Eyes. A deep, dog-legged inlet of the sea, blue as sapphire in the sun, it lay between fair hills on either side. They had arrived after a journey that from Aran onward had been one of fair weather and—mostly—convenient wind. When they had turned inconvenient, the bard had been able to soothe them into gentleness on the strings of Golden Singer. Such had been Befind's vision, and so it had turned out.

"Indeed, so it usually does," Muadnait told him. "When her predictions are to do with the sea, I have never known her mistaken."

"Nor I," agreed Odhran.

His own awareness of the sea's moods had been useful as they rode the waves. He had been more than useful the day one of the younger monks, Sochal, had toppled over the side in a sudden blow. Sochal was a weak swimmer and his fellows had been wholly occupied for a while keeping the curragh safe, so there was soon a perilous distance between the ship and the man overboard.

Odhran had cast off his kilt and donned his seal-skin in a moment. His transformation began even as he leaped into the water. Being a man of middling size, he made a small bull seal, but swifter, more clever, and large enough to support Sochal in the waves. He bore him back to the curragh's side. Getting Sochal inboard again in his sodden robe was easy; doing the same for the selchie was not. In the end he swam playfully next to the vessel until it made landfall again.

Muadnait, the bard saw, had been delighted by his antics and several times laughed aloud at them—a good thing, as she had been a sober presence aboard until then.

It pleased him well that the last part, the longest, of this journey had been light. His strained back had recovered before they left Aran, but he had not wished to weather any more wild squalls, and still less lasting storms. On his mother's recommendation, and his own memories of Befind, he had trusted her advice. Now he was here, in Cenél nEógain territory, the greatest—or the second greatest, depending on who was talking—of the Uí Néill kindreds.

The Lake of Eyes. He found the name apt. His bardic senses told him that ancient, watching presences haunted the sea-lough, among them ghosts of the ice giants whose grinding tread had scoured it out ages ago, the ice giants who were the everlasting enemies of the gods, in the belief of Nordic folk like the Danes. More recently, but still centuries past, human folk had raised the stone forts and monuments that looked down from the blue hills, and their ghosts too watched the curragh that skimmed past them, ephemeral as a mayfly. Nor were ghostly eyes the only ones that watched them. Enough human, mortal observers from hidden vantages were thinking they might be pirates.

"King Muirchertach will welcome a bard and a band of monks," Odhran said, his dark eyes on the shores ahead, "but it's less kind he may be to a selchie, and we are wary of human kings and lords."

"With cause," Felimid agreed. "You wish to leave us?"

The seal-man absolutely bridled. "Not for good and all! I'll be nearby in this lough, let you see, and you have but to call my name, or play on Golden Singer by the shore." He spoke to the bard, but his gaze strayed to Muadnait, and she looked frankly back. "There are other selchies here, too, and even you constant denizens of the land can tell us from utter seals by looking. There is a tribe of us entire in the Lake of Eachad, bear in mind, and its western shore is part of Sunspear's borders. Maybe your conflict with him will take you that far. The monastery of Armagh is nearby, also, and you may even find you must be visiting there."

"I reckon those fools, like the ones at Skellig Michael, call selchies soulless beings and will even try to exorcise them someday," Eichra predicted.

The bard thought with a pang that, yes, someone would one day, and if he waited until the power of the Cross had advanced, and that of the old gods waned further, he might have success.

Odhran stood then, and pulled on his sealskin as he had done before, changing in a few heartbeats. His manly shoulders narrowed, his hands shrank, his arms became flippers and his legs clawed vestiges. With a bark he lolloped over the curragh's side, splashed in the water, rolled and vanished.

A couple of the monks crossed themselves, and Tuathal muttered, "I'll never grow accustomed to that." Muadnait stared in wonder. Brother Sochal acknowledged it was a marvel. "But a marvel of God, surely. The day I fell over the side I'd have been lost but for Odhran. Sad am I for his departure. His company is well worth its space."

"On the sea," Eichra conceded. "Not on the land, and he knows it. We may not see him again; they do forget easily."

"It's his right to come and go as he likes," Felimid said.

He gazed ahead. Fishing boats rode at their moorings, two longships, a few curraghs, all larger than the monks', and even one surprising round-bellied merchant ship whose like Felimid had not seen since he returned to Erin. Probably it had come from Leinster with foreign goods. Whatever its origin, its most likely cargo was wine, that ever-welcome maker of glad hearts, and would find a good market here because of the wealthy kingdom Ruarc had made out of Airgialla.

In just three years. How, how did he do that? Sorcery's in it, surely, some gift or power that Dicuil bequeathed him. And I'll find out what it was or I am not the grandson of Fergus and Umai.

Muadnait, thinking along the same lines, said speculatively, "I wonder if Sunspear has spies in Aileach?"

"If I were Sunspear, I would make sure I did!" Eichra assured her.

"I don't know," Felimid said. "Sunspear is proud, and makes quite a parade of being so great that he has no need of subterfuge or deceit."

"What he says and what he does may not be the same," Tuathal offered, and Eichra's sardonic snort agreed.

"No . . . and Mathgadro or, from what I have heard, Taladh Teisne, would be well likely to place spies yonder on their own initiative, if their lord did not. There'll be open envoys and messengers of Sunspear's at Aileach, in any event. He will soon have news of our coming, if he does not know now. I hope it irks him like an itch he cannot scratch."

"A prospect of delight," Eichra agreed. "He's proud, though, as you say. Be careful he does not come here and challenge you himself."

"Well, I must just meet that chance as it comes, and practice each day till it does."

Sea-stained and itching with salt, they went ashore with their belongings and were promptly greeted by itinerant folk with horses for barter or hire. The travelers chose pack and riding beasts, and made their way up steep hill slopes clad in bracken and turf to the fortress of Aileach. Its grey unmortared stones rose above them, closely fitted, the three concentric ramparts so vast they had surely been the work of the mighty Dagda in the age of bronze, even as legend declared.

Or maybe not so surely, Felimid's gibing, irreverent side whispered to him. *Maybe not. You saw the ruins of many a mighty structure in Britain, the wall in the north and the sky-tall lighthouse in Kent, and others, and they were built by Romans, not gods.*

No matter. Aileach was awesome. It crowned the hill royally, each entrance more like a tunnel through the triple ramparts than a doorway. The legions of Rome in their pride would have had no easy task taking it.

Outside, on the hill-slopes, cattle grazed and riders on fine horses guarded them. There were byres and huts and at least one carefully dug well. The interior could not be seen. Felmid knew, though, that an imposing hall occupied the centre of that circular space. Its slate roof showed above the ramparts. Half a dozen warriors walked those ramparts, watching the countryside and the steel-blue Lake of Eyes. Some were bare-headed; a couple wore hard leather caps. Their spear-points glittered.

Two more men stood before the main entrance, a gateway with a massive stone lintel. They wore saffron tunics edged with red under iron-studded leather vests, and their round shields carried the famed Uí Néill emblem of the red hand. Besides their spears, they bore long swords, always a sign that these were men of high rank, likely two of the king's companions, his personal war-band.

"Welcome," one of them said. Seeing the harp on Felimid's back, he asked courteously, "May we know your names and families?"

Felimid and the others gave them. When they heard the name Felimid mac Fal, the warriors' eyes changed and one of them even started. They looked at each other. Then they looked back at Felimid with a grave gaze.

So, the bard thought. *Now it truly begins.*

Chapter Eight

"It is what I think," said Fingan, "you will hardly see the calves that are following your cows at this time grow to be yearlings; or if you do itself," he said, "it will not be much use your life will be to you."

"That is what all the others said to me," said Cethern, "and it is not much profit or credit they got by it, and it is not much you yourself will get." —The Awakening of Ulster

"It's a delight to see your honest smiling face again, Mathgadro."

Felimid smiled himself while he said it, as winningly as if he'd been sincere. They sat with the other poets and bards in the wide booth for that class of men—and women—in King Muirchertach's hall. There were others for monks, lawyers, smiths and the rest.

Gazing into the pale pits of malice and jealousy that were Mathgadro's eyes, he felt, trivially enough (knowing how gladly the other would knife him), pleased that he sat there vastly better clad than the other bard. He had bathed as soon as he arrived—Golden Singer in her case close beside him, his companions on guard—and dressed in garments from his chest, garments Pendor had created for him by his own peculiar sort of magic.

Mathgadro, despite his own fine tunic, looked shabby by comparison. More importantly, being now a lower rank of bard than Felimid, he had not the right to wear as many different colours on a public occasion. That sign of lesser status rankled. He smiled, as Felimid said, but the smile was steeped in adder's venom.

"I do not think so. I think you remember the promise Ruarc made you, three years gone."

"Hmm, somewhat, now that you mention it." Felimid yawned ostentatiously. "Unfriendly and fierce and hateful the promise was. I am told he has established himself in a pleasant little kingdom hereabouts, though, so I think he should be content with that."

"He will never be content until our master Dicuil is avenged," Mathgadro spat. "Dicuil whom you murdered!"

Felimid met the poisoned gaze with a level one of his own. "That matter was settled in a Test of Truth before a tribunal of bards. I'd have been stricken deaf and dumb had I lied thereat. You were there—you and Ruarc Sunspear—before you left with Dicuil's shrouded body. Do you say that is not so, Bluetongue?"

"A tribunal of bards in the *south*." Mathgadro said, as if the word *south* was foul. "Under the influence of your teacher Suibni! What is that worth?"

"Suibni neither headed the tribunal nor was part of it. You well know that. Had I lied, the ban of the bard's pact with truth would have come on me. I never slew Dicuil; I slew his demon instrument, not knowing Dicuil had such a bond with it that he'd die too, in consequence. Two attempts on my life had he made by then, and was preparing a third. He fell on his own acts. Say that I lie, honest Mathgadro, and I'll accept that you believe it." Felimid smiled more winningly than before. "But I'll also invite you to fight me to back your belief."

Eichra the Eel exclaimed later, "Oh! My grief that I missed hearing that! And missed seeing Bluetongue's face!"

He missed hearing it because he, and Tuathal, were seated in the booth of the warriors, not among the bards. Besides weapon-men of Aileach, and guests from foreign parts, they shared that long table with two of the Fir Dicuil who had accompanied Mathgadro from the Red Branch House, first cousins named Senan and Cathal, alike as twins, tall rangy hard-muscled fellows, their chestnut hair shot with pale copper streaks and a dark patch at the crown. Not a contrast naturally seen, it still owed nothing to dye and everything to their heritage from an inhuman great-grandsire. Eichra, contrary as usual, disbelieved that, no matter what Felimid told him or anyone else said, but he refrained from picking a quarrel and so, he found with a certain regret, did Senan and Cathal.

Mathgadro was the one giving his spite free rein. In the poets' booth he stared disdainfully at Felimid—and at Muadnait, who was there also, as a *banfili*.

"Fight, eh? Yes, you would liefer do that, I know, than undergo a new test, a tribunal of bards not aligned with you and your kindred."

"A tribunal of bards in the *north*?" Felimid said, words and tone the precise echo of Mathgadro's, mocking him. "Influenced by Ruarc Sunspear? What is that worth?"

"What does your companion say, then?" Mathgadro challenged. He stared at Muadnait with ostentatious scorn. "Mighty silent so far. So, well, I do not suppose you brought her on this journey to talk, but even you could do better for a bedmate than this half-burnt tree, surely."

Muadnait stiffened, but she did not turn pale. It was Felimid who did that, and he whitened, the sudden glitter of his green eyes all the more conspicuous for it. Muadnait had not come to the table wearing her cowl; she had boldly exposed her face, daring comment, and none until now had made untoward remarks, not even in wine. None until now.

She had brushed her brown hair until it gleamed and dressed it in an ornate coiffure. *Pride*, Felimid thought, and he approved, as well as admiring her courage in doing it. The burn scars on cheek and jaw made a horrid contrast to the rest of her face. She had seldom been in any company but that of the *banfilidh* for years, and this was an over-king's dun. Nevertheless she held her nerves and her voice even.

"My face is a memento of your master's kindness, Mathgadro Bluetongue. I am King Ibair's daughter, the one who survived when Dicuil—a curse on his name!—called fire spirits on Ibair's house. Only I. My brother carried me out of the blaze and died for his courage. The fate of Dicuil was past due and I am glad I lived to hear of it."

"I ask your pardon," Mathgadro said. "I did not know you for a king's daughter. And who would? I took you for a *cumal*."*

"You did not," Felimid said in a voice like honey, "unless your usual fine perception failed you, and that I cannot credit. So it must have been an intended insult. Unlike you, I take no delight in satires that injure, but truly I think you should ask this *banfili* of Aran's pardon, or I may forget that."

"*Banfili* of Aran! Even if that's true, shall I, the Airgialla king's companion, take notice of it? Aran! A seaside coven of witches who are said to lure ships to the rocks and devour drowned sailors' corpses that wash ashore! At best a kelp-stinking hut of driftwood where hags live on better folk's bounty." Snarling the words, Mathgadro worked himself into a blacker rage. "You would both be stunned mute if you set eyes on the Red Branch House."

---

*A female slave, whose value was estimated as that of three milch cows.

"All of the first part is lies and the last part unconvincing to me," Muadnait said calmly. But only her voice was calm. Her body was tense and her legs quivered, as Felimid, seated beside her, could tell better than any. "I've no more words to waste on you."

"I have a few," Felimid said. "You have not asked Muadnait's pardon yet. Unless you do I shall call you forth for a combat, of poet's satire if you are as deadly a satirist as they say (but remember how Tachdan mac Lugo fared when he tried), or with swords if you prefer."

"Oh, Tachdan," Mathgadro said. "Yes. He lives in hope of encountering you again."

He smiled broadly, he who seldom opened his mouth more than a chink. His tongue, unpleasantly long, mobile and narrow, showed for a heartbeat, indigo like his palate and gums. Some, intimidated, said the poison power of his satires caused it, while others averred it was a childish effect he brought about by chewing woad. But the second group did not say that to his face.

"Tachdan must be patient yet. In the meantime I'm not inclined to quail before an extortioner's discoloured grin. The small matter of combat by satire or sword? We were discussing that. If you refuse both, and won't ask pardon, I will proclaim you a coward, north and south, in all forms of verse, until you can show your face nowhere, least of all in Airgialla among your friends."

"Senan and Cathal are two sworders here who would cut you in pieces, saving me the trouble! And Ruarc the king, if those two failed, which is not likely."

"Oh, by Lugh of the Long Hand, from whom Ruarc claims descent! This to me? To me, who overthrew Koschei the Deathless and proved that Dicuil was far from deathless? You threaten me with Dicuil's mere grandsons? Or Dicuil's mere pupil? Let that come if it comes. My dispute here and now is with you. I advise you to ask the *banfili*'s pardon."

"You know little of Ruarc Sunspear," Mathgadro said more quietly, though his pale eyes still seethed with rancour. "He has powers that even great Dicuil did not exert."

That rang unexpectedly and wholly true, and there was a note of gloating in it. Felimid took notice. He told himself to give thought to it.

"Still it is no secret that Ruarc cherishes you for himself," Mathgadro continued, "and will be angered if I cheat him. I ask pardon, then. For that reason only."

"Bold words," Eichra said from the corner of his mouth, "but he shrinks just the same from facing the mac Fal's sword *or* his satire."

Muadnait made a scornful nod. Mathgadro subsided into silent vexation, perceptibly dreaming of what Ruarc would do to Felimid when the time was opportune.

Perhaps it was best that a servant in madder-red tunic approached at that moment.

"Nobly born Felimid," he said, "the king desires to welcome you and the *banfili* Muadnait."

Felimid gave Muadnait his arm. They stepped into the long aisle on the northern side of the hall, and walked past booths of smiths, shipwrights and warriors. In the latter Felimid noticed—they were hard to miss—the parti-coloured red heads of Senan and Cathal. They marked his passing. Under that three-toned hair, their eyes glittered colder than ice.

He ignored the pair.

He had not entered a royal hall—unless the shadowed abode of Donn, the Grey Man, or the king of Leinster's huge long pavilion at Oenach Carman, counted as such—since his return to Erin. Muirchertach's was ruggedly built of oak pillars, with closely jointed planks in between. The rafters had been adzed out of reddish-brown deal hauled from bogs, skilled carpentry such as only chiefs, and great ones, could command or pay for. Above the rafters were the roof's thick slates, which Niall of the Nine Hostages himself, it was said, had ordered brought from Dumnonian quarries by sweating shipmen in the days when none, in Erin or Britain, mocked a request of Niall's.

This place was neither a common royal hall, nor one with any precedent in Erin. No. Not though Aileach had been built long before the clan Uí Néill was founded or even imagined. The Uí Néill were no tribal chiefs, nor the lords of some loose confederation of *tuatha*, coming together and then whirling apart like smoke in the wind, to be forgotten in a year. They were a dynasty, lasting as the rocks of Aileach fortress, and what they took they retained. The madder-dyed tunics and the device of the red hand around Felimid stood for more than vaunting, hot-blooded pride and personal glory. They stood for union and power. The Cenél nEógain of Aileach, here, were only the third part of Uí Néill strength, with the Cenél Conaill immediately to the west making another third.

Further, there were the southern Uí Néill, between Airgialla and Leinster, the last third, and like the Cross-worshippers they were something new, something that might shatter the ancient, sacrosanct concept of the Five Fifths of Erin, the *Coic Coiceda*, headed by five equal kings who even within their own borders could be rejected, in lawful method, by their people should they prove autocratic or unjust.

But maybe autocracy was coming. Ruarc Sunspear surely intended that there should be autocratic kingly rule. *His.*

Muirchertach of Aileach was Niall's great-grandson. He gazed from his kingly seat at the newcomers. Forty or thereby, he had been black-bearded once, but those days were past and his facial hair was grey, though still thick as a furze bush. His hair too was greying. Thick-limbed and powerful, he wore a calf-long maroon tunic sewn with golden discs, and grey trews. Two tall brindled hounds couched at his feet, and neither took food from any hand but his, or bore caresses from any other. Muirchertach, Felimid had heard, prized his hounds and horses and was good-humoured in general. All that seemed promising.

Duinseach, his queen, namely for generous hospitality and magical weaving skill, had enough ordinary human vanity to dye her own greying hair. She had borne Muirchertach a daughter and four sons who lived. She looked at their new guests with interest and some concern. Their presence could well presage trouble, though she knew trouble was apt to come in any case, and from Sunspear's direction, in the end.

The cup-bearer on the couple's left held a flagon, the royal spokesman on the right a wand of office. He owned a good voice for his function, strong and deep as a drum.

"Felimid mac Fal, grandson of the Chief Bard, and Muadnait of the Aran College, *banfili*, you are welcome in honour," he said, and the queen pledged them with a draught from a gold-mounted glass cup.

They responded with courtesies. Muadnait had already presented her college's guest-gift, or rather the monks had done it for her, a giant ivory narwhal horn that Muadnait could not have lifted. Their own gift was a fine scroll of ramskin parchment bearing Muirchertach's genealogy, coloured, illuminated, finely calligraphed in Latin, the work of months, in a cylindrical copper case. Felimid, with a bow, offered his own guest-gift now, a white doe-leather satchel pricked with interwoven indigo patterns, its hasps silver. It bulged. Opened, the budget proved to contain that which made even the king's eyes widen a little; amber, jet and ivory, skeins of many-coloured silk, a flask of scented oil so fine the Emperor at Constantinople would not have disdained it, efficacious, Pendor had sworn, for the stiffness and pain of old battle-wounds, of which Muirchertach had a number. Felimid didn't doubt he would be pleased. Pendor, whatever else he was, had high and deserved repute as a herb-doctor.

The satchel also contained a jet and ivory chess set in a silver-bound case, ornamental even if the king never took to the game. He maintained a kingly gravity where the satchel's other contents were concerned, and said of the chess set, "I've heard of this game you brought to Erin from abroad. Like *fidchell*, is it?"

"Yes, lord, somewhat," Felimid agreed, "though *fidchell* is a hunt game, pack against the quarry, and this derives from battle, with kings, horses, Druids and warriors, each piece moved in its own fashion."

"Roman?" Muirchertach examined a *ceithern*, a naked common soldier with his mouth stretched wide in a battle-roar, his weapon a short axe. Like the other pieces, it showed uncommonly fine detail.

Sunspear

"Persia is where the game started, I was told. I was taught to play by a madman, and while that surely was interesting, it had its dangers, lord. If he found me too contemptible and weak an opponent, he might have had me throttled in disgust, and on the other hand he might have been displeased if I won too often."

"Hmph! I felicitate you on having lived to come home, where the lives of bards are decently held sacred. But I'm told many in the south are coming to love this game. You must play me a round or two."

"Gladly, lord. Yea, it is becoming liked. When you will."

He doubted the king was quite that taken with the game. Looking into the shrewd if short-sighted blue eyes, he suspected Muirchertach was making a pretext for a private conversation or two, on the matter of Sunspear's desire to have Felimid's head on a fence-pole.

As private as any conversation could be in this crowded and communal place.

The king spoke to Muadnait, also, with words of appreciation for her college's aid to many a mariner. She responded in kind, stood tall and spoke clearly. Felimid admired her for it. But as she spoke he remembered her cogent question, "I wonder if Sunspear has spies in Aileach?" and Eichra's answer, "If I were Sunspear, I would make sure I did!"

Who might the spies be?

Mathgadro certainly would know, and never be so maladroit as to associate openly with them. The spies might even be trusted, but suborned or terrorized, members of Muirchertach's household. The cup bearer? The spokesman? One of the bodyguard? A kinsman who wished to be king himself? *That* was a frequent situation.

If it existed here, the spiteful, devious Bluetongue would be one to take advantage of it.

Chapter Nine

"I ask you, Emer," said Cuchulain, "why I may not have my turn in the company of this woman; for in the first place she is well-behaved, comely, well-mannered, worthy of a king, this woman from beyond the waves of the great sea; with form and countenance and high descent; with embroidery . . . with sense and quickness . . ."—The Only Jealousy of Emer

Felimid and Muadnait, wrapped in big four-cornered cloaks against the wind, stood on the highest of Aileach's three ramparts. The bard, as usual, carried the harp Golden Singer, and he wore Kincaid at his side. Within the king's hall he carried no weapons, for that would imply mistrust, but outside it, with Mathgadro and two of the Fir Dicuil in Aileach and bearing a bitter grudge, none, including the king, would question Felimid's wisdom in going armed, or take offence—unless he was the one to provoke violence, and that he meant to avoid. The sword's silver pommel, shaped like a cat's head, glinted beside his hip.

The two looked towards the Lake of Eyes. It had a steely sheen in the afternoon light. The ships moored at the margin were not visible from where they stood.

"I wonder if the seal-man is there," she said.

"No knowing, but he may have chosen well not to be *here*. He'd be vulnerable, and if some vessel of ill-will stole his skin, he'd be at that person's mercy, have to do his bidding."

"I'm sure that was in his mind, though he did not say so." Muadnait knew which "vessel of ill-will" the bard had in mind; it was no subtle or deep question. "He would not wish to work treachery upon us."

She turned to look at him directly, a certain challenge in her face, and he realized again that it was brave of her to leave her Aran sanctuary, facing the stares of oafs. "Treachery," she said again. "We know who will work it, but not in his own person, I think. He's too crafty. He will have tools here in Aileach that we do not know."

"Yes, that's so. We do know his object, though; it is to get his hands on this harp and take her to Ruarc. He desires her even more than revenge on me. That he can always seek, but Golden Singer—can invoke the power of the air, and the earth, and maybe the other elements. I am chary about doing that, for it has consequences, but Ruarc would be reckless and inordinate in pursuit of his ends. He'd roll the seasons like dice."

"He must not have her! But if he wants her so badly, Mathgadro may just have his two attendants, those red men, seize her and flee."

Felimid frowned over the suggestion.

"No," he decided. "I might expect it from Tachdan the Sudden. A sudden attack, me slain—if they can do it—the harp taken, fast horses waiting, a race ahead of

Muirchertach's men to Airgialla—that would be Tachdan. From Dub Dothar, I'd await a challenge to fight. Maybe some sly fellow waiting to steal the harp while we battled and all attention was on the combat. Mathgadro will try something subtler. Treacherous, as you say."

"Can you guard against it?" she asked. She looked anxious.

"There are ways. I had better use them, too. Dicuil the Fiery wanted the harp before he met his end, and Sunspear wants her now." Felimid spoke more vehemently then than was his habit. "He must never have her, Muadnait. Never! There is power in the harp of Cairbre even I did not know before I rose to fourth degree. In your close vicinity she can change the seasons, and once in Britain, I harped a raging torrent to flow gentler. Under Suibni I lately learned her music can open Gates to the Otherworlds, even Gates that have long been reckoned shut forever. Or Gates to the past."

"The Gates *are* closing, more and more," Muadnait agreed. Felimid saw a flash of grief in her eyes. "We know something of them in my college, in especial the Gates in the sea. Golden Singer can open them again?"

"Some of them. Some are shut forever now, and some, especially on the sea, are mighty difficult to find but by accident. I can make a close guess as to one that's on land! Sunspear has built his royal hall on the very site of Emain Macha, seeking to copy the glories of the Red

Branch. It was abandoned since its burning, until he came. Even in Erin there can be few places where the past is more present and forcible. If Sunspear played on her, on Golden Singer, in the right manner—*there*—I can scarce imagine what might occur."

"It's a fearful notion." Muadnait laid a hand on his forearm. "And yet would Sunspear know? He's a rank below you in bardic training, true? *You* were not aware until wise Suibni taught you."

"Sunspear's teacher was Dicuil," came the answer. "That wild Archdruid, as he styled himself and maybe was, could have taught him things he has no business knowing, things he was not ready to master. Our fine Ruarc has many traits, but not patience."

"And he has not pursued his bardic training much since Dicuil died. We know that. He's more concerned with kingcraft and power in these days. And battle."

"And alliances. He's seeking a queen whose kin will serve his purposes. He wants a fair one, too."

"The women talk about that. Sunspear has asked this king and his daughter to visit him at Emain Macha. Manannan mac Lir, it never ceases to irk me that he calls his dun that! Emain Macha was destroyed long ago. No man can restore its glory. I have never been there, but I'd wager a herd of cattle it is a poor imitation, if I had a herd of cattle!"

She clenched her teeth and her fist.

"Inclined I am to agree," Felimid said, laughing. "This daughter of King Muirchertach's—what is her name, now? —"

"Fiadh, I think. But Muirchertach will know—the sparrows know—that Sunspear has a leman named Aivene the sight of whom ravishes the eyes, and he's dangling the Ulaid's king on a cord with the hope of marriage to *his* daughter, Caragh. And the women say Sunspear even makes overtures to the king of Connacht with a prospect of marriage ties."

Truth of the gods! Felimid thought. *Muirchertach will be ill pleased by that, if it happens! Connacht and the Uí Néill have clashed in battle before this. Muirchertach and Eógan Bél are on the verge of a blazing feud! But what's Sunspear about? Is he offering the hope of marriage to half the royal women in Erin? Is Caragh of the Ulaid no more than a distraction, and this of Connacht maybe meant to spur Muirchertach into wedding his daughter to Sunspear, to prevent any ties forming 'tween Sunspear and Connacht?*

Whatever the purpose, it's surely not going to affect his intentions towards me.

"A question," he said. "Where would you look for Sunspear's observers and agents here in Aileach?"

"I have thought about that."

"I am mighty sure you have."

"I'd look first and sharpest," she said consideringly, "at the men who talk most often against Ruarc Sunspear and his kingship, and the error of allowing it to flourish.

For it's a rare and gullible woman," she added, "even one as little practised among men as I am, who has not learned to beware of the ones who protest too emphatically."

"It's a good thing to watch for. I'll take care not to protest too emphatically in your ear."

She gave him a sideways look and coloured a little. "Then do not be arch."

The bard thought he discerned some archness in the way she had mentioned—unnecessarily—being little in practice among men. He did not say so. Bad enough to have a marred face if you were a man, and ten times worse for a woman. He had observed on the way from Aran to the Lake of Eyes that she could be shy and touchy. Any trace of the light raillery he might have used with another woman would humiliate her.

"I'll try to avoid it."

"You put that cur Mathgadro in his place." She turned her scarred cheek towards him. He conceived the terror and pain that must have meant for her when she was so young she did not remember the day now. "You do not look away from this. You do not stare at it either. It doesn't matter to you?"

"It matters whenever I think of the fire your goodly brother saved you from, and *who* kindled it. I'm glad my actions finished him. What was his name, Muadnait? Your brother, I am meaning."

"Loghan. I was too little to remember him. Whenever I am in the *tuath* where our father was king, though, I visit his grave, keen for him, and make an offering. Each Samhain Eve I set a place at table for him and believe I feel his presence, that he has come." Her eyes flooded with tears. "I try to make him proud. I'd not have his ghost think he wasted his life to save me."

"My oath as a bard, I am sure he does not."

Felimid lifted his hand, without haste, giving her time to move away. She did not. Gently he placed his open palm on her burned cheek, covering it and the side of her jaw. Nothing but the slightly tilted eye now indicated what had happened to her. Her mouth had a tender, generous shape, her eyes were bright, the unburnt skin smooth and her body graceful.

"Your brother will have no cause to be angry with me either," Felimid promised. "I'll see that no harm comes to his sister, and if I must be away from you, be sure you stay close to my foster brother and Eichra. There may be those who would see an advantage in threatening you."

"Crude that would be."

"Crude. But some are crude."

Felimid took his hand from her cheek. He fancied he saw a flash of regret in her eyes. Perhaps it was just that, though—fancy.

"I have a knife," she told him. "Maybe better yet, for a woman, I have a scream that can be heard from here to

Dealga. There are no quiet secret places for wrong-doing in Aileach. None that wouldn't be seen, none out of earshot of a dozen warriors, bard."

"Given I hear a scream, or even a stifled outcry, I'll come running and leaping. And my ears hear all. Nevertheless, watch your back, Muadnait."

They looked then in silence across the land that was now Cenél nEógain land, down the hill-slope to the grassy, flowering plain that swept to the Lake of Eyes in one direction and to more hills in the other, covered in green oakwoods. Southward lay the realm they were both thinking about, Airgialla, Ruarc's kingdom, and the restored Emain Macha, a name of enchantment and power to all Erin. The enchantment that lay on it was perhaps of bad omen to Sunspear. Its king of old had forced an otherworld woman, a goddess, to run a race against his horses even though pregnant, because of her husband's boast that she was swifter than any horses. He showed her no mercy though she pleaded. All Erin, likewise, knew the story of her curse, that the men of the kingdom should suffer the weakness and pain of a woman in travail whenever their need was most dire, and be unable to fight, generation after generation. Ruarc might sorrow yet, that he had chosen to build his kingly house on that site, to take advantage of its mighty associations. They were not all good.

Sunspear

They left the ramparts and walked among the crowd in the fortress. Aside from the hall there were no buildings of consequence except a crescent-shaped stable under the ramparts and guest quarters on the opposite side. Aileach had, in truth, little room for any others. Muirchertach's barns and byres stood on the hill-slopes without.

Felimid had seen them all at his first approach and entry. Now he saw Mathgadro, before the guest quarters, his pale stare on Felimid and Muadnait, his mouth sneering, and he cared little. Felimid had snubbed Mathgadro's sharp nose when he ventured to affront the woman, and if it became necessary again, why, so much the worse for Mathgadro.

Maybe Muadnait had given a small hint of interest to the bard. A kind of shy overture. Or maybe not. A man could read too much into a woman's behaviour. He surely had other things to think of, as did she, but . . . perhaps . . .

Since Gudrun Blackhair's death the bard had been with few girls, and none had deeply engaged him. He still, when he thought of women, thought first of the pirate, so strange a mixture of ruthlessness and generosity, and often she haunted his dreams. One other, and only one, stayed strongly in his memory, the bronze-haired enigmatic British sorceress Vivayn. Sometimes he went so far as to ask the winds from the east for news of her, but even the winds seemed ignorant. Vivayn might almost have vanished from the earth; he ought to acknowledge that he was unlikely to see her again. Unless she had died—the thought caused him a pang—she was most likely somewhere in Gaul, one of the great cities, though the coarse brutal rule of the Franks would fill her with disdain.

Och and ochone! What kind of dreamer fool am I, then? I'll see neither Blackhair nor Vivayn again. Come, son of Fal, think of Muadnait and what needs to be done here, now, as your father, whatever his faults, would do.

He did think of Muadnait, and the scarred face over which she often wore that deep cowl, and sudden, crackling rage filled him. Dicuil was extinct, yes, and good riddance, but fire would blaze as many a dun and monastery gouted sparks, if Ruarc Sunspear carried out his intentions. Therefore, he must not, and Muadnait, who could warn Felimid if fire magic was practiced anywhere nearby, must not be hurt further.

Muadnait at the time was giving herself a like lecture, as it happened.

The gods help me! What a fool! I was flirting with the bard, a little, or more than—when we are on Ruarc Sunspear's threshold and men of his are here in Aileach, children of danger. What, am I ten years old? And don't I know what this face of mine is like?

She ordered herself sharply, then, to stint that indulgence. Three-quarters of her face was fine. Some women had their entire countenances ugly, born that way by sheer bad luck, and also lacked the kind of abilities which bring respect. Muadnait had been endowed with those, by birth and training, for which many a mariner was thankful. Luck. The blind wild way the dice rolled.

Still it had been some time since a man's arms were around her. And—Angus the Young God, whose kisses became birds!—the bard's green eyes and lithe form were enough, surely, to give a woman thoughts best kept private. They intensified when he opened his mouth. He had a good voice, mellow and manly, but gentle as a rule—though it could bite when he wanted.

He hadn't been the only man aboard the curragh she found of interest. No. The brown-haired selchie was comely too, with a good face, a powerful, well-muscled swimmer even as a man. Her heart had pounded to see him rescue the monk from the waves. It had been merry to watch him keep playful pace with the boat afterwards. Besides, there was some fellow-feeling. The selchies were truly at home on neither land nor sea, and they were mistrusted. So were the women of Muadnait's college, by the ignorant, accused of causing storm and wreck, called down as sea-witches—by some Cross-worshipping monks in particular. Not Brandon and his fellows, true...

Oh, enough, she scolded herself. *Enough thinking about men, at least in that way. Think about the men in Aileach who are spying for Ruarc! Eichra has the right of it, there will be some, and if Ruarc Sunspear didn't appoint them, no doubt Cuanach or Taladh Teisne did! Look for them while Felimid talks with the king.*

Instead of mooning!

Chapter Ten

I stood by the knee of Amergin the poet, he was my tutor, so that I can stand up to any man, I can make praises for the doings of a king. —The Courting of Emer

"Let the southern bard play for us!"

"For us and the king!"

"Let's hear if he be as good as even the poorest northern bard. I doubt it."

The latter utterance, said with scathing malice, came from Mathgadro.

King Muirchertach had an amiable nature, though said to be pugnacious in battle. Flushed with drink as were most others present, his queen, the skilful Duinseach Ingen Duach, included, he raised his cup towards Felimid. The throng quietened.

"We should like to hear. Will you oblige us, grandson of the Chief Bard?"

"Honour it is, great-grandson of Niall Noigiallach, and I will gladly."

A square four-legged stool was shoved forward below the king's high seat, and the bard accepted it. Golden Singer's frame of time-blackened oak sheened like silk as he drew her forth, ancient, filled with power, fashioned by

Luchtaine the wood-worker for Cairbre the bard, both of them gods in the age of bronze, when the mysterious Tuatha De Danann had been lords of Erin, then called Tir-Tairn-Gire, Land of Promise.

Briefly, Felimid felt an urge to mischief. He could fashion a song that told the unflattering truth about the Uí Néill dynasty, risen to great power through the deeds of a pirate in a mere hundred years. Despite the proud claim of bards to be vessels of truth, they adapted it—and euphemism—to suit their hearers. Indeed, their training did bind them to truth, and when they submitted to a supernatural Test of Truth they must honour it or suffer supernatural penalties—but when they celebrated the ancestry, appearance, and deeds of their patrons, that was another matter, and truth was often eclipsed.

"I am giving you, as is fitting in this good company, the Tale of Niall's Kingship."

They cried out cheerfully, but when the first harp chords sounded they hushed, even Mathgadro, though the sneer remained on his mouth.

Now let restraint go, Felimid said to himself as he plucked the golden strings. *Scatter it afar. For this audience there's no such thing as fulsome or extravagant, not on this subject. Oh, Muirchertach, by the time I finish, the legend of Niall will be bigger!*

"Eochu the king had five strong sons,
Eochu the lord of unconquered duns,
Master of herds and wide green fields
Guarded by fighters with spears and shields,
Riders of steeds that were steady and true
Though the red fight roared and the javelins flew—
And whenever an insolent foe imposed on Eochu the king's wide lands,
Whenever one would not take a rebuke but from iron in bold men's hands,
Eochu the king was first to fight
When the spearheads shimmered blue.

"Four of his sons were from Mongfind's womb, a queen of malignant pride;
Most of her rivals vanished, and most of her enemies died.
Brian the brawny was short and wide and never the worse for wine;
He could shape a mass of iron by bending it over his spine.
Ailill had thoughtful foresight and the deftest hands of the four,
Whether to carve an image or steer a longship to war,
While Fiachra was harsh and jealous, his mother's son indeed,
And those who admired his courage could not but deplore his greed.
Fergus the mild and easy had seldom his own intent,
But would back his brothers' exploits and go where his brothers went."

Yessss ... not bad. So for the setting, the lesser folk. Now the heroine, the mother of Niall.

Sunspear

New music rippled from Golden Singer, no longer male but feminine as a young girl's walk, with an element of passion and strength ringing through it.

"Last of the sons of Eochu was born of a second wife—
Carina, a British princess, that he won in the crimson strife
When he waded ashore from his galley, his gleaming sword on high,
Shouting his name, "Eochu!" for a dreaded battle cry—
Carina, his noble captive, of a royal British line,
And descent from the Roman purple, imperial and divine.
In Erin he called her Chasdub, for her curling midnight hair,
And her eyes were blue as summer, and her skin was sea-foam fair."

Felimid paused for breath and a swallow of blood-red wine. The sound of stamped feet and cheers was considerable; he also saw professional heads going together among the poets for serious discussion. Some looked approving, some envious. Either was a compliment.

He resumed. With a brief glissando he turned to the shorter strings and brought forth a cold, sinister ripple of sound. Then a veritable crash of notes that sounded like the essence of hatred.

Now comes the wicked villain.

"Queen Mongfind thought of murder from the day Carina came,
And learning she carried Eochu's child made her rage a consuming flame.
She dared not slay in the open day, but she forced the girl to work
From the first faint glimmer of morning to the grey descent of mirk—
Yoked with a weighty burden to stagger up from the well,
Or scrape a hide by firelight in the tan-pit's reeking smell,
All for a single purpose, to make her lose the child,
But Carina Chasdub was hardy as winter storms are wild.
The child remained within her and kicked with promising force,
Yet should it survive the birthing, the simple, cruel course
Of clandestine infant-murder was there for Mongfind to take,
Since newborns die full often, sleep and then fail to wake,
Of causes unknown to any, a natural halt to breath,
Or smothered by a witch-queen from the Otherworld of death."

Snake fangs and cat claws. Next the loyal saviour.

"King Eochu's poet was Torna, a clever, prophetic man,
And Chasdub pleaded, 'Oh Torna, will you save my child if you can?'
Torna the poet answered, 'I'll surely devise a plan
That shall save your unborn infant, and read his future withal,
For his fate should not be meagre, and that demon queen should fall.

If you can bear him in silence I will dare dark Mongfind's curse;
I will take him away to hide him with a worthy woman to nurse.
Mongfind may send her searchers! My verses will tangle their minds
In a shifting net of confusion, in flurries of dust that blinds.'
Carina Chasdub carried her child to the day of his fated birth,
And suffered her labour alone by the well, on the wet unyielding earth.
No common omens presented, the stars were strangely aligned,
And Torna the poet saw mighty things in his deep, prophetic mind."

Good, Felimid thought, *good. They are in raptures. The king is not so easy to impress, but he likes it. As to whether any prophecies were truly made when Niall was born, or there even was a poet called Torna, there is no knowing. But by the gods there should have been!*

Torna's prophecy, real or invented, was known word for word throughout the north. Felimid halted his music. He pitched his voice to portentous depth and made the phrases resound through the hall.

"Welcome, little guest!
"He will be Niall of the Nine Hostages!
"In his time he will redden a multitude.

"Plains will be increased, kingdoms overthrown, battles will be fought,

"Longside of Tara, host-leader of Mag Femin, custodian of Maen-Mag,

"Revered one of Almain, veteran of the Ruirthech, white-knee of Cadal!

"Thrice nine years will he rule Erin,

"And Erin will be inherited from him for ever."

A sweeping claim, he reflected. None alive would be able to refute it, though, unless some man or woman was reborn in other shapes forever. And even Tuan mac Cairill had not been reborn *quite* forever.

"'Niall,' Carina whispered, as Torna wrapped him round,
And wild with rage though Mongfind searched, he never by her was found.
He lived to grow to manhood, to train with weapons and fight,
And the crimes against his mother were crimes he lived to requite.
Far had he ranged as a reiver, winning both fame and wealth,
Until he reckoned the time was ripe and returned to Erin by stealth.
Young was he yet, and angry, as he came to Chasdub's side:
He said, 'You shall serve no longer, and now let Mongfind hide.'

With his iron hand in her roughened palm and his anger growing more,
He led his mother up to the hall and the warder who kept the door.
The warder would have stayed them, and Niall struck him dead;
A champion rushed against him, and Niall took off his head."

Laughter and approval, again, greeted that. King Muirchertach joined it, to the bard's pleasure. It was more than a tribute to his art. It signified that the king might listen to other things from him than a rhymed story.

"He led Carina Chasdub to a high proud honour-seat,
He flung the dark queen sprawling in the rushes at her feet,
He wrapped his mother in purple that Roman empresses wore
And made his oath by the gods of his race she should never be slighted more –
With a glance at the dark queen's champion where he weltered in smoking gore."

The rafters rang and creaked. Felimid thought of interposing a section anent the test of the burning smithy in which Niall vied with his half-brothers to qualify for kingship, but decided against it. The story was so well known it might bore them. He had no wish to lose them when they were with him now. He brought the story to a close.

"Mongfind was driven to exile and Niall plundered the sea,
Raiding Britain and Gaul and Spain in despite of Rome's decree!
He lived to take nine hostages as the bards and harpers sing,
Nine of the proudest nobles—he lived to become a king.
The dynasty he founded is a word in every mouth,
Pre-eminent in the sleety north, a power in the misty south!
Honour to mighty Niall, the strong trusty anvil of rule,
Forebear of kings until time shall end, and truth's abiding renewal."

Those present loudly approved of that finale, too, and Felimid basked in their applause. He knew well enough there was not another harper in Erin to equal him—not, at any rate, another as young, and assuredly not Mathgadro. The king should wish Felimid to stay, for his own honour.

"Well played," Muirchertach said. "Well devised. You must remain with us awhile and play again. And you must show me how to play this new game you brought as a gift."

"I will well, lord. When you wish."

He assumed this was something of a pretext to speak with him in seclusion—or all of it that could be had in Aileach. Kings and queens never did have much. In the deep of night they did sit at the chessboard, two bright lamps spilling light on the pieces that a skilled man had carved in the likenesses of king and queen, Druid and chariot-car and naked common warrior. Felimid could not wholly dismiss uneasy thoughts of the way he had learned this eastern game, in the palace of Koschei the Deathless, with pieces made of ruby and diamond, on a board of red garnet and white quartz, and his fingers trembled a little. Was Koschei truly deathless, and did he writhe now in his wrapping of chains, buried under that huge grave-mound in Obodrite country? Would fools disinter him someday?

He strove to forget that and set his mind on chess strategies.

"Not a hunt game, but a battle game, eh?" Muirchertach said as he studied the board. "That may be fitting for you and I, Felimid mac Fal. There was a battle, not on a board, at Ocha. My father against Ailill the Ram. Your grandsire and your father were there, too, fighting for Ailill."

"Yes, lord, and the Ram lost. My grandfather Fergus was Chief Bard already. His satires might have carried the day for Ailill, except that someone poisoned him the night before the two hosts engaged. He almost died, so."

"I'd heard that." Muirchertach frowned intently over the board. "It's lawful, you said, to move this front-rank piece, a *ceithernach*, two squares on its first move?"

"It is."

Muirchertach moved it. His gaze met Felimid's.

"My father would never have countenanced poisoning a bard, even to win a crucial battle."

"No, lord. My grandsire never thought so. It took him a month to recover, but he never reckoned your father was responsible. Someone did it, some treacherous cur who thought it would be a service, without telling him. Fal discovered who it was and sought him out."

And killed him.

"Carefully expressed," the king said. "True, it was thirty years gone and more, but I wonder, now, if it comes to a battle between me and the present king of Connacht—we are not friends—which side you will espouse. He's Ailill the Ram's grandson."

"Truly, lord, I do not care whose grandson he is, and in the event I suppose I would be on the same side as my people. But Sunspear, it seems to me, is a more immediate concern, and his power is great for a young man, as young as I, who was not even king of a single *tuath* the day I returned to Erin! That's a mighty sudden rise. He does not appear content with it, either, and I wonder and wonder and wonder how he achieved it."

"That's why you came to the north, eh? Because he is your enemy? You might have been wiser and safer to stay by the banks of Sinann."

"Then he'd come looking for me at last. Will you tell me, lord, how he ever became king of Airgialla?"

"One step at a time, that is how, as if you do not know! He appeared with his war-band after Dicuil the Fiery died, and took service with the king of that first *tuath*. The king died." Felimid did not ask how. "None was then eligible by blood for the kingship, and Sunspear prevailed on the freemen to accept him as king. He had wealth inherited from Dicuil, and Dicuil's fierce breed followed him without question, even accepting that he should control their sire's treasure. He increased his wealth and theirs by cattle-raiding, led them with success, and they are not a normal folk; they care little for wealth or power, only for fighting. He's a better fighter than any two of them. So it went. He gave generous client-fees to a couple of weaker neighbours to own him their lord. He made sure that everyone round about saw that they did not lose by it. His next step upward."

He paused, frowning, as though deliberating whether to say more. In the end he did.

"It was strange in a way. To be sure it is done all the time. But other kings seemed almost eager to become his clients, even on terms not to their kin's advantage. There were protests and even lawsuits over it, but the litigants always seemed to settle to young Sunspear's profit, not their own. As if they could not resist his requests. Maybe it was fear at work. Yon Mathgadro has the power of satire, like the others, though theirs are not as virulent, and then, the Fir Dicuil serve Sunspear, ready at any time for a harvest of heads."

"Was he not opposed with spears at all?"

"He was," Muirchertach grunted. "There were bloody battles! On the losing side, and the losing side was not his, few survived. He and Dicuil's offspring made themselves useful to us of the Uí Néill now and then, most notably at Druim Derg last winter."

"What if he thinks, in the end, to play you against each other and increase his power further that way?"

"It would be his mistake," the king said flatly. "We'd unite against him and crack him like a nut, Fir Dicuil or none." His tone declared that was the end of the matter, but Felimid saw unease in his deep-set eyes. His broad hand reached out to touch one of the pieces Felimid called Druids. "How are these moved again?"

"Always diagonally, lord. Always staying on the same colour square they started. Nor can they jump over other pieces."

The game continued, with Felimid talking no more of power or politics. The blunt king of the Cenél nEógain had said as much on those subjects as he wished to. From what he did say, Felimid had plucked forth eight words as being the most significant.

As if they could not resist his requests.

Chapter Eleven

"There is the young man you sent out," he said, "and this is the treatment Cuchulain will give to every other man that goes out against him." And Maeve came out of the door and spoke high, angry, loud words: "I had put great hopes in that young man," she said, "and I did not think it was under bad protection he was going, when he went under the protection of Fergus." And Fergus said: "What business had he going out at all, to meddle with Cuchulain? And if I went there myself," he said, "it is well pleased I was to get back again safely." —The War for the Bull of Cuailgne

Muadnait disliked Eichra the Eel. He had hardly uttered a word to her the entire voyage to Aileach, and she supposed it was because her burns repelled him, though even without that, he had demonstrated his scornful doubt of the skills of her college. It seemed to her he had scornful doubt of most things. In itself that only meant he was something of an oaf. His evident jealous pride was a different matter, one that might affect their mission. She knew nothing truly dishonourable about him. By all accounts he was loyal to Lacth of the Booming Shield, one of her best warriors, but they were far from Lacth's dun, and among these northern strangers Eichra's pride might lead him to pick a quarrel. A disastrous one.

She did not think he would desert them, go over to Sunspear, although even that was possible. But Sunspear was a powerful young king now, with a name for battles, and the feared Fir Dicuil in his entourage. He could pick and choose from fighters more famous than Eichra.

Muadnait stayed within sight of him, though, for all her dislike, or of Tuathal the Bowman, whenever she was not with Felimid. None of those three made her as uneasy as Mathgadro and his bodyguards. Bluetongue's store of spite was a byword.

She tried to watch them without drawing notice. They were often by the big circular hearth in the middle of Muirchertach's hall. Cauldrons simmered there and carcasses roasted, in the normal way, but in time Muadnait observed something else. The stones made a perfect, meticulously constructed ring which looked new, perhaps not even a year old. Nor were they limestone, but some dark fire-born rock.

The *banfili* gritted her teeth and went closer. There, surely, where fire was maintained day and night, though often banked, would a fire spirit be summoned. If at all.

Feigning to warm her hands, she approached the hearth. The scar tissue on her cheek tightened, prickled, then itched unbearably. So did her calf and heel.

Magic, fire magic!

She wanted to turn and run.

Instead, taking hold of her courage, she stretched her hands to the hearth and warmed them, gazing into the coals where little flames wavered. They shifted, of course, changed shape constantly, as fire does. She focused her *banfili*'s senses. Something in that hearth hissed and crackled with more than the ordinary random noise of fire. Something moved, well camouflaged among the other flames, elusively blending with them, but just slightly brighter an orange-yellow—if it was not her unnerved fancy.

Her stinging cheek and foot said otherwise.

She saw it altering shape, a tiny pennon, an unstable face, a lizard (now stubby, now long, thin and nimble), a flower . . . a fire imp.

She moved away from the hearth, carefully. Only an agent of Sunspear's could have conjured the thing. Someone must be working magic to contain it in the hearth, or it would escape, after its natural inclination, and quite likely set the hall ablaze, to express its pique at being confined. That must not be what its summoners wished, or it would have happened by now. Maybe in the future? At the right time?

They were hopeful if they thought to restrain a fire imp that long. Such beings were restless, and quick. They were lucky it had not broken free as yet.

Muadnait whispered to her companion the archer. The pair went outside, out of the Grianan entirely, to the hillside where Tuathal practiced shooting at targets. She watched him, and went back and forth recovering his shafts. Felimid soon joined them, resplendent in his patterned cloak, an enameled bronze pin gleaming at his shoulder. Muadnait did not suppose he had joined them on a whim, or that he thought she was merely out for exercise. He might be comely, but he had a brain.

She told him succinctly about the fire imp.

He neither wasted time nor tried her patience by asking if she was certain.

"The one who tends that hearth will be the one who watches over the imp," Felimid said. "A tricky task. If the fire were quenched that little imp would be quenched with it. If it escaped—"

Muadnait shuddered. "I cannot sleep in that hall again! I dread fire! I've had one rooftree burn above me."

"I won't ask it," Felimid assured her. "Away from Aileach right hastily, you. Indeed you must not sleep another night in such danger. Or better, it is the fire imp we could remove away!"

"How?" Tuathal asked pragmatically.

"We'd have to convince the king. It's with his royal hearth these liberties have been taken, and he will not like that. I wonder why Ruarc—it's his doing—risked Muirchertach finding out? What is the gain to him?"

"He must have conjured the fire spirit in an enchanted blaze at Emain Macha, then surreptitiously sent it here,"

Muadnait offered. "A mighty useful spy. Whatever the imp sees and hears in Aileach, Sunspear can read in the parent flames at Emain. He will have that much skill in divining by fire."

"Pyromancy," Felimid said. "So the Greeks call it. With the Brotherhood of Britain I knew a man named Palamides, a man of some learning. He taught me the word.

Yes, Ruarc was Dicuil the Fiery's pupil for years. You have it, Muadnait."

Tuathal listened closely, but having small knowledge of such things, he only listened. Setting another arrow on his string, he aimed at the thick plank fifty paces off, and hit it breast high. The next stuck a hand's breadth below.

While his foster brother went to retrieve his shots, Felimid looked around him, and saw Mathgadro Bluetongue coming their way. His constant companions of the Fir Dicuil flanked him, girt with their swords, long well-forged blades with shining hilts. Eichra the Eel had noticed them leaving the hall, and sauntered along at a useful distance behind them, very blithe and innocent, very much there by merest happen-so—with two round bucklers tucked under his arm and his own sword-hilt showing above his left shoulder.

"Not bad shooting," Mathgadro hailed Tuathal. "Adroit you are with that coward's weapon, indeed."

"Imagine, now," Tuathal said. "Although I do not see any four-footed dogs, I hear a dog yapping."

"Perhaps it was a bitch," Mathgadro suggested. "An ugly bitch, yapping in heat."

"With two dogs sniffing around her," said Cenan, the taller of his companions.

"I," said Felimid, speaking with lively scorn although in truth he found this sort of exchange dull, "see three dogs, two of them reddish and brindled, one with a blue tongue. My grandfather Fergus would say a potent *aer* is wasted on them, but I am generous." His sea-green eyes held an amiable, easy look as a rule, but not then. To Mathgadro he said deliberately, "Unless you ask Muadnait's pardon like a man, you and I will compete face to face composing satire against each other, and we'll see whose disparagement is more deadly. I wager on myself to afflict your face with larger, redder wens than my ancestor Cairbre gave to Bress, despite your reputation. Maybe tremors of hand and foot withal." He smiled at the notorious satirist, sweetly. "Meet me with weapons if that's your preference. We're both wearing swords. It would not trouble me at all to send Sunspear your head in a bag."

The other bodyguard, Cathal, Senan's cousin and his elder by three years, burst into a laugh that was not genial. Like the rest of the Fir Dicuil, these two reckoned any day on which they killed no man as a day to lament. They had been sent with Mathgadro as his guardians, what was more, and would not scant that duty.

"Any gathering of heads will be done by us," Senan said, grinning. "You fight us first."

"We will name you a coward from shore to shore if you do not," Cathal added, with a grin as wide. "We've no fear of the supposed curse on Ogma's sword. The one of us who kills you will take Kincaid as a trophy, and your harp will go to Emain Macha for the king."

"A splendid gift that will make for him, and deeply honoured he should be when he gets it," Felimid said.

"He will," Cathal said with conviction, "and that, no matter how it distresses this charred bit of driftwood whose sisterhood, I hear, pastures on the corpses of drowned mariners."

"Rot your low uncouth tongue!" the bard flashed, his air of patronizing tolerance gone. Muadnait, properly, had not deigned to respond, but Felimid saw how her burn scars turned crimson and the unmarred skin of her other cheek whitened. "You might have had the fight you crave without saying that. But fight me now. Eichra! Go tell King Muirchertach that he may come see it if that pleases him."

"Ah, no. You cannot be greedy enough to fight the pair? Let me have one!"

"Not on this day. The Fir Dicuil should learn who they are dealing with. I am thinking there will be enough others for you in the near future. Will you go to the king, now?"

"Right you are," Eichra said, disappointed.

"But Cathal said the truth," his cousin declared. "Only the truth. The sea-witches of Aran raise storms and wreck ships to replenish their larder, so. All men know it. A shame our grandsire did not roast her thoroughly when she was small."

Felimid said softly, "I am the man who made an end of your triply cursed grandsire, and it's a matter of pride with me."

"Then let's fight," Cathal said, no less softly.

"Lir of the Green Sea!" Muadnait exclaimed. "I was afraid that Eichra would do this thing, not you. These boors are not worth your attention."

"No. But they insulted you."

The antagonists shortly faced each other on level ground, each with his sword and a round oak shield, iron-rimmed, Felimid's covered with green leather, showing the device of a white running horse, Cathal's black with a golden sun-wheel. Both wore hard leather casques, the bard's with cheek-pieces. King Muirchertach and his queen came out to watch, with many other spectators. Eichra, Tuathal and Muadnait stood close together, the woman pale and tense, Tuathal *an Seighdeoir* frowning in worry, Eichra smiling openly.

"He's practiced with me for a while, and with the king's champion since we arrived here," the Eel said. "Let's hope it was enough."

Tuathal did not answer. His bow was on his back, and several arrows in his belt. Grimly, assessingly, he eyed the men with parti-coloured hair.

If Felimid falls, he promised himself, *I'll shoot these two, though all Erin is watching.*

Cathal pranced forward, his long double-edged blade a bright wheel about his head, flashing left to right. Then he struck overhand in a savage, downward chop. It looked flamboyant and reckless, but Cathal's shield covered his belly the whole time, never shifting. Felimid parried the overhand stroke with Kincaid, and felt the impact jolt him to his heels. He slanted his shield, and struck at the side of Cathal's knee with the iron rim.

Cathal sprang away like a grasshopper, extravagantly high, landed with knees bent and came straight at Felimid, sword, arm and body extended in a line, point aimed at the bard's throat. Felimid raised his shield in time to block the point, again was rocked back by the other's strength, and retaliated by cutting down hard with Kincaid's edge at Cathal's long blade. The swords rang.

Felimid knew well that his sword's toughness and temper exceeded those of any other weapon in Erin. Cathal's blade was good, and strengthened with a central rib, but not equal to Kincaid, and he struck with fierce impetuous strength. That might undo him; his sword might snap. Felimid forcefully parried Cathal's strokes at every chance, with that object, while using his shield as a weapon of offence. Once, ducking low, he swept the shield around and got home with the iron rim, hitting his adversary below the knee hard enough to have broken most men's shinbones. Not Cathal. He was Dicuil's grandson. An eighth of his physical heredity was demonic. His swift response to that blow almost removed Felimid's head for a gift to Sunspear, as Cathal had promised.

The bard parried Cathal's blade again, directly, both swords taking the full force of the impact. Again Cathal's sword survived the clash. No, it was not going to break. Felimid abandoned that notion.

"I'll take your *head*!" Cathal snarled. He doubled his onslaught. His celerity was beyond the common, and he used the point as readily as the edge. Saxons' and Goths' idea of swordplay employed the edge only, and that, when he fought them in his years abroad, had given Felimid an advantage—but this was Erin, and Cathal was one of the fell Fir Dicuil.

Not quite superhuman, though. Felimid thought he saw a weakness now. He lacked supreme coordination; his movements did not always flow smoothly. Several thrusts, though sudden and strong, had seen his point go a handspan wide of his intended aim. Also, fighting a left-handed man seemed to irritate him.

Against a descendant of Ogma, dear man, you need a cooler head than that.

Cathal ran his point like an adder's strike at the bard's throat. When Felimid did just what the other expected, raising and tilting his shield to deflect the thrust, Cathal cut even more swiftly at his adversary's hip. Just as sudden, but more precise, Felimid drove his point to the inside of Cathal's elbow. It arrived first, thwarting Cathal's cut, jolted on the bone, and sliced all the way to the shoulder. Cathal's sword arm was laid open. Keeping hold of his sword, albeit with a badly weakened grip, and snarling like a wildcat, he aimed the spraying blood at Felimid's face to obscure his sight.

Felimid yanked his head aside. Cathal made a swift attempt to break his neck with his shield-rim, and Felimid, displeased, blocked the blow with his own shield.

Striking his enemy's temple with the flat of Kincaid, he dropped the other unconscious on the grass. He lay bleeding from his nose and ears as well as the filleted arm.

"You should . . . see that he does not bleed to death," Felimid said.

"Do!" Senan snapped to Mathgadro. To Felimid he said in rage, "It's you will bleed to death. I'll see to't."

Bending, he seized his cousin's fallen blade and sprang at Felimid with a sword in each hand, each one a glittering blur. But the weapon Cathal had used was slippery at the hilt with Cathal's own blood. Senan paid no attention to that.

Felimid met the attack with cool defensiveness, turning slashes and thrusts that came like a double whirlwind. It hadn't escaped him that the grip of one of Senan's swords was blood-greasy. Again and again he parried that blade with his own until its edge notched, while that of Kincaid stayed flawless.

With a beast's howl, his eyes frenzied, Senan cut at the bard's neck with his right-hand blade. It thundered on the green shield. With the other he made a great overhand swing that would have split Felimid's head, leather cap or none, but Felimid met the descending edge with a direct parry. He was jarred to his heels by the impact and brought to one knee. However, the result for which he had worked came at last; the other sword broke. The point flew yards and stuck in the earth. The bloody hilt spun from Senan's hand. Felimid seized the moment—the bare heartbeat, and both hearts were beating fast indeed—to deliver a long ineluctable lunge, still on one knee.

It slid into Senan's belly an inch left of the navel. Muscle divided. Soft pulsating loops of gut split along the keen edges. Senan neither fell nor staggered; his iron-muscled legs thrust him backward, away from the point, and he grasped his remaining sword's hilt two-handed. With a wild shriek he brought the blade over and down in a diagonal stroke at Felimid's shoulder.

The bard lifted his shield, and that saved him, though Senan's blade split it across the middle. Felimid's legs, the legs of a horseman and swift runner, thrust him to his feet, and his sword, a blue-white blaze, met Senan's long weapon again and again. The bard ignored the pain in his shield arm, though it blazed like a lightning bolt from fingertips to elbow. He opened that hand with difficulty, pulled it out of the shield-grip, and shook half of the riven shield loose. It fell to the earth. Backing away slightly, the swords ringing together, Felimid tossed the other half of his shield at Senan's shins, hoping to make him stumble.

Senan sprang over it. Landing, even after that small leap, must have sent lances of agony through his pierced guts. His teeth showed to the gums as he ground them together, but he never groaned, or paused in his attack. Like all his breed, in a fight he cared not for life or death. Neither combatant had a shield now, and each possessed only a single sword.

Felimid fought on the defensive again, waiting for his stricken opponent to fall. Not even Senan's vitality could sustain this onslaught long, with his belly wound. He knew it, too. Eyes glaring in a ghastly fashion, he sought to close with Felimid and hurl an iron arm about his waist in an embrace of death. Twice the bard barely slipped aside.

"Don't play with him, you fool," Eichra called out. "*Kill him*!"

"Quiet," Tuathal *an Saighdeoir* said, in a tone that brooked no contradiction. "He's the one fighting, leave it to him."

"But Senan has nothing to lose," Muadnait said softly, urgently, in Tuathal's ear. "He's a dead man, with that belly wound, and he might still slay before he dies. Eichra is right."

Then she closed her hands into fists, and her lips to repress a squeal of consternation. Felimid had tried a low cut from the outside, and Senan caught and held it, then responded with a thrust like the stab of a cormorant's bill. The power of it should have been impossible, wounded as he was, but Felimid had no time to waste marveling. He brought his weapon over, forcing Senan's blade aside despite his snarling resistance. The grandson of Dicuil showed himself, finally, human enough to stagger, and Felimid struck the sword from his weakening grip. The weapon flew out of the fighting circle, to lie innocuous in the grass.

Senan, astoundingly, even now remained standing, did not fall in the grass himself.

"Kill me," he spat. "My clan will have your head yet."

Breathing in pants, Felimid leaned on Tuathal, who had come to his side, as had Muadnait on the other. Senan had a hand pressed to his belly. His face was white. Killing him would be a kindly favour, the bard thought; men always died with belly wounds like that, and such deaths were more horrid than most. But he was shaking where he stood with the effort of two gruelling combats, and with reaction.

"They may have my head, as you say," he gasped. "But you should not—have given gratuitous insult—to Muadnait, so. I have killed you. Your cousin should see that you die swiftly."

"He won't die of these hurts," Mathgadro sneered. "The Fir Dicuil are not like other men—or women."

"It's true," King Muirchertach said gravely.

"It is true," Mathgadro echoed. His mouth twisted in something like a smile. "Their kinsman Fothad took a worse gut-wound than that at Druim Derg—his entrails were exposed to the sunlight! He lived and he healed well. He's eating now as heartily as ever, walking about fit for battle. He and every one of his kindred will cast dice to challenge you first when they hear of this."

"Hmm," Felimid said with interest. "My understanding was that I am Sunspear's meat. Has *he* beaten these two?"

"And not one after the other," Senan rasped. Grey faced, dripping cold sweat, he stayed obstinately on his feet. "He's fought mock combats with both of us at once. We've yet to best him."

It might have been mere talk. Felimid found he believed it. Accordingly, he shrugged it off.

"In the meantime, you'd better avail yourselves of the best physicians in Aileach, would you say?"

"Oh, come away," Muadnait said to him. "Will you bandy words with these all day? Have a care to yourself! He sundered your shield on your arm. Is't broken?"

"It could be," Felimid admitted.

"Come on, then." Muadnait passed her own arm around his waist and supported him on that side. Tuathal offered the same on the other, but Felimid shook his head. "Thanks, brother. One is enough."

Behind the king and queen and their attendants, he moved towards the grey fortress.

Chapter Twelve

The growling of a lion; a flame that can cut like a sharpened stone... —The Championship of Ulster

His arm was not broken. By nightfall, though, it was black with bruising from wrist to shoulder. His elbow hurt like a demon's kiss.

"Battered you have become since you started this," Tuathal observed with a grin, as Felimid lowered a cup of wine with his good arm and a physician examined the other.

"A little," he agreed. "Oh, a fine restful three years it was while it lasted—not so restful in spots, but mostly. Just a couple of rough interludes. Well. Nothing is permanent."

"They might have killed you," Muadnait said, her look at him soft with favour, and her voice also. "Was it worth it?"

"They all wish to kill me, the friendly Fir Dicuil, and they will try. Now, though, they are after knowing it will be difficult—and they may be careful how they insult my companions in future. What they said of you, *banfili*, they should not have said."

"It's in my mind that the others will leave you alone, now," Eichra opined. "Not from fear. They will see you as Sunspear's meat, as you said. So will he."

Felimid's mouth formed a derisive shape. "Mighty comforting. Think you it's true, what Mathgadro said? That those two practice-battled often with Ruarc without ever besting him?"

"I reckon it is. There are witnesses, and not his companions only, that he cut down Failge Berraide. That one was no easy prey."

"Och, then it's as well I beat them. Tuathal, I saw you standing ready with your bow strung. Good it is that the Fir Dicuil know nothing about bows! You only string it to be ready for business. If I had gone down and you had shot Cathal and Senan, not much good would ha' been done."

"No." Muadnait smiled broadly, though she cupped a hand to her scarred cheek in concealment. "But I hazard you have done yourself some good in Aileach by winning, bard. The warriors are talking about it respectfully, and the king, I think, is happy enough that the Fir Dicuil were humbled a little. Fighting those two was more impressive than a chess game."

This was proven a little later, when the king's leech Brona, a pot-bellied, sharp-eyed man with white hair, came to examine the bard. His arm had neither broken bones nor damaged muscles. Liniment and time ought to help the bruising, but in the meantime, it would hurt, Brona said perfunctorily, his manner that of one long aware the world abounded in idiots who courted harm from weapons. Felimid assured him he expected no less.

The pain was rather damnable. But Felimid's time in exile, among the Brotherhood of Britain, Gudrun's pirates, and others, had caused a certain amount of harsh warrior pride to seep into his soul like a dye. He never flinched, though the physician's knobby fingers hurt like fire, especially as they palpated his elbow-joint.

"Nothing broken," Brona pronounced. "Nothing is chipped or cracked, even, that I can find. Keep the arm still. If the pain grows rather than subsides, tell me. By Nuada's silver hand, you escaped lightly, battling the Fir Dicuill!"

"That's wholly true," the king agreed. He was present, with Queen Duinseach, a sign of favour lost on nobody. "Or maybe not. Maybe they are the ones who came away lightly, since you gave them defeat and they are alive."

"It will hurt their pride," the queen cautioned. "They will want to battle you again, if Sunspear does not claim the right, as he may."

"I'm grateful to be warned, royal person. Nevertheless, I was bound to have trouble with him someday. He holds me responsible for his mentor's death, and he swore to take up that matter with me again when it was convenient. He was never going to forget."

"He's an over-king now, and our neighbor," Muirchertach frowned. "But you are a bard and our guest. We'll prevent any harm befalling you. I advise, with my whole mind, that you go nowhere near Emain Macha. You would not leave it with breath still in your lungs."

"If I went to Emain Macha, I'd be *his* guest, surely? And still a bard. He could not have me openly killed."

"No."

Openly was the word that mattered, as they both knew. Someone would have to do it surreptitiously, a pretext found. Ruarc mac Amalgaid would wish for a way that did not violate his vainglorious sense of honour, but he was clever enough, and strategist enough, to find one.

"He must not kill you, openly or otherwise!" Muadnait declared. "He must not get his hands on the harp of Cairbre, either. He has power enough without that."

"By the old gods and the new, I agree," Muirchertach grunted.

"He's making overtures of marriage to our daughter," the queen said. "Not that she is the only one receiving the honour. So too are royal women of Connacht, and as we hear, Caragh of the Ulaid. The splendid Ruarc is a bull of many heifers."

It's one and just one he must choose for a queen, Felimid thought, *and present power or future gain will decide the choice he makes. It will not be Caragh, then. Ulidia's reduced and shorn of power.*

Many men his age would have dismissed the question at that. Felimid told himself to inquire further into it. The more he knew of Ruarc's plans, including dynastic ones, the better his chances of outwitting him.

Muadnait gave little attention to that. She said, still incredulous, "You let them provoke you to fight. They might have killed you. Was it truly because of their insults? To me?"

"Why is that amazing? I'm a rogue to the core if I lie. It was. Their words to you were past allowing."

"It was not wise, was it?"

"Maybe it wasn't. They had me too angered for thought. Cairbre and Ogma, I was almost stammering with it."

"It did not show."

"Bardic training is useful."

Bardic training also practiced a man, or woman, in the skill of modulating one's voice (partly by mastering tone, partly by magic) to be heard only by the person addressed. That could be *very* useful, in a place like a royal fortress where private speech was hard to obtain. Felimid had subjects he wanted to remain in confidence—to keep from Mathgadro, anyhow, and maybe even from Muirchertach and his queen.

"The little fire sprite in the great hearth, now. You are sure it is there?"

"I wish I were not. I'm as sure of it as I'm sure that I limp, and why! It is there, and some creature of Sunspear's put it there."

Muadnait said nothing of the horror fire elementals gave her. The bard knew. She had trouble containing her bladder if she even sensed such a being was nearby. She supposed he did not actually *know* that, although he might guess, and for her pride's sake she would be buried in a midden before she'd inform him.

"So. It's there," he said, accepting. "Then those tending the hearth must know, and work cantrips at dawn, midday and sunset to confine it there, even though nothing loathes confinement more. If it gets free—"

"Yes. It will burn this hall, this fortress entire, and grow big. Those supposed bondwomen tending the hearth must be adroit in fire sorcery, to prevent it. More than they seem. Sunspear, or his agents, introduced them here."

Muadnait bit her tongue at that point. She perceived she was rattling along, and saying the obvious. The fire imp had shaken her.

"I did ill to bring you near that imp," Felimid muttered. "I am thinking you must leave, Muadnait. At least go down to the shore and the ships while I deal with it."

Muadnait looked at him with some trepidation. She had begun to know the bard's impulsive side.

"Deal with it . . . how?"

"In the simplest way. By telling Muirchertach. He cannot receive the news kindly that a fire imp has been installed in his royal hearth, and it'll surely be plain to him that the most likely one to do that was Sunspear."

"And what will happen then?"

"It depends on the king. He's a man of steady sense. If my advice prevails, all will be handled with care and discretion, but it may go wrong. I'm not wishing you to be there if a fire imp misbehaves; once in your life was enough. Go down where the ships are moored, Muadnait, and take my good foster-brother for an escort. I'd as soon he was not there if the elemental breaks free, either. Try to call the selchie if he is nearby. I'll need to talk with him."

"If you're alive!" she said fiercely. "What about yourself and Eichra?"

"We'll take our chances. Isn't that what gods and heroes do? Go quickly now. If I must implore, I do!"

She nodded, pale as sea-foam. Despite her longing to stay, her belief that it was cowardly to go, her courage failed, and as soon as Tuathal was beside her—not having been told everything, anent which he would say much, outraged, later—she fled the fortress.

She made a point of chatting to Tuathal in order to sound as ordinary as possible, and fought constantly against the urge to look back at the Grianan, her mind aflame—appropriate word!—with visions of the hall and outbuildings gouting fire, sparks whirling high above the stone ramparts, with a dread mutable shape exulting, leaping, and *growing* amid the conflagration—a vast bird with flagrant wings, a red-tentacled octopus, a prancing giant in a pyrotechnic cloak, growing, constantly growing, and bursting loose to seek more food.

Chapter Thirteen

The people praise my honour, my bravery, my courage, my wisdom; they praise my good luck, my age, my speaking, my name, my courage, and my race. Though I am a fighter, I am a poet; I am worthy of the king's favour... —Birth of Cuchulain

The harp Golden Singer rode on Felimid's back in her leather case as usual, but of particular necessity now, as he sought King Muirchertach. He held the broad strap to steady her, with his right hand, also as usual, though that arm hurt savagely. The stroke that smashed his shield had been no love tap.

Well, he had given better than he got, and to the Fir Dicuil, no less. He wasn't so lamentably out of practice after all. Or perhaps he had been. If so, everything had come back to him in time.

He found Muirchertach at the stables, a tall stallion's damaged hoof in his hand, working on it with a rasp and double-edged trimming knife. He treasured his horses and hunting dogs. Felimid felt glad he had found common ground with Muirchertach there, and that he had taken to the game of chess which Felimid introduced to Erin. It all helped. The king's reservations concerning Ruarc Sunspear and his purposes helped even more, and Felimid's fight with the Fir Dicuil cousins might be for the best after all. Muirchertach had rather liked the result.

"Pardon me for being peremptory, mighty king," he said, with a salute, "but I have discovered a thing that places the fortress of Aileach in danger. I should say, the *banfili*, Muadnait, did. It's immediate, or may well be."

"So!" Muirchertach methodically finished trimming the hoof, examined the stallion's frog, and released the foreleg. "Where is she?"

"I made bold to send her down to the shore. This is a menace of fire, and she has suffered enough from fire. The lord of Aileach can summon her later, if he sees fit."

"Fire?" The king was all attention. He had lived through the years in which Dicuil the Fiery's magic made all the north of Erin afraid. Dicuil was gone now, but his protégé Ruarc was very much a present power. "Speak on, bard, and don't waste words."

He did not.

"In your hall's great hearth there is a fire spirit, introduced there by design, I think. It remains surreptitious, and that is not the nature of them unless they are confined by magic. I think the hearth itself has signs of power cut on the stones, where they do not show, and for that purpose. When was it made, lord? Who made it? And who tends it?"

"Not so fast!" the king warned him. "You say the fire spirit is there, in my main hearth, and the *banfili* discovered it. I know how she came by her scars and her limp. She may be mistaken. I have magicians and Druids in my hall. Why do none of them know it?"

"I can't tell, lord." Felimid used a diplomatic tone and filled his eyes with innocence. "Surely they are wise, but maybe they did not discover it because they did not expect it?"

That, or they were successful place-seekers who could not tell an elemental from a rushlight. From the king's sour smile he was thinking the same.

"Muadnait can feel a fire elemental's presence in her flesh, and she is not one to make presumptuous claims before kings. I'd implore you, lord, not to send for her at once. Try my words first—and try the two bond-women who tend the hearth. How long have they served in Aileach?"

"My queen would know surely. I am thinking it is less than two years." Muirchertach's eyes widened. He did not show open signs of astonishment often. "That hearth was built just five seasons gone. Indeed, we were best to have a word with these bond-women."

Queen Duinseach Ingen Duach listened, and proved more ready to show open feeling than her husband. Her jaw muscles tightened like the cables of a plunging ship. "Those two? You don't remember when they came, Muirchertach, and their looks so strange? The king of Dalriada brought them here as a gift, Midsummer before last."

There was no need to exchange looks or say "Aha!" The bond-women of strange aspect had come to Aileach a few months before the new hearth's construction. Sunspear could have influenced the king of Dalriada.

"Suppose this is so, and a fire spirit lurks in the coals," Muirchertach said. "How did it come there? Did some wizard conjure it out of the flames, dare do so here at Aileach?"

"I doubt that could be done without drawing notice, great king. I doubt it much. It would take rites and chants. But once conjured, the being might have been carried from elsewhere in a fire-pot, with spells to contain it."

"Risky," was Muirchertach's frowning comment. "Fire yearns to break free, and will if it has the chance. Has it fretted unseen in the hearth for maybe months?"

Felimid's view was that they had sufficiently discussed that aspect, but he quelled an impatient remark. The royal couple . . . was royal, and he, their guest. This matter was more novel to them than to him. Best let them consider it at their own pace.

"Someone, if that be so, has made a careful job of curbing it," the queen murmured. "Someone has been vigilant. The foreign women are always tending that fire, crooning chants as they work. They cut and lug the firewood most industriously. Twice have they kept a blaze from running away. I was well pleased, then; now I am not so sure."

"What if we confront them and they set the imp loose?"

"If they're the ones who have kept it prisoner all these days, they will hardly wish to do that," the bard said. "It will resent them. Also, I believe I and my harp can keep it quiescent, until it is back in a fire-pot and away to distant parts. Maybe it were better to quench it out entirely."

"First let's discover it."

Very shortly then, the two bond-women from Dalriada were quailing before Muirchertach's fury. One, Felimid saw, having seen her like before, belonged to the Atecotti, the "very old people" of north Britain. Short and gnarled, with sunken eyes that shifted as though looking for a way of escape, she crouched low. The other, much taller and straighter-limbed, had a face like adzed timber. Ash and sweat stained her tunic, dyed with blackberry juice but otherwise plain.

"We've come to know," the king said grimly, with no preamble, "that a fire sprite occupies the great hearth. Do not waste our time with expostulation. I trust those who told me."

Trust us more or less, Felimid thought.

"This is wrong!" the taller woman cried. "There could be no fire sprite there without our knowing. We tend the hearth!"

"Yes. And I commanded you to waste no time in protest. Do not ignore my word again."

"You concede," the queen said, "that no such imp could be there, and you ignorant of't. Thus far, so good. Ah, Gartan." A fat servitor approached with a leather bag in his hands. "You searched their belongings as you were bidden?"

"Yes, great queen." Gartan looked at the women, who glared pure hate, then at his rulers. "I discovered a fire-pot with oghams cut in a circle around the lid—a charm, surely. I cannot read them—"

"I can," Felimid interjected. "Have you the thing in that bag?"

With a nod, Gartan produced it, handing it over as though glad to be rid of something accursed. It looked most ordinary, a container of fired clay, shaped like an egg two hand-spans high. Round holes, pierced while the clay was raw, were spaced equidistant around the lid, and written characters—oghams—ran around the pot just below the lid. But these were the ancient, original script, like those on the sword Kincaid, not the second-rate cipher derived from them and cut on memorial stones in the present. To Felimid's bardic sight, they flickered orange and yellow like tiny flames. They held immediate, perilous power.

"This was made to hold a fire spirit safely," the bard said, "tiny, and innocuous."

"And why not?" the tall woman rasped defiantly. "We are skilled at holding fire. My father was a blacksmith. We have tended the royal hearth since we came to Aileach, and tended it well, too."

The sunken-eyed woman of the Atecotti, who spoke Erin's tongue only in mangled accents though she understood it well enough, growled, "We have that."

"None says otherwise," the bard conceded. "Suppose you come to the hearth now, and we take your efficacious fire-pot, and see if a fire imp is there or not. I have it in mind that my harp may induce mild behavior in him."

Muirchertach, with no good humour in his face now, took an old spear from the wall behind him.

"If there is an imp in my hearth, and it bursts free to burn this hall, you will both die," he told the women. Then he turned his gaze on Felimid. "If there should not be one—then you and I will talk, and you will not enjoy the conversation, though you were ten times a bard."

"So be it, lord." Felimid drew forth Golden Singer and held her in the crook of his right arm, the one that hurt considerably. They approached the great stone hearth, and Felimid's mind was uneasy. Maybe even the warrior king's heart stumbled. As for the bond-women, they shook between fear of Muirchertach and fear of Ruarc Sunspear.

The deep coals in the hearth lay banked and quiescent. Nothing cooked over them at present. That something as volatile as a fire elemental could have lurked there for months, kept under control, never making itself known in spectacular fashion, said much for the diligence of the two women. One began a series of arcane gestures, the other a chant in what Felimid recognized as the Atecotti tongue. He felt in his flesh and bones they were meant to soothe, to mollify—for the nonce—but he did not trust the women. These in all probability were Sunspear's creatures.

"Lord," he said sharply, "have them cease this."

Muirchertach did not question him. He barked the command, and brought his spear-point to one woman's breast by way of emphasis. The queen took fierce hold of the other and showed a glare as daunting as any spear-point.

Felimid's left hand ran over the golden strings. Notes that hissed and crackled burst on the air. Something stirred, deep below the surface ashes, and Felimid turned his flagrant music on the longer strings. It shifted to mellow, appeasing measures.

The bard sang as softly.

"Spirit without a shape,
Fire imp without a name,
You who rage at confinement,
Be yet confined and tame.

"What carried you here may hold you,
And carry you whence you came,
Even to Emain Macha,
Which once was set in a flame.

Sunspear

"Say you to fiery Sunspear,
This king will not eat shame;
Not he nor the Queen of Aileach
Play his presumptuous game.
"Tell him the bard Felimid
And a woman that fire made lame
And Tuathal called the Bowman
Are one in saying the same.

"I send this bardic word
Through Golden Singer's frame –
If fire imps trouble Aileach
We shall know who to blame."

Something appeared, moving across the coals. It was bright, flickering yellow in hue, shapeless as Felimid had called it, with a hotter, paler core. Very briefly it seemed to have definite form, like a fledgling bird crying for food, but it shifted as pictures seen in fire always do, became shapeless, then a blind sharp-featured face, then shapeless again. If it sprang to the garments of any one of them, Felimid thought, it would set them ablaze and grow.

He struck harsh, forbidding chords with his nails. The being shook. Beckoning with gestures, the gnarled Atecotti woman spoke to it, and the tall one held forth the fire-pot with its circle of symbols. The imp arched into it as though drawn. Dry scorched linen, several times folded, gave it food there. The tall bond-woman clapped its lid on the fire-pot and fastened it with thin iron chains. She began sliding twigs and chips through the holes in the lid to feed her captive, little and helpless now, dependent—and not liking it—but able to devastate a kingdom if given the opportunity.

"By the Red Hand," Muirchertach said in a shaken voice. "My gratitude is yours, Felimid mac Fal. You two!" He scowled at the women. "Take this back to Emain Macha. Ten of my riders will see that you don't swerve from the way. Tell Ruarc Sunspear that, just as the bard sang, I take this act of his as an impudence and I will not forget.

"Now go!"

Chapter Fourteen

It was Levarcham, daughter of Aedh, the conversation woman and messenger to the king, that was there at that time, and was sometimes away in the hills, was the first to see them coming.
—The Boy Deeds of Cuchulain

The massive rooftree of Aileach loomed darkly above the booth where Senan lay stoical in his pain. His kinsman sat beside his couch, and Mathgadro stood, pale hair hanging lank about his discontented face, harp in his hands. He looked a little unkempt, a sign that he was worried. His respectful salute to Muirchertach was manifestly insincere, his look at Felimid malign. Felimid grinned in his eyes.

"No sign of infection, warrior?" Muirchertach asked the supine man. "My physicians say not."

"None, lord." Senan looked derisively at the bard. "My breed is not prone to't."

"So I have heard," Felimid agreed. He had doubted it, and so had Muadnait. She had been sure this man would die. "It's well. I desired to teach you to be just the smallest thing wary of giving offence, not slay you. But the combat grew hot."

Mathgadro sneered. "You haven't seen heated fighting yet, betrayer. Ruarc Sunspear will show you some.

You are beneath his attention, but he has promised to give it you, nevertheless."

"I travelled north that he may have the chance."

"In the interval," Muirchertach said with a look, "I am king in Aileach, and I have sent the two bond-women back to Sunspear, with the fire-spirit they fetched here, and the message that if a second one comes to my fortress, in secret or in the open, I'll see it as a most hostile act, and the one responsible as a declared foe. Once Senan and Cathal's wounds mend, they and you must depart also, Bluetongue the satirist. As swiftly as you can."

"As the king wills," Mathgadro said.

"Smirk like that again, and you will indeed leave. But your head will stay here. Bard or not."

Mathgadro bowed very low.

Tempted as he was, Felimid made no comment. The king was in a curt mood. Besides, the state of Senan's belly wound—free of sepsis—reminded one that the Fir Dicuil were not wholly human. They bred fast, grew fast, and were hard to kill. They might present trouble to all Erin in future, whether as Ruarc's war-band or on their own account.

A concern for another time.

He rode to the harbour to give Muadnait the news. She was waiting there, by the long steel-coloured sea-lough, and Odhran the selchie with her. It gratified them both to know that she had been right. The fire imp had been discovered, made prisoner in a clay pot, and sent back to Emain Macha with a warning. Muadnait especially trembled with relief.

"I am sorry to be such a child," she said, angry with herself, "and to have run away. I couldn't—couldn't—face being in the hall if that living flame should escape and go wild."

"Cairbre and Ogma, no! You were better here. And a child you were not. You discovered the fiery imp. Now it is prisoned in a clay pot, and conveyed back to Emain Macha under guard. I wonder what Ruarc will do with it."

"Who knows?" Odhran shrugged his scarred shoulders. "Glad I am that I was in the lough while you dealt with the thing, lord of the harp. Right glad. No more than the lady do I love fire imps."

"Now it is gone, you can return to the hall and receive credit," the bard said cheerfully. "Na, don't shake your head. It will do you good to be the cynosure of admiring eyes and receive the thanks of an over-king. Nor will that vessel of spite Mathgadro make any disparaging remarks, not after what I did to Cathal and Senan. He's not my match with either weapons or words and he knows it. Come. Lift your head high, and come. At my side, if you will."

Muadnait coloured a little, but she looked Felimid straight in the face and agreed.

"Yes. I'll come."

She entered the hall again, as Felimid had said, between him and Odhran, to a sudden respectful silence. Each last ember in the hearth had been drenched out with water, to incantations from the king's Druids, and now the stones were being removed one by one. Some had potent symbols cut on their inner sides—cut not with chisels, but with spoken words of power—and these were carried out of the fortress to be broken. With her back to the hearth and her face to the royal pair, she received the thanks Felimid had predicted she would get.

"Our gratitude is yours," said the king, and his big voice rang. "You are our esteemed guest. Harm or insult to you is harm or insult to us. By my name and my queen's name, by the red hand of our *feine*, you are to be honoured in this hall as you were our daughter."

"And take this for my gift, *banfili*," spoke Queen Duinseach Ingen Duach, unpinning the gleaming mantle she wore. Woven in Erin, from silk that had come across the sea with traders from Spain, and before that, to Spain from Byzantine Egypt, it was purple, bordered in green and gold, and carried the Tree of Life design in the same colours.

"Munificent queen," Muadnait stammered, taken aback, "this is glorious—and—more than I merit."

"There is truth from her, this time," Mathgadro muttered, tone carefully low, "and more than I looked for. Corpse eater."

Felimid had not been intended to hear. He heard. Assuming a time came when larger matters did not take precedence, he thought he and Mathgadro might clash.

"This fortress might have been consumed in flames one day—one not so distant day—but for your warning," the queen reminded her. "I will decide what that merits, yes, and be offended if you refuse."

She clapped her hands. Two attendants removed Muadnait's cowled cloak and put the precious silk on her instead. Her body grew tense as hammered steel at the exposure of her face, but pride kept her head up—pride, and knowing it was unwise to slight a royal gift. Seeing that burned cheek exposed, one of the attendants sucked in a shocked breath, and the other glared at her for the lack of discipline.

"I'll wear this gratefully," Muadnait said.

Odhran, lithe in kilt and sandals, his sealskin on his shoulders, looked around him with liquid dark eyes. "I am still uneasy in the hall of a king of men," he said. "Their wine I do like, though. It is in my mind that I will get drunk with Tuathal and Eichra."

"No reason why you should not," Felimid agreed, seeing no danger to the selchie in that, apart from the likelihood that Eichra would play a joke on him while he was fuddled. "Bluetongue is treacherous, but until his bodyguards heal and can assist him, he'll do nothing."

"For now, I would rather not think of such things." Muadnait's grey eyes cleared of trouble. "For now we are secure. There are no more fire spirits hidden in this dun. I'd know if there were."

"Of this I am sure." Felimid thought of her waiting by the harbor, wondering if Muirchertach's hall was ablaze. The journey there and the journey back, in one day, had been demanding. "Come and rest."

"Come and rest," she echoed, with a small laugh. "Off Aran I have rowed all day, at times, in a rough sea, till my hands bled and I saw visions. And I could still do more, for soft I am not. I'll come, though. It's kindly thought of."

Like other individual guest apartments in the hall, Felimid's was a neat oblong against the wall, with oak panels, wicker screens, and leather curtains. Its couch boasted a feather mattress, linen coverlet and furs, with rushes and sheepskins on the floor. Despite her claim to strong endurance, Muadnait shed her shoes and stretched on the couch with a sigh.

"Ahhh, there is grateful," she said.

There were burn scars on one foot and calf. That ankle tendon was shrunken, the cause of her limp. Felimid did not avoid looking at it. Unless he misread her, there had been a challenge and test in the way she exposed her foot. Any grimace or other sign of distaste would have closed her face and her mind to him, regardless of his fight with the Fir Dicuil.

He discovered he did not wish that to happen.

"Not pretty, is it, hey?" she said.

"No. It was foul that it ever was done." He looked her in the face. "I'm glad, again, that Erin is rid of Dicuil."

"It's in my mind that you will have to rid it of Ruarc too. He's young yet, but he's wholly human, and so has it in him to become greater, more perilous than Dicuil. And you or he must die in the end. He will have it no other way."

"Yea, he was overt and expressive on that score, so he was. I reckon his pride will impel him to some sort of response at once. Not a surreptitious one. He's not Mathgadro. We must just wait and see."

"We could wait in worse company," she said.

"I've thought so," he agreed, "more than once."

He sat beside her and passed an arm around her waist. It felt excellently supple and warm. Their two faces were close and her grey eyes looked into his green ones. She coloured a little.

"Do not kiss me," she said, "unless you mean it."

He did kiss her. And left her in no doubt that he meant it. After the first long moment he did not find her shy. In her arms he forgot the terrible sundering axe-strokes that had killed Gudrun Blackhair, and Muadnait forgot her horror of fire. They reveled in life instead, in mounting sweet pleasure and passion, and they learned more about each other, without words.

Words were called for, in the end, though. Running his hands over her smooth shoulders and back, Felimid said, "Earth Mother Danu, sea-wise woman! It appears you needed *that*."

Muadnait laughed into his neck. "It has been some time." She seemed to debate with herself whether to say more, and to be doubting the wisdom of it. In the end she gave her thoughts utterance.

"There was a skipper, a brisk fellow, and I thought he liked me. It wasn't so. He desired a charm against storm and reef. He supposed I was so desperate for love I would give him one if he tumbled me. When he asked for the charm, and gods but he was brash about it, I saw through him, and was angry that he held me so light. I'm not without pride. I told him to thank his stars I did not ill-wish him, but he was not worth it. If he wanted a charm for sea-luck, he must get it from the college by paying for it, like any other mariner. I said a deal else, too. So did he. I must have been deeper hurt than it warranted—a trifling thing, really—because I did feel a strong urge to curse him and his ship, but I know better than to be promiscuous with curses. There's danger in it."

"There is truly." Felimid thought he had a picture of that fellow in his mind, fine looking but coarse and shallow. He'd become vindictive when denied the charm he sought, no doubt, and hit back in the obvious way, bawling at Muadnait that with her face no-one would want her unless he had something to gain. "What is his name?"

"What? It's of no weight! It isn't, surely, in your mind to go seeking him out?"

"There are greater things to hand, no question, but if I survive them, I may run across this oaf someday."

"Let it be. I took it too much to heart. There was nobody since him, not until you. Well." She awarded him a very female smile. "Worth waiting for, it was, Felimid mac Fal."

"Splendid it was. And moved I am that you wished it."

"Then," she said with her breath coming fast, "might we do it again?"

Chapter Fifteen

"It is a fine setting out you are having," said Bricriu, "but maybe the coming back will not be so fine." "It is a journey that will be heard of in every place," said Maine. "I suppose," said Bricriu, "it is but a day visit you will make there, for you will hardly stop to feast through the night in a district that is under Conchubor." "I give my word," said Maine, "we will not turn back..."

—The Wedding of Maine Morgor

Ruarc mac Amalgaid, known as Sunspear, lay on his royal couch at Emain Macha. Like Felimid in the same hour, he held a woman in his arms, his languid paramour Aivene. Not quiescent when they coupled, or she would not have held his interest long, but she drifted in a kind of detached warmth else. She stretched atop him with her satisfied loins straddling his powerful thigh. Running her fingers through the golden hair that pelted his chest, she kissed him and studied his face.

"A message and gift to the king of Connacht, then?" she said. "You keep him, and his daughters, guessing."

"For the present, it suits me. And I never would willingly exchange you for any of Connacht's daughters."

She accepted that, and his reciprocal ardent kiss. She accepted too that he kept her for her beauty and passion—what other reason?—and that even had she gifts of sagacious political counsel, and greater prophetic power than Taladh Teisne, Sunspear would reckon it an outright insult to his manhood, to take a woman's advice.

She accepted his remark about the daughters of King Eógan Bél also. They *were* a plain lot. A link with the fifth of Connacht would have value, but it would anger the Uí Néill, a thing Aivene could see even though she took small interest in her land's tangled animosities and alliances. They changed from one day to the next.

No matter who Ruarc made his queen, Aivene felt sure she would remain in his bed. That was no ill thing. Being Sunspear's leman carried a cachet, even if renown and power meant more to him than anything wearing skirts.

Having no royal kinship, she would never be his queen. That too was fine. Her father was a cattle-chief, prosperous enough to have always a vat of milk, a vat of ale, and a candle on the candlestick, but as his fourth daughter Aivene had no fortune other than her face and shape. She had become the leman of an over-king, handsome and mighty, which was far better than stepping in cow dung every day.

She watched the big golden man don kilt and sandals and—for he cared as much about his grooming as any son of Erin—coil his hair. He was folding his cloak about him when Cuanach, overt spokesman and messenger, covert spymaster, entered his presence. The face of Cuanach was pale.

Ruarc observed his tension. He said, "Let me hear."

"Lord, the women who tended the fire at Aileach are back, with the imp," Cuanach told him. His eyes and tone conveyed that he would rather be somewhere else. Not all Ruarc's adherents were at ease around fire elementals. "Ten weapon-men came with them to make sure they would not leave the road. They wait in the banquet hall. They say they have a message from Muirchertach for the king's ears, and no others before the king."

"Do they so?" Ruarc smiled broadly. "And you are concerned about it? Maybe Muirchertach mac Muiredaig *is* irked. Let him be. He'll not be wrathful enough to try conclusions with me and the Fir Dicuil. I'm indulgent. I'll listen to the word he sends."

Taking his long, gold-hilted sword, he strode to the hall, where he beheld the ten men from Aileach, bereft of their spears and shields but truculent in their stance, scowling. In the midst of them stood the two women, the taller one holding the fire-pot, with leather wrappings about it to shield her hands from the heat.

"I welcome you, men of the Uí Néill," Ruarc said in his mellow, ringing voice, the voice that could arouse men to reckless fury before a battle, or make women catch their breath. "Are you here in friendship or war?"

"Not in war, king of Airgialla," answered the leader of the ten, a scarred warrior a decade older than Ruarc. "Not in friendship either. We come at our own king's command, to return the gift he did not ask for, and that you did not let him know you were sending. It's in this firepot."

"You puzzle me," Ruarc said, indulgent and kingly.

"King Muirchertach did not think I would, lord. The pot holds a fire-imp. Muirchertach's message is that your act in placing the thing in his royal hearth was an impudence he will not forget. And a word more. But first the bard Felimid mac Fal sends a word of his own to King Ruarc."

"Felimid?"

"Felimid, lord. The two fighters who accompanied your friend Mathgadro quarreled with him. He fought them both, and beat them both. They are hurt, but they live."

Sunspear believed it. He breathed deeply, controlling his ire. These were his men, and their defeat harmed his honour. But silence had more dignity than a volley of oaths.

"Felimid's word is this. Senan and Cathal are fortunate that he does not send you their heads. If he had done that, he would have sent you Mathgadro's head too. King Muirchertach's word after that, which he bade us convey, is that if Felimid had chosen such a course, he'd have given it his sanction, and that you should keep your fire elementals away from Aileach."

His gilded scabbard creaked in Sunspear's big hands.

"Muirchertach says that? *They* say that? Lugh of the Long Hand! That calls for an answer at once! I will make it! Saddle my red roan. Bring firewood here and pile it high. The imp shall feed and grow. Bid Sirega arm herself and choose a troop of men. We ride for Aileach, and I'll be there by sunset, or be displeased."

Aivene heard him shouting, and dressed without haste in her second-best gown. Going leisurely to the hall, and finding Ruarc no longer there, she sought him on the open space outside. The firewood he commanded had been stacked head high. Although tranquil by nature, not easily shaken, Aivene looked at the pile and shivered. She had seen the fire elementals Ruarc could summon.

Ruarc had not gone to the *liss* either. He had repaired to the great central chamber, where none might go in his absence, or unless he himself called them to enter. The ceiling, as fine an imitation of King Conchubor's fabled silver dome as art could contrive, glittered above him. A ring of red yew pillars, each clasped with bronze circlets, upheld the shining dome handsomely. Ruarc, pressing hidden catches, opened one of those bronze circlets to expose a hollow space within the pillar. He reached inside, his expression solemn and avid at once, to bring forth the twisted gold collar he wore when giving judgement, or presiding as king in other ways.

Closely watching the curtained entrance to the chamber, he donned the collar. Then he closed the bronze circlet around the pillar again. None knew about that hiding place but he and his magician-seer, Taladh Teisne. The craftsman who had made it was dead.

Ruarc strode forth again, fine to behold, the torc in his hand. Taladh Teisne awaited him beside the pile of firewood. His look was sombre, his bearded mouth set grimly.

"Powerful lord, this is not lightly done," he said.

"I am not doing it lightly," Sunspear assured him. "Not lightly at all. No more lightly than I promised Felimid mac Fal I would take his head to the White Isle on a spear for his mother to see, before I burn that cursed holding. I'll meet him sword to sword yet! I promise it on my pact with nature and the blazing spear of Lugh! Now bring the fire elemental and my harp."

The last was addressed not to Taladh Teisne, but to the women fresh come from Aileach and a young attendant of royal blood who stood nearby with Ruarc's instrument. For a common person to have touched it would mean death at Sunspear's court. Once, a like penalty had attached to handling of Golden Singer, but down the centuries it had softened.

"Let the imp free," Sunspear commanded.

They lifted the pot's lid and spilled, with care, its contents on the heap of fuel. Swiftly, deftly, they fed the little flames with straw, bark and twigs until they caught on the wood. Green or old, ash burns well.

Something bright yellow moved amid the flames. It flexed the semblance of wings, like some fledgeling bird. It chirruped, hissed, and grew. Hungry, wild in its freedom after close confinement, it fed and grew larger.

Sunspear watched it closely, and struck the strings of his harp in swift, crackling cadences. The music rose ardent as fire itself. His rich voice joined the notes, his tone commanding.

> *"I am a lord of fire in the mind,*
> *I am a child of the life-giving worshipped Sun;*
> *I have made songs and I have fathered life,*
> *I have made music and I have awarded death.*
> *I am a king above kings and a champion of war,*
> *A benefactor of Druids in the secret groves,*
> *A child of the worshipped Sun that spawned you,*
> *An elder brother to the progeny of fire."*

The fire-being devoured the wood and waxed greater. Its form constantly changed. From a thing of roughly avian form it became a dazzling golden orb wreathed in ribbons of orange ignescence. In another moment it had the form of a six-legged reptile, finned on the back with shifting fire. In that shape it lay briefly quiescent atop a log of fuel, and it seemed to be listening—giving heed to Sunspear's claim to be its elder brother.

He went on in rhymed quintains.

"I summon your like from bright Brigid's fane,
I call and dismiss and I may not be slain,
Not even by you of the bright ardent mane –

Yet your very being needs fuel to maintain,
And can vanish in any wild tempest of rain.
So follow my bidding and blaze in the sun,
And burn, if I order, a proud royal dun,
Sparing not farmer or chieftain or nun –
But until I unleash them your flames may not run
E'en in timber or pitch or the driest flax spun."

The fire elemental swelled in resentment at these strictures—but it did not hurl itself on the man who presumed to direct it, and burn him to cinders. It crouched where it was. That in itself acknowledged Sunspear's mastery—for the moment.

Caragh, princess of the Ulaid kingdom—what remained of it—watched in fascinated dread. Even her father, a hard man, maintained his composure with some effort. They did not behold fire elementals every day.

Ruarc finished giving orders to his various folk, and then turned to his royal guests, his manner stately.

"King of Ulidia, noble princess, pardon this uncouth commotion. Muirchertach of Aileach has sent me a message—and with it this fire spirit—that insults me roughly. The bard Felimid who murdered my teacher Dicuil has been more malapert still. They hold me too lightly. Their affronts call for an immediate answer, and I will not be sending one by the tongues of messengers. I'll speak it with my own mouth into their faces. I'd not be leaving in this precipitate fashion else." He saluted them, and gave Caragh a look so ardent that she lost countenance. "My sorrow. When I return I shall make amends."

"Let them know it is ill to trifle with Airgialla," Caragh's father growled. He hoped to see her as Ruarc's queen and the Ulaid's prestige renewed. Withal, he had no love for the Uí Néill.

"I shall," Sunspear laughed.

He hadn't ceased laughing as he passed Taladh Teisne, but he said swiftly, "That matter of Armagh's bishop, my friend—put it forward at once. When I return, I wish to hear that he's a captive in the grove."

"It will be so."

Chapter Sixteen

"It is best for you to tell it at the king's desire," said Cuinaire, *"before you get your death through refusing it, as many a champion from Alban and from Britain has done before now."*

"If that is the order you put on us when we land here, it is I will break it," said Conlaoch, *"and no one will obey it any longer from this out."* —The Only Son of Aoife

"He's coming, and with a cavalcade," the Queen of Aileach said, cloaked in fringed green and black on the highest rampart of her husband's fort. "You were right, Felimid mac Fal."

"Any man can be right when a sprite of the wind brings him news, lady," Felimid answered. "The king and you predicted it without that."

"We know Sunspear," King Muirchertach said, and laughed, but with an edge of unease. "Jab his pride and you'll get a response, by the red hand! There he rides."

Sunspear rode tall, in the lead, on a roan stallion whose harness glittered with gold. On his own person, at arms, throat and waist, the dazzle and flash of gold could be seen from furlongs off. Behind him, the powerfully muscled Dub Dothar bore a green banner with a golden sun-wheel worked upon it in stiff bullion. Niall and Tachdan, on black horses, rode to either side of him, and behind them, a fighting tail of the savage Fir Dicuil. The woman Sirega rode first among those, on a sorrel mare fierce as she was, spinning and tossing up her barbed spear, she who had waded in blood and torn out entrails when she fought at Druim Derg.

The horses had been pacified with a calming draught in their water. They would have galloped all ways in mad panic else. Above them, above the whole fine cavalcade, flew a shape of light that dazzled, especially its core, a white globe of radiance. The form around it shaded from hot yellow to vermilion. Now it was an orb surrounded by streaming prominences, now a dragon-like being with fiery wings, now an equine shape with a flaming mane and tail, heart incandescent, hoofs glowing, rampant in mid-air.

Muadnait made an appalled choking sound and fled. Felimid saw her stumbling along the rampart to one of the stairways leading down. This was bad. The stone steps were not perfectly even and some had become worn over time.

"She may fall," he said rapidly. "Forgive me, my lord, my lady."

"Surely," Muirchertach agreed. "*Go.*"

Felimid sped after her, racing as though his life hung upon it. The sword Kincaid caught between his legs and he almost fell, himself, but got back his balance and overtook the *banfili* just as she stumbled on the topmost step. Bracing a foot on the step below, and clutching Muadnait hard, he felt the frantic rigidity of her muscles. Her entire body was one rictus of terror.

"I have to get out of here. That fire will burn . . . everything!"

"Yes," Felimid panted. "Right you are. Not that it'll burn everything . . . it's in my mind that Ruarc just demonstrates power, seeks to frighten . . ."

"He has!"

"And you must go."

He aided her down the stair, for her lame foot still endangered her. He smelled urine, and the front of her skirt clung wetly to her thighs. She was an infant again, with her whole known world ablaze. The bard felt rage that she should suffer such humiliation because Sunspear was arrogant. He'd remember that.

Queen Duinseach and her lord, staring at the thing in the sky, as rulers of Aileach were more outraged than Felimid. The king ground his teeth. Anger overcame dread of the fire spirit, and he motioned to one of his bodyguard, a dour scarred seasoned fellow.

"Obtain four other good men with javelins, Marudd," he said. "Have them within range of Sunspear, but not obtrusively, from the time he enters. If yon fire monster goes wild, even wholly by accident, Sunspear is to die, and yea, have *an Saighdeoir*, Felimid's foster brother, ready also with his bow, to the same purpose. He's gone beyond what is seemly, has Sunspear."

Such was Felimid's view. Beneath the ramparts, he said in Muadnait's ear, "Listen to me. Find Odhran, and go back to the harbour with him. Stop for nothing. I'll come to you later, and do not fear for me, or for Aileach, I am thinking. Sunspear does not wish to burn it, unless he's a fool—but he may fail in control of that living conflagration he leads. Muadnait! You hear me? You understand?"

"Y-yes."

"I'd go with you, it's right, but I cannot. While I carry Golden Singer, Sunspear will treat me like gold itself; he wants her, undamaged. So did Dicuil in his day. And by Earth Mother Danu, I want *you* undamaged. Get to the water-side with Odhran."

"Yes," she said again.

It was the best counsel and most safety he could offer her with Sunspear at the gate of Aileach. Even the bard had not expected him to come bringing the fire elemental, in a larger and more menacing form. Indeed, he had his prideful gall. And what trees and houses had the creature fed upon while it made the journey? There might be a trail of ashes across Muirchertach's kingdom to answer that question, and Sunspear in his pride and defiance would be careless of the offence.

Their imminent meeting should be provocative.

Muadnait hurried to find the seal-man, and Felimid watched her depart. This was the second time in a nine-night she had scurried in dread to the Lake of Eyes, because of a fire imp. (More than a little imp now.) Because of Sunspear! Self-indulgent rages had small appeal to the bard, but he gazed at the eye-hurting glorious fulgour of the elemental, then at the rider on the splendid red roan, and his pulses beat hard and scalding.

Being Felimid, and having noted Ruarc's magnificence of dress, he made sure his own garb and grooming was superb before making for the main entrance of Aileach with all the impudent sang-froid he could express in his gait. It was not closed. Sunspear's pet could have burned the portal clear in a moment, and barring it in his face might have looked fearful.

Tuathal and Eichra joined the bard, the former with bow on his back, arrows in his belt and King Muirchertach's instructions in mind. Ruarc Sunspear saw them approaching, though he had attention only for Felimid. His eyes widened, he hissed a soft, drawn-out "Ahhhh," and felt a great urge to spur his steed forward, riding the other man down. He quelled it.

The fire-being hovered above, its energies blazing about it. It flashed, too swiftly for the eye to follow, left and right and into the zenith like some lesser sun, coruscating with wild power. The weight of Golden Singer on his back was reassuring to Felimid, very much so. That fragile frame of oak with its silken gleam was so coveted—yes, and held sacrosanct—by Ruarc that he would not damage it. Felimid hoped he could maintain control of the volatile entity he so arrogantly led like a pet.

Three years of increasing power lay on Ruarc like his mantle. Collar, armlets, cincture, and saddle ornaments flashed gold in the sun, and in the shifting radiance of the fire elemental. Yet it was in Sunspear's face most of all that Felimid saw the solar gleam remembered from three years ago, finer and more intense. Indeed, he'd acquired kingship and mastery, too soon, maybe, but—he possessed it.

"Give you good day, Ruarc Sunspear," Felimid said courteously. "I believe you have improved since I last saw you."

Ruarc smiled like a lion unsheathing its talons. "It's pleasant to see you again. Fourth bardic rank now, I believe."

"Yes. I took some extra time and repeated some training. I'll attain to the fifth in a couple more years."

"I do not think so."

He meant that Felimid should not live so long. However, he did not overlook the presence of Tuathal with his bow, or miss the Aileach men with their javelins, unobtrusively within throwing range. He showed no sign that he had even noticed.

"I am here to visit Muirchertach," he said. "He perhaps misunderstands me. When kings misunderstand each other it is a weighty matter. I'll talk to him now."

He did not say it as though that was a thing for Muirchertach to decide.

Before long, he stood in the presence of Aileach's rulers, who greeted him from their high seats with cool courtesy. He smiled, unabashed, and offered them polite honours in return. Muirchertach took those for precisely what they were worth, with a fire elemental darting back and forth above his fortress, and surveyed Ruarc without love. Still smiling, the younger king seized a chief seated in a place of honour, hauled him out of it even though he resisted and was no weakling, and took his place with studied nonchalance.

"As King Muirchertach did not invite me to sit, I do not suppose he will be offended when I require the recognition due me, and seat myself," Sunspear murmured.

"King Ruarc mac Amalgaid supposes wrongly." The lord of Aileach reddened, but kept his dignity. "I was offended when you surreptitiously placed a fire imp in our royal hearth. I was more offended when you came to our royal seat bringing—I take it—the same fire imp in greater, more threatening form. I am a third time offended when you manhandle a chief of this kingdom in my presence. Give him back his seat, now."

Ruarc made a show of considering the order.

"Well," he said, shrugging, "my point has been made. Standing or sitting, I am Ruarc Sunspear. This is King Muirchertach's dun."

He stood. His stance was insolent, his expression one of barely contained ascendancy. Muirchertach was having none of it.

"You surreptitiously placed a fire imp in our royal hearth. Why?"

"I am a king. A king must know what his neighbours do," Ruarc said condescendingly. "The fire from which I called the imp—more than an imp now, as you rightly said—still burns in my dun at Emain Macha." *Now there,* he implied, *is something worth calling a kingly hearth.* "I could read in its flames what transpires here."

Pyromancy, Felimid thought. The long word might be Greek, but the skill was known in many places, from Persia to the Celtic west. Sunspear would have practised it for years under Dicuil's tutelage.

"And if for some cause you ever wished to lay Aileach waste, you had only to release the imp from your two witches," Muirchertach said. "You spied on us. You placed our household in danger. The elemental might have escaped their check at any time whether you wished it or not, were they careless. You are within my walls and safe conduct applies. Else this would be your death-day, Ruarc Sunspear. You may even feast and drink here this night. I never refused any traveller that. You may have the place due a king." His voice rose to a roar. "By the gods my people swear by, though, I would not be long about leaving tomorrow!"

Calmer, more measured, but no less definite, Queen Duinseach added, "This fortress will be the cleaner when you take Mathgadro Bluetongue and Senan and Cathal with you."

"Are they fit to travel?" Sunspear asked. "They had best be."

"They can travel," Bluetongue assured him. "Not in litters, either. It would take more than this mudlark to incapacitate them long."

"True, but crude," Ruarc murmured. "Let's be gracious. He did well to survive them. Better than most would do." Briefly, his gaze moved to Felimid, and there was murder in it despite the mild words. Then he smiled at Muirchertach. "I accept your hospitality for the night, mac Muiredaig of the Cenél nEógain, with appreciation. We depart in the morning as you request. I am shattered to have displeased you. May I make amends for it in the future."

Muirchertach forgot kingly gravity and snorted. "That will take a little doing."

Ruarc said imperturbably, "It took a little doing to become king of Airgialla. I have hopes." He glanced at Felimid. "What, you leave us? Where would you go?"

"The ship haven by the Lake of Eyes."

"That does not amaze me," Mathgadro sneered. "No boarding the nearest vessel and fleeing for home, pirate's get."

"I'd never think it. My errand there is my business, and I'd have you fully comprehend this thing. Tuathal comes with me, and if any creature of Ruarc Sunspear tries to follow, he will meet an arrow."

Ruarc lifted his golden brows, pained, and asked Muirchertach, "Do you sanction this?"

Muirchertach did not reply to the question directly. To the bard he said, "Take horses. It's something of a walk."

Chapter Seventeen

"But if it is in the House of the Red Branch you are put, then he is going to do treachery on you."
—The Fate of the Sons of Usnach

There were no vessels at the haven now but a few fishing boats, and Brandon's large curragh. He and his brothers still abode at Aileach, but Felimid had seen little of them lately, and they were far from his thoughts now. One person who occupied them was Sunspear, and another was Muadnait. She waited in the shadows of the rugged sea-rocks. Water sucked and swirled among them, smelling of weed. Seabirds cried forlornly.

"I was afraid," she said in his arms. "Lir! I am ashamed. I wet myself when I saw that fire spirit. I could not run away fast enough."

"You were wise," he assured her. "I knew I was safe. More or less. Sunspear does not wish this harp to burn. He cannot be sure of restraining the elemental, though, and if it escapes his rule—"

"He may be the first one turned to ash."

"It's predicted that Ruarc Sunspear can only die by a triple death—three ways at once."

"It does not sound likely," Odhran contributed.

"While he keeps that fiery being near him, on such a fragile leash, he stands in sudden danger of burning at any rate."

"What should I do?" Muadnait asked. "I cannot go back to the fortress. I dare not."

"And it's best you do not, I am thinking. I mean to advise Brandon and his monks to get their backsides out of Aileach as well. They can fare east to the Giant's Causeway. It's navigable for a curragh like theirs, up the Bann to the Lake of Eachad, is't not? And from the lake they can reach Armagh, the See of Padraigh, if they wish to."

"I have been there," said Muadnait, with no huge enthusiasm. "From the southern shore it is three leagues or less. The monks at Armagh are not like Brandon and his brothers, while . . . the bishop . . . "

"Yes, I hear he's a harsh, narrow-headed man. But the Armagh foundation is dead ground for magic, and the fire elemental cannot approach it. That's the thing that counts. You will be safe there, the monks too."

"What about you?" Muadnait gripped his arms. Her gaze searched his. "Will you return to Aileach? With Sunspear there? He hates you."

"He'll do nothing against a bard. He'll do nothing against the power of Golden Singer either, *a ghrá geal*. And I have to know what he does mean to do. He has only one night at Aileach to do't, whatever it might be. Muirchertach has told him roundly to pack out in the morning."

"And you are going back? Yes. I see that you are."

"The Lake of Eachad is a good destination for us," spoke Odhran. "It's very good. A tribe of selchies lives there. We'll find a welcome and safety with them. Yes, the bard advises well, *banfili*. I am thinking neither we nor the monks can do much good biding here."

"Nor can Felimid!" Muadnait cried. "Nothing but ill can come of your returning to the stone fortress! Come away with us, Felimid, to the Lake of Eachad or any other place, but not to Aileach or Emain Macha. Do that, and by the waves of the sea, it's in my mind that you are doomed."

"Listen to her," Odhran told him urgently. "Come with us. You will be safe on the sea, or on the big lake. Fire elementals dread water."

"So they do. Odhran my friend, Muadnait, it's well I would like to come away with you, but I cannot leave Eichra or fail to advise the monks, and there will be men dead in their blood if I run away from Aileach. Muirchertach has been a noble-hearted host, he deserves better. But neither of you fret. I will see you by the Lake of Eachad, or here again, depend upon it."

By the sombre look in Muadnait's eyes, she gained no comfort from his words, and she was a *banfili*. Yes, but she was a woman, and he had become her lover, and she was afraid for him. That often enough brought convictions of doom. He searched for words to reassure her.

"I have a harp that can summon the power of Earth Mother Danu," he reminded her, "and the powers of the air, and I know Ruarc's inordinate pride. It makes it possible to handle him. In any case I would have to handle him someday. He was never going to smile and forget me." He kissed her on one cheek, then on the other, and last on her mouth. "Now I must be getting back to the Grianan, before Sunspear begins to say I have fled and Eichra takes hot offence."

"True is that," Tuathal agreed. "If he challenges Sunspear or one of the Fir Dicuil it will be the end of him, and he perhaps would."

They said farewell to the woman and the selchie, and made for Aileach's grey ramparts at a trot.

"I am growing tired of dashing back and forth between the fortress and the ship-haven," Felimid remarked. "Yes, the least bit tired. It's almost good that Sunspear decided to come here."

"Almost," Tuathal said. He fingered his arrows.

When they entered Muirchertach's hall again, they looked at each other and wordlessly altered that view. The barely contained hostile rage between Muirchertach's warriors and the red-headed Fir Dicuil could have been chopped with knives and hung like crimson meat. They had, under command, left their weapons outside the hall, save the knives in their girdles. The Fir Dicuil were well capable of using those knives for other purposes than eating, of course, and most of them had killed with their bare hands, or beef bones or wooden stools, the woman Sirega quite notably. She stood glowering, bare above the waist except for bull's-hide epaulettes warding her collar bones, and the rancour in her scowl was all for Felimid. Senan and Cathal stood near her, recovered and healing swiftly, silent proof that their partly inhuman descent was no mere chatter. If Sunspear bade them unleash their rage, there would be a redder evening than the storied one on which Da Derga's hostel was destroyed.

He did not. Looking about him, he said in a reverberant voice, "There will be peace in word and deed this night. We are guests of the king. Courtesy will prevail. Who fails to observe it shall have my harshest displeasure."

"Peace?" a huge man with hair patched russet and black, and a flowing beard similarly piebald, echoed in loud disbelief. "In that false bard's presence? All gods curse the word!"

He drew his knife and rushed at Felimid with a wolf's celerity. Felimid dropped a hand to his own knife, a short sax from Britain. He never needed to draw it. Ruarc Sunspear moved even more swiftly than the bearded man. He took three long steps, bent, and picked a great sweeping blow all the way from the rush-strewn floor. The heel of his open hand met the angle of a russet-bearded jaw with an impact heard a table's length away.

The man fell dead with a broken neck.

"When I command peace," Sunspear said, and added softly, "or *war*—I will be obeyed."

One blow, Felimid thought. *Not even with a closed fist. And it killed a man of the Fir Dicuil. The others stand quiet and accept. Even Sirega, she of the barbed spear.*

He had known that Sunspear was formidable and a menace, but this was a sharp reminder.

"Felimid mac Fal," the young king said, "I will own that you did well to inflict defeat on Senan and Cathal both, and I am pleased that you forebore from slaying them. You were, and you remain, the grandson of Fergus Chief Bard, and it may be that you have high Danann descent also, though once I doubted it. Sorely though it goes against my urges, I am a king, and I have a purpose for Erin, so for the paying of Dicuil the Fiery's honour-price to his *fine,* I and they might content ourselves, cease seeking your life. It is the law."

"It is, so. I value the magnanimity of the offer," Felimid said, believing not a word.

Sunspear, no fool, was aware of the mockery. "Do not mistake me. It comes hard, to me and my master's offspring, to give up vengeance, but we have a purpose, and great Dicuil himself hoped you would join it—to restore the great days of Erin and the Red Branch heroes, drive out the Cross-worshippers. You are a bard! Would you not have the bardic mysteries, the bardic powers, the bardic class itself, respected?"

Respected was one thing, Felimid thought. Dreaded and extortionate was another. Ruarc appeared to believe the men of Erin would stomach that without limit. But let him talk. His love for the sound of his own voice might cause him to say too much.

"I would so."

That answer committed him to nothing.

"Then come to Emain Macha with us when we depart in the morning!" Ablaze with enthusiasm, he rose, one hand, the hand that had just killed, making an expansive gesture, the other closing on the magnificent torc around his throat. "As a guest, and a bard, sacred on both counts! See Airgialla for yourself, see the Red Branch House restored, hear the things I propose! Not a hand will be raised against you, not an insult spoken. You shall go in peace no matter what your answer to me in the end, but come, guest with me, harp and chant under my roof, and hear my words. What do you say?"

He hadn't one thought, it appeared, for the man he had just struck down, even though the corpse was yet warm and was still being dragged out.

Felimid cursed rather inventively, though not aloud. This was the thing he could not decline, the asking he must accept, by the terms of his birth geas. He did not suppose Ruarc knew that, or could have learned it, either through mundane spying or pyromancy, but when a man, any man, called on Felimid to guest in his house, he was bound to accept. He must accept now.

He struggled to keep his brain clear. There was more to this than his own magical obligations, his own bonds of behaviour. Another compulsion was at work. He felt it assail him. Its power was overwhelming, and its source was Ruarc Sunspear's voice. Felimid had been taught from childhood to perceive the power of speech, to discern and use it. He needed to know more, hear more, to form a conclusion.

He said as though incredulous, "This is truly your wish, Ruarc Sunspear? You would have me guest in your palace, the new Emain Macha?"

"By the gods of earth, air and sea, by my own all-competent forebear, Lugh of the Long Hand, I would have it! I ask it! And in asking, I concede more than I ever did believe I would. What do you say, then?"

"Tell him to—" Eichra muttered in Felimid's ear, and the rest was excellently vulgar.

For Felimid there was only one answer he could make. He looked upon Ruarc, in his hero's dimensions and golden adornment, great and dangerous yet with something child-like about him. The words he uttered held power. Felimid, trained in magic, had an inkling of that power's source, and with each heartbeat in grew clearer. It was foolish to leap to conclusions, yet this one explained so much, fitted as neatly as a shoe cut to the measure of one's foot. He had to believe it. Unless he met with conclusive disproof. He did not think that he would.

"I accept with a will," he answered.

Chapter Eighteen

"I will stir up strife," said Bricriu, "between the kings and the leaders, and the heroes of valour, and the swordsmen, till every one makes an end of the other, if they will not come with me to use my feast."

"We will not go for the sake of pleasing you," said Conchubar.

"I will stir up anger between father and son, so that they will be the death of one another," said Bricriu; "if I fail in doing that, I will make a quarrel between mother and daughter; if that fails, I will put the two breasts of every woman of Ulster striking one against the other, and destroying one another."

—Bricriu's Feast, and the War of Words of the Women of Ulster

"You fool, Felimid, you blind witless addled fool!" Tuathal raged. "Why? Why did you take that invitation? An invitation to die is what it was! Any one of Ruarc's companions, and Mathgadro in especial, or Ruarc's seer Taladh Teisne, or that spokesman and messenger of his, that I hear is truly neither of those, but his master spy, could arrange your death in some way that will bring no blame upon Sunspear himself, and you are fully knowing it. Why?"

Sunspear

"A question needing an answer," Eichra said. His lip twisted. "And glad I am to see *something* can move you to fulminate, bowman. Gods! A child would refuse that. Are you counting on his, Sunspear's, honour and your right as a guest? He'll find a way around it, or his underlings will find it for him."

"He will, and I think I know the way he'll find. Calm, though, calm. This is something I'd as soon explain once, and merely the once, with the king and queen hearing." Then he reconsidered. "No. Not that pair. I don't wish Ruarc to see us with our heads together, and the wrong ears might catch our colloquy. Eichra? Oblige me, slippery eel. Find Brandon and say I'd speak with him on the ramparts, the first chance that offers."

Eichra looked at him narrowly. "You do have a purpose, there's more than meets the eye. That's good to know, at least. I will do't. And here comes a word from the king, unless I err."

He was not mistaken. A servitor in saffron frieze approached, and asked if the bard would attend the king, with a glint in his eye which suggested the king was ill pleased. Felimid went at once, and saw by Muirchertach's frown and the queen's lack of expression—but tapping foot—that they both were.

"So we are to lose you in the morning," Muirchertach said grimly. "Let me counsel you, Felimid mac Fal. If you go to Emain Macha as Sunspear's guest, you are not as wise as I supposed."

"You are not wise at all," the queen said. "*Why?*"

"It's needful that I learn what happens at the rebuilt Emain Macha," Felimid answered. "He's given his word that nothing will be done against me. He cannot overtly break it. Every bardic college in Erin would be against him then, northern or southern, and every king who honours the bards."

"If he *overtly* broke it," Duinseach Ingen Duach repeated. "And if one of the Fir Dicuil broke it for him? He could be greatly outraged and exile the criminal. He could even pay your honour-price. He likely would. Little good that would be to you."

"I've had before this to take care of myself in royal duns where I had enemies, honoured queen. And it's late for misgivings now. I have said that I will go."

They were not concerned only for his life, he could perceive. They had begun to wonder if he might truly go over to Ruarc Sunspear. Maybe Sunspear himself was toying with the idea, wondering if it had possibilities yet. But Felimid knew that even if he responded, it would never last, for Ruarc would never forget or forgive Dicuil's death, and he coveted the harp of Cairbre as his mentor had. It always came back to that.

It concerned Felimid that Muirchertach and the queen now had doubts, but it was beneath him to reassure them.

Sunspear

When eating was done and the drinking far from done, Felimid sought the monks at their long table, opposite the magicians' booth. Brandon and his fellows were drinking the king's ale as freely as any, and Oengus the steersman, Felimid noticed, was ogling one of the women who brought it around. Why not? His monastery was not one of those whose rule forbade monks to marry. They were cheery and talkative, which was all to the good, for their loud converse would cover what Felimid had to say to Brandon.

He did not leap into that revelation at once. Brandon, too, appeared to have much on his mind that he was not saying immediately, and no doubt it was about the bard's consent to guest at Emain Macha among his most unappeasable foes, which Brandon, like others, would deem madness. Yes, and maybe he was correct.

After a time, Felimid leaned forward and said, "I depart with Sunspear's party in the morning, to see the glories of Emain Macha. You know this, Brandon the seawise?"

Brandon nodded his tonsured head. "I do. All Aileach knows it. I will not say if this be wise or not. You surely have reasons."

"Oh, politely put!" Felimid said, quelling laughter. "Yes. 'Tis true. Now I have those reasons to impart to your ear, and I ask that you will try to believe. I ask also your word of honour that, when Sunspear and I are gone, you will share those reasons with Muirchertach, and inform Muadnait and Odhran. I can tell none of them with Sunspear and his entourage about. But they must know. So must you."

"My word you have. My oath to God if that will make you surer. It seems this is sufficiently important."

"Your word is enough, mariner. Prepare your mind to believe something strange! I accepted the bold Ruarc's invitation because I could do nothing else. He may think I do not know why. I suppose he does. He sometimes forgets, I think, that he's not the sole fellow in all Erin with instruction in magic, and that I too know it when I encounter it. Magic is with him, Brandon. The source of this particular sort is that great gold torc he wears. When he puts it about his neck and fastens it, those who hear his voice—*can refuse him nothing he asks.*"

Brandon crossed himself, but made no foolish expostulation. He asked softly, "How are you sure?"

"I'm sure. Magic's in my heart-marrow and blood. You might as well ask me how I know the difference between wine and water. I know a work of magical craft when I'm near it, and I can feel it working as you can feel the wind blow. Sunspear, as I say, may not be giving me so much credit. He overlooks things in his pride."

Brandon tugged on his thick beard, thinking hard.

"Don't doubt it," Felimid urged. "Cairbre and Ogma! There is no time. It explains so much—how he never loses a lawsuit, why none refuses to become his client, why every arrangement he proposes is accepted, and in short, how he became the lord of nine tuatha, over-king of Airgialla, formidable even with the great Uí Néill, in just three years."

"It does explain it, so. But where would he get such a thing?" Brandon gave the answer himself. "From Dicuil, surely, before the red magician died. Dicuil! But then why did he not make Ruarc, or himself, a king long since?"

"I am guessing, but my guess is informed, and it is that Dicuil made the torc, strand by golden strand, while he trained Sunspear from childhood. I reckon there was no other sorcerer in Erin with the knowledge, the power, in these days, and even Dicuil could not do't quickly. You know the story of Nuadu's silver hand. Perfect, as good as the hand he lost fighting, it took seven years to fashion. Maybe that torc took longer. Maybe Dicuil was intending to use it himself, but he died first, and so Ruarc received it."

"So much," Brandon murmured, "it does explain so much, and from your lips I must credit it, for if any man would know it is Felimid mac Fal. None can refuse him? All must bow to his asking?" Brandon shuddered strongly. "That is wickedness essential. Why, he might take you hunting, and command in your ear before leaving that you fight a bear on foot, with nothing but that sax at your girdle!"

"He might require of me a number of inventive things," Felimid agreed. "We're on common ground that Muirchertach must know this, and that I must destroy the torc no matter what else may transpire, right, holy Brandon?"

"None so holy," Brandon said dryly. "A sinner like any other. My brothers and I could be tempted by the thought of that devil's collar being used to further the faith in Erin—but the more I look beyond that, the more I see its use leading nowhere but to disaster. There's no mere fallen man or woman who could be trusted with it. That your first thought is to destroy it makes me trust you, though."

"I'd become bored very quickly with none able to refuse me anything. And turn into a much worse man, as you say, within a year. The thing must be destroyed. It's mere gold. Kincaid's steel will cut it in pieces. I'll destroy that cursed collar if it costs me my head, Brandon. I must. Let you never go near Sunspear while he wears it, and advise Muirchertach to the same effect. You may desire to warn the Primate of Armagh also."

"I shall!" Brandon promised, with fervour in his tone. "On Padraigh's holy bones I shall. Sunspear has vowed thunderously, so, to destroy Armagh one day, and he promised to deal likewise with the White Isle and your own mother. He hates the Cross."

"I know," Felimid said, his green eyes uncharacteristically cold. "It's never far from my mind now. But I reckon we should leave the subject."

They ceased speaking of it, but both men continued thinking. They thought hard. Brandon thought of Ruarc's enmity to the faith of the monks, and his passion for eradicating them from Erin. He did not believe that could ever be accomplished by any mortal man, but with the sorcerous collar about his neck and the kingship of Airgialla to exploit for his purpose, Ruarc might come closer than any other personage. Before his final failure many a monastery and church might burn, many a red battle be fought, many a Christian die.

Felimid thought of the growing arrogance of many bards, their extortionate misuse of satire, and the way Ruarc Sunspear encouraged it. Mathgadro Bluetongue was just one of that faction, though about the most spiteful. Niall, Dub Dothar and the rest thought all folk bound to defer to them and meet any demands they made—a posture that would get them a sharp lesson in the end, for Erin's people had no submissive temper. The class of bards might be brought down to the mud. And that was almost incidental to the high chance of implacable hatred sprouting between those of the new faith and those of the old beliefs, father turning against son, brother against brother, red division within royal clans—when more than enough of that occurred already. Sunspear might loose a tide of blood that even he could not foresee. None would do well out of it but Badb the War Crow.

"Here's my counsel," he said. "Take your ship and your brother monks. Take Odhran the selchie, and Muadnait, and get safely away from here."

"Back to Aran?" Brandon shook his head, and the long locks at the back of his crown shook likewise. "The notion does not sit well with me. Too much like running away. As you said, the Bishop of Armagh must hear this."

"What's the best way to reach him? By way of the Lake of Eachad?"

"So I think. Were you knowing that a tribe of selchies dwells in that lake? It's so. They are not Odhran's tribe, but he has guested among them. They will welcome him. There's a river that flows from the northern end of that lake to the sea. We can navigate it. The Bann; I've done so. Yes, that will be best."

"You are the sailor. Just so that you go where you are safe."

"As you are doing?" Brandon said, sticking his tongue in his cheek. He grew serious. "Nowhere is safe at this time, and surely not Armagh, but go there we must. We will see you again, Felimid, and I will pray for you."

That could do no harm. His mother, surely, was at the same exercise daily. Both prayers would be honest.

Felimid nodded. "With all you have."

Chapter Nineteen

"On with us then to that dun," said Cuchulain. "No good will come to you through saying that," said Ibar; "and whoever may go there I will not go," he said. "Alive or dead, you must go there for all that," said Cuchulain. "Then if so, it is alive I will go there," said Ibar, "and it is dead I will be before I leave it."
—The Boy Deeds of Cuchulain

Ailill of the Uí Bressail, Bishop of Armagh in succession to the blessed Padraigh, was accustomed to shave his crown in a circle, the so-called tonsure of Peter. It grew around his head in coarse black spikes aggressive as his proclamation that this style was the one true holy tonsure. His eyes smouldered and smoked with that and many other convictions.

Neither the tonsure nor the supremacy of Rome concerned him over-much at present. Kneeling in the stone church Padraigh had founded, he prayed fiercely for God to confound and destroy the young king of Airgialla, who had promised destruction to the foundation of Armagh and all its monks, Bishop Ailill in especial. Sunspear's power and pride had advanced so fast that surely no power but the devil's could be in it, with Sunspear such a hot declared foe of the Cross.

"May the plagues of Egypt fall upon him and his followers if they dare move against this holy place, this thrice-holy place, of Padraigh!" the bishop cried. "May the pain and weakness of a woman in childbirth afflict them in the hour of their greatest need, he and his followers, as it fell upon the men of pagan Ulster for their cruelty to Queen Macha, if they dare move against this holy place of Padraigh. May the cry of the dread banshee that infallibly presages death fall upon their ears, if they dare move against this holy place of Padraigh. May their heads and arms be broken as the image of the Philistines' god was broken, when they dared place the ark of the covenant in the heathen temple of Dagon, if Sunspear and his warriors dare move against this holy place of Padraigh. May they hang from higher trees than Haman or Judas, disgraced before the world, amen."

Breathing hard, he left the church and gazed over his extensive community, stretching down a green ridge protected by two stone walls, two defensive ditches, and a wooden rampart. Within lay the usual structures, well, cisterns, kitchen, eating house, dormitory, the monks' individual cells in scattered rows, workshops, and the greatly prized library. Padraigh had valued the Latin learning in which he well knew he was deficient.

"Bishop Ailill!"

A long-limbed monk came running uphill, breathless and stumbling. His breach of discipline brought a scowl to Ailill's brow. Maybe the brother had cause, though, and Ailill resolved to hear him before he imposed a penance.

"Be still!" he snapped. "Get your wind and some decorum back. Then explain to me. What is toward?"

The brother, wild-eyed, drew several ragged breaths. "Hell is toward, bishop! Ruarc Sunspear, or his wizards, have conjured a fire demon, and he leads sixty of his fighters, maybe more, to the Grianan of Aileach, the demon, the fiend, blazing in the sky above them as they travel. I ... witnessed ... I saw! It changes its form constantly. I saw it descend on a rath and burn the outbuildings. Afterwards, it was bigger. Fith the tanner saw too. He follows as fast as his short legs will allow."

"God's mercy!" Ailill breathed, assessing this. "Yes. It's believable. Sunspear was instructed by Dicuil the Fiery. He goes to Aileach, you say? Why? Unless it is because Felimid mac Fal is guesting there. So have we heard. Sunspear has vowed his death, as he has vowed the destruction of Armagh."

"Neither pagan demons nor pagan magic have power in this holy place. The fire spirit cannot assail us."

"I need not be told that. Yes, it's so. And Sunspear cannot assail us with his warriors, either, unless he wishes to fight all the chieftains whose kin are monks herein. Too many even for him and his Fir Dicuil—so far."

"Besides, he is going to Aileach, the other way."

"Nothing lets him from coming back *this* way," the bishop said grimly, "if only in some attempt to terrorise us. He does not understand that faith is our strength." He named one of the monks of Armagh. "Send him to me."

The brother in question was clearly of Cruithin stock, and he had been working, his robe kilted above his knees. Blue spiral tattoos adorned his calves and arms. His tonsured hair was rusty-red, not brindled like that of the Fir Dicuil, his round face freckled.

"Aye, noble bishop?"

"Your clan is royal," Ailill said without preamble.

The brother nodded with pride.

"Go to them swiftly, and say that their warriors are needed here, fifty at least. Ruarc Sunspear is rattling his weapons. Fifty cannot withstand him, but an attack on Armagh and your clan would embroil him with the church, and your kindred and their allies, which should make him pause and reflect. There is time for them to march here. They are close by. Ruarc has ridden to Aileach and must ride back, which is a longish way. In the meantime," he added with a touch of mordant humour, "we shall pray hard."

With no hesitation or ceremony, the brother went. For a space Ailill stood alone, outside the long stone church, eyes shut in intense musing. The chanting of a group of his monks came melodiously to his ears.

Sunspear

". . . King of the Tree of Life with its flowers,
The space around which noble hosts are ranged,
Its crest and its showers on every side,
Spread over the fields and plains of Heaven.

"Glorious the flock of birds upon that Tree,
Singing perfect songs of purest grace,
Upon that never-withering Tree
Which gives choice bounty ever of fruit and leaves.

"Lovely is the flock of birds which keeps it,
On every bright holy bird a hundred plumes,
And without sin,
With pure brilliance,
They sing a hundred tunes for every feather."

Ailill felt love and pride rise in him at the singing. Then came a great surge of rage. By nature an irascible man, he had always to work hard at overcoming it. In his youth he had killed two men in his wrath at the same time.

Is this, all this, the work and legacy of holy Padraigh, to be broken because a prideful young king seeks power?

No. Never while stone stands or water runs!

Not so far distant, among the splendours of Emain Macha, Taladh Teisne also looked outward and brooded. His deep-set eyes under their shaggy brows were cold as midwinter ice, and within his beard the set of his mouth was harsh. He glowered down the slopes of the green knoll on which the royal enclosure stood. A lesser Druid standing with him misunderstood the reason for his dark scowl.

"It were better, indeed, if we could sacrifice the bishop here in the temple, Taladh Teisne. Better. But that would become known and we could not deny having done it."

"The king and I settled that a nine-night ago," Taladh Teisne said curtly. "No. The sacred grove is more secret and just as auspicious a place to offer him. In time we'll do this openly, but for now we must be surreptitious."

He stood silent, brooding. His heart burned with anger. It was intolerable that the church, the monastery, founded by that slave Padraigh, should stand a bare few miles from Emain Macha. Why had the kings at Tara not heeded the Druids when the slave preacher had impudently lit his paschal fire before the Beltaine blaze was kindled? They had warned the kings then, and Loeguire the chief of those royal men. "If that fire is not extinguished, and the one who lit it killed, it will burn forever."

It had not been extinguished, and the kings had not slain Padraigh. They should have done. But the fire he had kindled would not burn forever. It could still be quenched out. Ruarc mac Amalgaid was devoted to doing so, and he was one of the few men able enough—with the collar of command about his neck. Taladh Teisne's smile was malevolent as he thought upon that.

More certainty was needed, though. Despite Taladh's repute as a seer—deserved—the future was clouded. Reading omens in the heart and entrails of Bishop Ailill would make it clearer. Almost as gratifying, if he vanished without trace or explanation, it would dismay other monkish communities. That must be enough until Airgialla gained enough power to ravage them with fire and spear in the open daylight.

First catch the hare, as the saying went. Ailill the bishop must be abducted. The king had ordered this to be done by the time he returned from Aileach.

The lesser Druid, still supposing he could anticipate Taladh Teisne's thinking, said, "Armagh is dead ground for enchantment. Else we could conjure the likeness of a dark sea with hindering waves inside those foul ramparts, bring a blinding mist upon them—"

His voice rose enthusiastically as he talked on.

"Fatuous," Taladh Teisne said. "All would equally know we had done it. Far better we abduct the bishop without magic, and quietly, and those plans are made, our folk prepared. Your thinking is behind the race."

The other looked sulky. He was the sort, Taladh knew, who wanted to have a hand in everything, and feel as though he was first with mighty schemes. He was more the sort who would do something half-baked and botch the schemes of others, if not supervised well.

"Come," he said. "We will bid our folk act."

Their folk, prepared for the work, had camped a league away, a dozen strong. Disguised as pilgrims to the church of Padraigh, they carried no weapons but cudgels and a couple of spears and slings, such as any travellers needed outside their own tuath. These would arouse no suspicion. Nor would their appearance. None belonged to the distinctive Fir Dicuil. Taladh Teisne and his companion came to their camp on scruffy ponies, in simple frieze tunics and leggings. This too was ordinary and occasioned no wonder.

"It is time," the Druid said tersely. "Do the deed tonight."

"Good," the leader of the false pilgrims said eagerly. "The followers of Padraigh have claimed for too long that he was first to preach his faith in Erin. When Armagh is levelled, men may see in it the justice of God, and own the precedence of Palladius."

Taladh Teisne was indifferent to who had been first to preach the Christian faith in Erin. He desired to see the last one. The followers of Padraigh were strongest, and so must be eradicated before they grew stronger yet. The Palladians could come later. This fool was able to say the right things at Armagh and gain duplicitous entry, so he was useful. Those with him were partial Christians at best, but they could pass, and they mostly bore the furious, scathing Bishop Ailill a grudge. This exercise would seem fine sport to them.

It did. They came in overt humility to the gates of Armagh and made pious signs in the stone church. They gazed on the bishop's staff of Padraigh and prayed and sang. If some of them sang clumsily, and made errors, a smile and the claim that they were new converts was enough of an explanation.

The guest-house was filled, but the travellers, courteous and humble, said they would sleep in brushwood shelters. Bishop Ailill was less comfortably situated than that. Immersed to his neck in cold water, he meditated and prayed while midnight approached. Two sturdy monks guarded the cistern where he disciplined his flesh, in case someone might attack. All in Armagh knew how close they were to the rebuilt Emain Macha, and the danger of it.

Despite knowing their duty well, the watchers fell, taken by surprise. One dropped with a soft grunt, the impact of a sling-missile smashing his insides. His companion bent over him instead of raising the alarm, puzzled for a moment too long. A cudgel in a knowing hand broke his head from behind.

Stiff and clumsy from his long soaking, the bishop was easily overcome. They hauled him dripping out of the cistern, gagging any outcry he might have made, and lowered him over the monastery rampart. A few at a time, the other supposed pilgrims followed them. They carried the bishop north through the remaining dark hours.

In the morning, they rubbed him dry, then warmed and fed their ecclesiastical captive. They did not intend that he should perish of a chill. The chill he felt was all in his heart, as he saw that the trees of a notorious old heathen grove surrounded him, a Druid grove, nigh as old as time. He had long intended to have these blood-nourished trees hewn down one day. One day. When his faith dominated the land sufficiently.

He had much to think about as they placed him in a wood-barred cage. The top had strong wooden bars also, well lashed together, and thatched over to shelter him from rain. Being irascible and brave, Ailill ground his teeth in rage, heaved at the bars until he knew this was futile, and then pronounced varied searing curses on his abductors. After venting his anger, he bethought himself of his faith and prayed, which brought some comfort. But afterwards, looking around him at the sinister trees that had been there before the sons of Usnach were born, he surmised what his captors wanted of him, and felt a chill invade his blood.

Chapter Twenty

"The sky is over our heads, the earth is under our feet, the sea is round about us; and unless the sky with all its shower of stars comes down on earth, or the earth breaks open under our feet, or the blue sea goes over the whole face of the world, I swear that I will bring back every cow to its own shed, and every woman to her own dwelling-house." —The Awakening of Ulster

Ruarc Sunspear's proud entourage left the grey citadel where he had stayed one night, a less than welcome guest. A deep grunting of bull's-hide drums and the wild shriek of pipes accompanied the hoofbeats of the riders. Shock-headed *ceithernachs* walked barefoot, naked but for kilts, most of them, sunlight leaping from their spearheads or honed axes. The blaze of the fire elemental darting back and forth above their heads caught in flashes upon the weapon-metal too. Ruarc's sun-wheel banner, held high, symbol of his descent from Lugh, shifted in the light breeze. His golden armlets, torc and belt shone no brighter than his hair and flowing moustaches. His skin seemed to gather some of the sun's lustre as he rode. He wore solar hues, orpiment, amber and crocus-yellow, with indigo spirals on his cloak, and when he glanced at the fiery being above them, he did so confidently, a man at ease even in this being's presence.

The bard rode by his side and took care not to gaze too intently at his torc.

The big young king allowed Felimid's proximity. He displayed a grave, gracious dignity, just a little to excess considering that he had promised he would destroy the bard, but suitable enough since he had granted him guest status. The destruction, Felimid supposed, was to wait until he was no longer Sunspear's guest, unless he was meant to have some sort of lamentable mishap at Emain Macha. Or be provoked into breaking hospitality himself.

The matter of Dicuil the Fiery's death hung in the air between them, burning like Dicuil's own nature. Ruarc never hinted at it. He spoke of numerous other things, and always came back to the order of the Red Branch heroes, which he claimed to be establishing anew.

"Did you ever walk on the hill of Emain Macha? I mean, before you left Erin, before I rebuilt it?"

"I never did," Felimid confessed. "I've heard much about it. You surely must have been served by the finest artisans, working day and night, if what I hear be true."

"*All* of it is true," Sunspear said flatly. "All. You are a bard of a very ancient bardic line, and along with tales of the gods, you drank the tales of the Red Branch with your mother's milk. You will see."

Felimid suspected a gibe in that reference to his mother. Ruarc was not so clumsy as think Felimid had forgotten his promise to destroy both the White Isle and Caithlenn. He let it pass.

"Indeed, I look forward to seeing. The glories of old should not be forgotten."

"No. More. They should be restored!" Ruarc's face shone with enthusiasm. So intense it was that it seemed to dispel the shadows of his enmity. "And you could join me in that. I could even forget what lies between us, if you would come to my court, devote your gifts and power to that cause, bring back the days of Emain Macha and the heroes, even the glories of the Tuatha De Danann. My forebear Lugh was of their number—became one, gained entry to their fellowship, as you know, and I vow before the glorious Sun, I do honour the goddess. I seek to secure the honour and prestige of the bards. You know, few better than you, that the cursed Cross-worshippers seek to erode that very esteem. You have never become one."

"I have not." They had some common ground there, though maybe not as much as Sunspear imagined. "I've heard a little too much in my travels of how they prescribe peace and deliver discord. The Franks in Gaul have embraced that faith. It hasn't made them less treacherous or bloody. The Vandals far south—my father went there in his day, and took a couple of their galleys—did the same, but another sort of Cross-worship, the differences being ones I've never comprehended, and they rack and burn other Christians because of them."

"Well, then! Why stomach their presence here? We may be sure it will come to that in Erin too!" Sunspear grew earnest. "You see, that is why—one reason why—I could accept you, if you'd help me clear them out of our island. Even my master Dicuil would wish me to accept you and forget avenging him, to this end."

A lie. Felimid did not dispute it. He gave a non-committal nod.

"You have travelled. You know these things you spoke about—better than I. What I see of the Cross-worshippers here in Erin is bad enough, and you confirm it! Unless we extirpate them, their poison will spread like mildew. Now you—it's a moderate man you are, Felimid mac Fal, known for it. You have appeal to those who are not so furious as my faction. With your help it can be done. Done within a lifetime."

The deep golden voice had persuasiveness even to Felimid. Ruarc had never led a battle host anywhere but to victory. The mounted warriors from various kingdoms who accompanied him now, bright-cloaked and bright-sworded, all seemed enspelled by him, and the Fir Dicuil, riding in a tight, cohesive group, scorn of the whole world in their bearing, would plainly have followed him against the walls of Constantinople. The common fighting men tramping at the rear, dogged and unimaginative, would follow him as unhesitatingly for gear and silver. The terrible fire-being that seared the grass on their left flank now, in the shape of a blazing tree, and then leaped completely over them as a shaggy, flame-furred wolf, changing in mid-spring, before it lowered on their right as a bizarre chimera combined out of four or five beasts, none earthly, threw a mad weird glamour over the procession and made a constant reminder of Ruarc's potential for devastation. Yes, and his essential disregard for consequence. A gambler at heart, he would gamble Erin itself for power and glory.

There was something to his blandishments. Something. Felimid did indeed dislike many things the new faith brought. But Ruarc overestimated what he could accomplish, and one practical, immediate reason against aligning with him was that no matter what he said with his lips, he would never forgive his mentor's death. When he judged the time right, and Felimid to be convenient no longer, the bard would be dismembered or incinerated, and Ruarc would toss a die nonchalantly to decide which.

Felimid prevaricated. It seemed best.

"Within a lifetime?" he repeated. "That's unsure, so. Emperors of Rome tried to extirpate Cross-worship and did not succeed. The last one—Julian was the name, I think—tried with all his power. He died when he had been Emperor less than two years." So Palamides had told him, and Palamides would know. "Speared through. None has tried since."

"Rome never conquered Erin! It never would have."

"No. That's a fine truth. Still—new things have come, Sunspear, and they will not leave. The monasteries sprout like mushrooms."

"We'll pick them like mushrooms, also, and make a stew of them for supper."

That was a boy's brag. The urge to deride him came swift and strong, but Felimid quelled it; Ruarc's reaction to that might be dire. He countered instead with facts everybody knew.

"They have kingly connections. Mostly they are begun with grants of land from the tuath's royal family, and the abbots are mostly cousins or brothers of the king. Begin burning them, and you will soon have half the high clans in Erin against you. Not even you can win against those odds."

"Look above you," Sunspear said, sure and cheerful again. "Any host that comes against me will soon have a third of it blackened, the other two-thirds scorched and fleeing. Well, unless I decide to meet it with my own host and defeat it with no help from yon living conflagration."

Felimid owned that this might be no frivolous brag. He knew about the battle of Druim Derg in detail. Ruarc Sunspear could perhaps do it, but he would have to retain control of the blazing elemental, and the mastery of such beings by men of flesh and blood was ever fragile.

Felimid thought of Muadnait, and how her father's dun had burned, leaving no survivors. He found himself struggling to bridle his temper. Although it had been Dicuil who committed that bit of haughty incendiarism, well before Sunspear became his pupil, there was no reason to suppose the pupil would hesitate either.

"Why not join me?" Ruarc wondered. "I truly do not understand. You know the monks oppose all stories but the ones they tell themselves. They will drive the bards and sennachies from Erin without ruth, or restraint, or exception, if we do not drive them first."

"Oh, enough," Felimid said. "They no more have ability to do that than you have to banish the Cross-worshippers from the land."

"Yet!" Ruarc said in loud anger. "Yet! When I become High King of all Erin and my word is paramount, then we shall see. It will happen, and I will bring it about, and nothing shall resist my purpose, until I make everything as it ought to be again."

"So that's your scheme. And will you encourage the bards to extort and oppress, not the humble folk alone but the chiefs and kings? I saw some of that with you and your friends on the day we met. Sunspear, take thought to that, if you would succeed in the long term, for the men of Erin will not stomach it. Don't you of all men know the breed?

Our breed? They are not tame. The monks and abbots cannot exile the bards, the people will embrace them dearly in any such event—but not if the bards themselves forfeit the people's love by arrogance. And you facilitate this if the reports do not lie. Or have your ways changed now that you are a king?" Felimid's horse stumbled, and he checked it, looking down to make sure its leg was uninjured. "Is't true that there are more bards than any other kind of maker in your palace, and they take what they please from all, even wives and daughters?"

Sunspear smiled broadly again, a cat playing with a bird. "Oh, well, yes. Respect for bards has been insufficient for too long. See how many scruples you have when you arrive at Emain; I'll watch and wonder."

"And I am most eager to see it," Felimid said politely.

They travelled on through summer's exuberant green, the pace far easier than the king and his entourage had set when they went to Aileach. Ruarc's pride was satisfied now, and he had what he wanted, Felimid accompanying him to Emain. They forded two rivers, the elemental darting high above in its fierce aversion to water. Swifter even than air, it could vanish and appear anywhere it desired in a heartbeat. The far side of a river, the far side of Britain, or the far side of the world, was all the same. It would have vanished so, to do as its whims led, except that Ruarc Sunspear's chanted poetry and the music of his harp (inferior though that instrument was to Golden Singer) held the being as though on a skilfully wrought leash.

The leash was fragile, though. It could snap. A perilous pet to play with. Did Sunspear truly think he had it mastered like his hunting dogs?

Perhaps. They passed a ring-fort with the usual buildings inside the earthen rampart, and Ruarc, casual as a boy, whistled to the fire-being, then made a sweeping gesture at the fort's timber palisade. The elemental flashed down and consumed the circular wall in moments, the tall old tree within for good measure, and then the criss-cross of beams that reinforced the rampart, the latter more gradually as it was not exposed to the air. As well as obeying Sunspear in this, it was acting as its nature required, for like any fire it must have fuel, and like any fire it was careless what it devoured. When they halted for the night, though, Ruarc played on his harp, and the being, its form ever-shifting, became like a leaping stag for a moment. Bending its head, it lit a camp-fire with its blazing antlers before writhing away in the next moment, amorphous. It would have been just as easy to make a fire by more ordinary means. Felimid smiled wryly. For a man of power and prowess, Ruarc was quite the ostentatious flaunter withal.

A weakness worth remembering.

He had inordinate appetites, too. His talk of becoming *Ard-Righ* of all Erin, and his word being paramount, made that clear enough. Kings in Erin did not rule as autocrats like the Emperors of Rome, some of whom had been both cruel and mad—or rather, kings in Erin never had heretofore.

Ruarc had used the power of his enchanted torc on Felimid only once thus far. Did he really think Felimid, with his bardic perceptions, trained from boyhood, was unaware of it? Or did he know that Felimid knew? Were his attempts to persuade the son of Fal to his cause a mere cloak, or were they at least partly sincere? The gods knew. Under his swagger and flash, Ruarc Sunspear could be devious, too. Of one thing Felimid was sure. In the long run, Ruarc meant to make an end of him.

He wouldn't do so on this journey, for it would be too obvious, and bring the curses of every southern bard upon him. Those of Suibni the Chief Bard would be first. Besides, Eichra the Eel and Tuathal rode close behind. Tuathal's bow could not be conveniently used from horseback—he was not a Hun—but he and Eichra had short javelins rattling in leather cases beside their saddles, javelins they could throw in a heartbeat. Sunspear was well within range, and Eichra at least would be instantly suspicious if the king rode beyond throwing range. So would Felimid.

He fell back a little to speak with his companions, his gaze on Ruarc's broad, richly mantled back.

"You bold fellows heard all that?"

"He said it loudly enough," Eichra fleered. "I'm in accord with his wish to kick the Cross-worshippers out of Erin. That would be fine if he could do it, but he cannot. You are right there. Torrents of blood would flow and nothing be achieved."

It struck Felimid that Eichra might take a different view if he knew the power of Ruarc's golden collar.

Maybe it was as well that he didn't. He acknowledged what the Eel had said with a word of concurrence.

"Even were't possible, and by Sunspear too," Eichra went on, "he won't live forever. He'd die someday, his kingdom would break apart, and the Cross-worshippers come back. In the meantime, it's in my mind that I would not like to see that bumptious lad as *Ard-Righ na Erainn*, giving me commands."

"Not even if he made you a chieftain?" Tuathal asked. It wasn't, it seemed to Felimid, said wholly in jest. It wasn't a good jest either. There was an edge of mistrust in Tuathal's voice.

"Cairbre and Ogma!" the bard swore, before Eichra could speak. His eyes had flashed and his face flamed. "Foster brother, that was ill said, and without cause."

"Mighty ill," Eichra agreed, very softly. There was readiness to fight in every line of him. "I am Lacth of the Booming Shield's man, not Sunspear's. And not yours, archer . . . not yours, for sure."

He pronounced the word "archer" as if it was an insult.

"No." Tuathal took a grip on himself. Plainly struggling, he said, "I spoke ill. Pardon."

Eichra gave a curt nod.

Felimid said, "It's enough."

He grew pensive, not about Eichra's loyalty, but about Sunspear's collar. Many men would be tempted by that monstrous object and what it could do. Many would not think of it as monstrous; many a one would jump to the conclusion that he could achieve much good with it around his own windpipe. Felimid was rather less sure of his own virtue, his own capacity to resist the lure of power. Besides, Dicuil the Fiery had made it—almost certainly made it, for Felimid knew of no legend or tale that mentioned it—a potent argument in itself that the collar was better destroyed.

It was odd, it was startling, that Ruarc could be ignorant that Felimid perceived the collar's power. He'd been subjected to it. He no less than Ruarc was trained in magic. Could Ruarc truly have so large a blind spot? It appeared he must. Were he aware that Felimid knew, he would wish Felimid dead as swiftly as might be, in case he told others. And if he became cognisant that Felimid had done so, had told Brandon and passed the same knowledge to King Muirchertach, it was doubtful that any consideration would stay his deadly wrath longer.

They rode on.

Chapter Twenty-One

He built it in the likeness of the House of the Red Branch in Emain, but it was entirely beyond all the buildings of that time in shape and in substance, in plan and in ornament, in pillars and in facings, in doors and in carvings, so that it was spoken of in all parts...

Good as the material was, the work done on it was as good. It took six horses to bring home every beam, and the strength of six men to fix every pole, and thirty of the best skilled men in Ireland were ordering it and directing it.

—Bricriu's Feast, and the War of Words of the Women of Ulster

One night they camped under the sky, and the second they spent in the hall of one of Ruarc's under-kings, Ninedo. This was a middle-aged man with a name for cunning, a bald head, and a whitish cataract in one eye. He was not overjoyed to welcome his lord and his retinue in from the road, if Felimid could judge, and that he could understand. The Fir Dicuil were quick to take offence, and to give it. Ruarc might request support in battle at any time, which in gear, gold and blood, was a costly business. Merely food and drink for such visitors strained even a king's power to supply. Ninedo knew too well that if

Sunspear's bards were not satisfied they would make him the butt of a vicious satire.

His own bards voiced fulsome praise that evening of his generosity, his courage in a fight, his strength and even his appearance, earning their pay. After that they started on his ancestry. This was rich in the presence of a man whose Danann descent went back to Cairbre the god-harper and Ogma the champion, and through them to Earth-Mother Danu herself, and of Ruarc who—believably—laid claim to being a scion of Lugh the all-competent Sun Lord. Polite and indulgent, neither man made reference to that.

Felimid was soon called upon. He did not eulogise Ruarc, but went so far as to please him by recounting to the strains of his harp the great tale of Lugh and his combat with Balor of the Evil Eye, as monstrous a personage as any in song or legend. Sunspear would have to be content with hearing praise of his ancestor.

Flagrant in the night, making many hearts uneasy, the fire elemental ramped on a great pile of dry wood, feeding like a hungry man at a banquet. The faggots and logs had been heaped by Sunspear's order. The being that had been confined in a small fire-pot, vulnerable to being quenched into nonexistence by dropping into any cauldron of water, now bellowed in the shape of a gold-maned lion, thrice life size, and many other shifting forms. Warriors of high courage avoided each other's gaze and drank deep for comfort.

Felimid thought of sudden incineration too. He also emptied a number of cups, though he kept close count, and gripped the harp of Cairbre closely. It was his best immediate surety of living, since Ruarc was wholly loath to risk that instrument burning, but if the fire spirit broke free of Ruarc's control, it would care not a wren's feather for that.

The king of Airgialla ran into peril there himself. Felimid began to think he was exhilarated by the gamble of keeping such a being at his beck and even felt in his pride that he could do so with impunity. That, by the gods, was conspicuous over-confidence! Felimid wondered if Ruarc's harp-music was the true means of his control over the being, or maybe his enchanted collar, if it was potent over other entities than mortal men. Dicuil the Fiery had made it, after all. That possibility implied a special additional danger in destroying the collar. Ruarc perhaps placed too much confidence in the prophecy that he could only die a threefold death. There were many possible meanings to that. And any number of prophecies had come true in unexpected fashion.

It would be as the dice might roll.

As they approached Emain Macha, that slid from Felimid's mind. Before he left Erin, the site of King Conchubor's palace had been long abandoned, a green ridge haunted by ghosts, and by Macha's dying curse. Felimid had never set foot there. He felt eager to see it now, especially to know what Sunspear had made of it, whether rumour spoke truly or just echoed big-mouthed vaunting. Something impressive was more likely; Sunspear was not the man to be content with a second-rate counterfeit.

The first thing that showed as they approached was a splendid tiered roof made of tawny tiles looted from some abandoned British town. It blazed like hot red gold in the sun. Coming closer, the cavalcade entered a long avenue, kept scrupulously clear of brushwood and potholes, leading to the legendary hill. To the left, on open ground, stood a temple with open sides and a large carved stone within, a head with three faces, one laughing, one sleeping, one angry. Riding up the ridge to the hill itself, they came to three imposing halls and some lesser structures, just as the stories described.

The *Craobh Ruadh*, the Red Branch, the round edifice with the tiled roof, held the king's sleeping quarters at the centre with eight large apartments around it where the heroes feasted. Bronze hinges and nails gleamed on the doors; on the chief door they were gilded. The house rose in two storeys, with a sun-parlour and balcony on the second, very spacious. Doubting his eyes at first, Felimid saw what appeared at a distance to be small round windows of brightly hued glass, and proved on closer viewing to be just that, though such material was all but priceless in Erin.

Even in Leinster, the province most closely in touch with lands beyond the sea, glass was rarely seen except as bowls, goblets and beads.

The other halls also accorded with descriptions in the hero-tales. One, the treasure room, was roofed with beech-wood shingles neatly cut, smoothly laid as the feathers on a bird's breast, and bright as feathers too, each painted in three colours shading into each other. The shingles on the third and smallest hall were white alternating with brown, and this, surely, was the "mottled hall" where weapons and battle-gear must be relinquished and stored before the heroes, all jealous and prompt to quarrel over status, went in to a banquet.

"Earth Mother Danu," Felimid said softly. "Surely there is nothing of the like elsewhere in Erin, north or south. Luchtaine, the Danann's worker in wood, and all of their metalsmiths, would not be ashamed of this."

"Wait until you see it closer to," Rarc told him complacently. "I believe every man should behold such a wonder before his end."

Felimid might have described to him the demon-built palace of Koschei the Deathless, where he had been an unwilling guest for much of one summer, and other castles he had seen in strange places. Sunspear would have been affronted, and most likely disbelieved, too. Thus Felimid said nothing. Over the past nine years he had learned to guard his too-ready tongue—a little.

Then he recalled that Ruarc had trained under Dicuil, been his especial protege. Maybe—no, surely—Ruarc had beheld Otherworlds and seen great wonders himself, even the mansion of Lugh the Sun Lord, from whom he claimed descent. Foolish to underestimate him for his swagger and bombast, when that was even part of his power with fellow glory-seekers. Not even the collar of command could have gained him his kingship unless he had some strategy and judgement also.

By Lugh and all the other gods! Even the Cross-worshippers'! I hope, Sunspear, that you do not know I know the properties of that torc you wear!

Among the outbuildings of Emain Macha were stables grander than the houses of many chieftains, the thatch so intricately laid that it was an adornment in itself, and every horse therein bred from royal herds. As for the mottled hall, its broad double doors were manifestly the work of masters, hung not so much as a fingernail's width out of true, with a great prancing stag carved on each, surrounded by leafy branches. The treasure room with its feather-bright roof boasted thicker, stronger walls than the others, the better to thwart thieves, and doors braced, barred and hinged with silvered iron, each piece the labour of a year to forge and temper.

The Red Branch house, the central wonder, was meant to amaze more than the rest, and successfully did. Oak and yew pillars, alternating, upheld the external sun-balcony, each carved all over with cats, serpents, birds and leaves, with copper circlets—a fortune in copper—around the top of each. The main door was a single broad portal, carved with threefold spirals and interlocking knots that baffled the eye.

"Indeed, the skilled men who devoted their talents to your stronghold must have been many, and their labour assiduous," Felimid said. He poured more honey on his voice. "Your fame must have drawn them from far parts."

"And the wish to be part of the new Red Branch too," Ruarc said. His broad chest swelled as he spoke. "It has drawn great warriors to me, as you will see, not the Fir Dicuil only."

He could not resist a vaunt, even to a man he fully intended to see dead. Felimid felt anger growing, not because Sunspear was toying with him, though that he did mislike, but because all he saw here was the fruit of this man's abuse of the same ancient laws and customs of Erin he claimed, loudly, to revere. High among those principles stood the respected status of the craft masters, the makers, the *áes dána*, and without any doubt he had used the power of the enchanted collar to obtain their services. No matter how he had gilded it with smooth-voiced flattery and a promise of renewed glory for Erin, it came to bond labour. Servitude. The carpentry, the carving, the metalwork, the fabrics and jewellery that surely dazzled inside, were the work of unpaid compulsion whether those who supplied it knew or not. From smiths and carpenters to poets, the law required they be dealt with honestly, respectfully, and Ruarc had ignored it. Given a choice between glory and honour, he had opted for the second.

The gods' blessing on Erin it was that only one such magical collar existed. No sorcerer yet living—belike—had the skill to make another now Dicuil was dead. And no matter what else happened, that one collar must be destroyed.

Part of its power, maybe the essence of it, must lie in the intricate twisting of its fine golden strands into the cable that encircled Ruarc's heavy neck. Felimid knew enough magic to be confident of that. And gold was soft. Steel would cut it. The steel of Kincaid, forged by Goibniu in old time out of a fallen star, steel that could slay demons, would be efficacious beyond any. Ruarc, of course, had to be aware of it. He would be very careful of the collar—but he might gamble with its safety in order to gain possession of Golden Singer, the one treasure he might crave more greatly.

The splendours of Emain Macha were not in the buildings alone. Ruarc, just as he boasted, had gathered the proudest warriors, the wisest jurists, the most qualified poets—and the fairest women—he could lure. Even the *cumals* or bondwomen were so pulchritudinous that, no matter how serious his mission here, Felimid had the passing thought that the risk was worthwhile to behold them.

The two fire-witches he had seen in Aileach were not comely—no—but they possessed the skill to contain an imp of flame. These women plainly were required to be decorative first.

"The splendid Ruarc is a bull of many heifers," Queen Duinseach had said. Felimid thought that if he were a potential bride of Sunspear's, he would draw unpalatable conclusions from this. And there were at least a couple of those in Emain Macha now.

Ruarc dropped lightly from his horse and gave the reins to a stable attendant. Some of his folk came to greet him, Taladh Teisne at the fore. Felimid recognized the harsh-faced greybeard from descriptions, and guessed the identity of Cuanach the spokesman by his smooth youthful face and yellow hair; he had heard this one described also. No mere functionary, he was known to the wise as a spy, skilled to bribe or suborn. And there was the black-haired leader of Sunspear's bodyguard, a Munsterman with scarred hands, watchful eyes and meaningless smile.

Taladh, presented to the bard, was the one who spoke. He said forbiddingly, "You slew one who was greater than you, and who taught me much, so on that account it is no fond welcome I give you. But you come as the king's guest and so you are sacrosanct."

"Nothing else is possible in Emain Macha under the rule of Sunspear, O Druid," Felimid said graciously.

He needed a sense of the currents that swirled in this glittering, highly coloured court, the factions, rivalries and loyalties that existed in all seats of power. That was expressed by the women as much as the men, and Felimid saw quickly that there were two who might matter where power was concerned, and surely would matter as sources of information. Aivene, Ruarc's leman, widely known to be such, and for her remarkable beauty, was one. Caragh, daughter of King Tadg of the Ulaid, last vestige of the mighty old kingdom of Ulster, was the other. Rumour said Sunspear was considering her for a queen. Cynics said he merely used that possibility as a game piece while he played for a more advantageous tie. With Connacht in the west, for instance.

Felimid gave Aivene an unambiguous greeting.

"She will be fair, comely, bright-haired," he said, quoting *The Fate of the Sons of Usnech*. "Heroes will fight for her, and kings go seeking for her. I had thought Deirdre lived long ago, but she's in Airgialla now, surely."

"I had thought Cermait the Honey-Mouthed lived long ago," she said, midway between come-hither and mocking, "but he's in Airgialla now, surely." She added for his ears alone, past a smile that went no deeper than her lips, "I'd have no share in murdering a bard. Steal the swiftest horse in these stables and ride fast for the south."

"I'll not be murdered *here*," Felimid said, "for that would stain Sunspear's honour. But it's grateful I am for the advice."

Aivene shook her head in what looked like regret.

Felimid wondered if she was ingenuous or cunning. She had certainly given him bad advice. If he stole a horse and fled it would give Ruarc his longed-for excuse to pursue Felimid to the death; the law of hospitality would protect him no more. Even if he escaped it would simply set him back to his starting place, with the certainty that he'd have to deal with Sunspear someday.

No good, that; no good at all.

Chapter Twenty-Two

And another time enchanted pigs came out of the hill, and in every place they trod, neither corn nor grass nor leaf would sprout before the end of seven years, and no sort of weapon would wound them. But if they were counted in any place, or if the people so much as tried to count them, they would not stop in that place, but they would go on to another. But however often the people of the country tried to count them, no two people could ever make out the one number, and one man would call out, "There are three pigs in it," and another, "No, but there are seven," and another that it was eleven that were in it, or thirteen, and so the count would be lost.

—Cruachan

Copper and silver lamps burned fine oil in the magnificence of Sunspear's feasting hall, an hour after sunset. All weapons but knives—for eating—were barred, relinquished to the third hall with its mottled roof. Birch wine and strong honey-mead flowed freely, with vintages from beyond the sea. The king's tumblers and jesters performed contorted acrobatics that looked impossible, juggled knives, swallowed hatchets and retrieved them without taking harm, walked on wheels with brimming bowls of milk in each hand, and played pipes standing on their heads. Other heads, trophies of battle, grinned from small niches high in the walls, ominous between the carved panels and woven hangings.

The women moving gracefully back and forth seemed unmoved by the heads. As Felimid had noticed, having excellent sight, they were the most striking group of beauties, and the most diverse, he had seen since he guested at the dun of the great pirate lord Cerdic, in Britain. Children in plenty moved about the hall, maybe a dozen under the age of ten with Sunspear's golden hair, and a few more who were older. Like Cerdic, he appeared to have fathered a prolific brood, but unlike the great Britanno-Jute, he had been well born, well reared, and possessed a gracious manner.

Aivene, the king's current leman, appeared to have the task of supervising the servants, but she also appeared to do a vague, lackadaisical job of it. She drifted about among them, dropping a word here and there, showing off her beauty and fine raiment. Felimid had heard she was ambitious to be Ruarc's queen, but to him, viewing her at a distance and having spoken to her, so far, only to pay a compliment and receive a warning, she seemed too indolent. There was more character in the face of Caragh of Ulidia.

Neither seemed to hold a key, though, to the kind of power Ruarc was craving.

Seated among the other poets, Felimid seemed to see the hall through a faint golden haze that made each textured garment, each gem, head-dress and dagger-hilt, look even finer. He wondered for a moment if this was partly enchantment, a false vision, but the suspicion was fleeting. He had the bardic sight that pierces illusion, had possessed it through heredity and training since he was fifteen or younger, and so did the other bards present. No, everything was real, and any haze of exaggeration was due to the light and the copiously flowing liquor.

Well for me that I know how to drink, the bard said to himself. *Ruarc would be overjoyed to see me under the table. I'd awaken without Golden Singer, if I awakened at all.*

"Come, our guest," Ruarc called out laughingly. "Harp for us and declaim. Your skill is known. But I do command, in no light way, that you shun entirely the magic strains of laughter, sorrow and sleep, and shun the music that changes the seasons' round too. I had experience of that at Rochusa! No, son of Fal. You will observe your obligations as my guest, as I shall observe mine as your host."

There was nothing ambiguous in the ring of his voice, and he wore the golden torc. Felimid felt the compulsion of that cursed thing settle heavily upon him again. This command, though, was not too onerous. He might not invoke the three strains that all men knew belonged to the harp of Cairbre, or the music to which the seasons came and went, but not for a heartbeat had he meant to try anything so obvious, so well-known to Ruarc, as to Tachdan and the others.

Ruarc had not commanded him to refrain from aught else.

Odd that he seemed oblivious to the notion that Felimid would be aware of the golden collar's power the first time it was used upon him. Ordinary men, untrained men, without magic in their marrow, would suppose they had been persuaded, or intimidated. Did Sunspear underestimate Felimid's perceptions so badly? Oversight indeed, if he did.

Or perhaps he placed reverential trust in the skill and power of he who fashioned the collar.

Felimid bent over Golden Singer and drew sighing, nostalgic music from her strings. Mischief glinted in his eyes. He'd been enjoined to harp and declaim, and that he would. His offering would prick Sunspear like thorns. He began the song he had created on the banks of Sinann but never finished.

"New faith has come from a distance untold
To this land of all lands enchanted,
And grey stone crosses stand carven and scrolled
Upon lands by proud kings granted . . . "

Ruarc's wide brow darkened when he heard that. He looked ready to stand in rage and shout Felimid down at the very mention of "crosses carven and scrolled", but he held himself mute. At the lines paying respect to the old gods he relaxed a little. Only a little. Felimid watched his reactions closely.

"The live old trees in the groves of oak
Too holy for fire or the axe-man's stroke
Remember the moon and the Druid's cloak
And the snow-white bull with its gilded yoke . . ."

Ruarc lost his kingly poise for a moment there. His golden head whipped around, and he glanced almost wildly at Taladh Teisne. Taladh, the Druid and prophet. Taladh himself looked startled for an instant. Then both men were composed again, and Taladh Teisne, still under his king's regard, shook his head slightly. The voiceless exchange had been intense, and Felimid knew it had been occasioned by his rhymed lines, but the *why* thereof baffled him.

Nevertheless, bold scion of Lugh, here's to finish the poem, and if it ruffles you, oh and ochone, too bad.
"This monks should know as they pen their script
In their workrooms devoted to learning,
With their quills and brushes in bright hues dipped
And pious devotion burning;
Life is not lived in a dark stone crypt,
Nor faith is the only yearning.
The old gods pass and the new gods rise

Sunspear

But the old are remembered yet,
And if time makes dust of the fair and wise
It cannot make Erin forget
Great Danu the mother of fruitful earth,
Or Cuchulain of the wondrous birth,
The Dagda's prodigious strength and girth,
Morrigu's fury or Grian's mirth,
While the earth and the sun are turning -
Though the wings of magic are slowly clipped
While the stones of time are querning,
And change has spears that are sharply tipped,
As bards of all men are discerning.

Sunspear was displeased.

"I will have," he said ominously, "no more words of that kind strung together in Emain Macha. This is the seat of the Red Branch heroes. Honour it. Honour the glories of Erin. As for new things coming and old glories fading—we shall see what fades when I visit Armagh, with a war-band behind me and the banner of the Sun above me! So far I've done nothing in that direction but forbid those accursed monks to approach my dun, and vow to take the heads of any who do. None, despite the faith they profess, has so far dared test that promise. Have a care of your own head, Felimid mac Fal."

He sat glowering. This had never been a usual expression of his. Ruarc Sunspear generally felt well content with life and himself. Felimid quelled the flippant words on his tongue (once, he would have uttered them and let the consequences be what they would) and gave a slight, equivocal nod.

Earth mother Danu and all her children, the wings of your arrogance need clipping, my Ruarc. I truly should have paid you a visit before this.

After a time, he played on Golden Singer again. The temptation to work a prank on Ruarc like the one he had played on the ferocious Tosti in Kent, causing his beard to grow astoundingly, was intense, but again he let caution prevail, groaning inwardly with the effort. He turned his bardic attention to King Tadg and Caragh.

First, he tickled the father with a satire comparing Tadg's kingdom, the rump of the Ulaid, with its rival and constant pest across the water, Dalriada. Not to Dalriada's laudation. He mocked without mercy the raids of Dalriada against the Ulidian coasts, making them a farrago of sorry seamanship, and craven bungling on such occasions as they even reached Tadg's shores without sinking, the Dalriadan king especially being contrasted with the strength, wisdom and valour of Tadg and his house. Tadg's efforts to maintain impassive dignity failed once or twice, as Felimid declaimed an especially choice line, to the extent of Tadg being moved to chortle and slap a massive thigh.

Then, reckoning the father had been sweetened enough, Felimid turned to the praise of the daughter

Caragh, eulogising her beauty, manners, accomplishment, the lawful behaviour and noble ways and grace of her, until she blushed—and the undeniably fairer Aivene, as she listened, pulled a disparaging face. Tadg swelled with pride.

Sunspear's anger (or sulks) seemed to wane somewhat as the panegyric rolled out. He even ordered his cup-bearer to take Felimid fine foreign wine, though the bard knew that sprang from Sunspear's aversion to seeming niggardly or graceless. His intentions towards the—indirect—slayer of Dicuil were unaltered.

King Tadg and his daughter seemed aware of it also. Caragh came to the bard, with care to walk in a stately manner, as he had described her doing, and since he already had a brimming cup, she gave him a gemmed brooch from the bosom of her gown, and a kiss on the cheek. With the kiss she breathed in his ear, "Go fast from here. Ruarc means you ill."

"My deep thanks, daughter of kings."

That made two very different women, Aivene and Caragh, who had given him the same advice.

He talked with Caragh and her sire later, finding Tadg a man of wit despite his curious appearance, a head oddly shaped due to a difficult birth. Rivals in his royal clan had objected to his kingship on that ground. He had prevailed, though, due to his skill in negotiation and proven courage in battle.

The bard interested him.

"If you desired a place at Ruarc mac Amalgaid's court, you made an error in singing the ancient ways' decline," Tadg observed. "But sure, you knew there would be small use in *you* trying to find his beneficent side."

"Not much, lord, no." Felimid smiled cheerfully. "I came north to find him since I also saw little profit in waiting for him to come find *me*. He promised he would one day."

"That is what I heard. For us to be friendly would prove difficult if he marries Caragh. Supposing you still walk the earth and breathe air on that day."

Felimid looked from father to daughter. "I'd not give offence, but is that likely? I have heard he is being somewhat profuse with his offers, or at least his overtures."

"It is likely," Caragh said simply. "Indeed, 'tis all but certain. Oh, maybe not because of me, I am comely, but there are others. Because of an alliance with the Ulaid."

That made little sense to Felimid. The Ulaid, in the north-eastern corner of Erin by the Giant's Causeway, was a truncated fragment of the ancient province. It and Airgialla were neighbours, the geography was convenient, but other than that he did not see much in the affiliation that Sunspear might deem worthwhile.

"I'm slow of thought today," he murmured. "Has Sunspear designs on Dalriada?"

"His designs are all in Erin," King Tadg told him forcefully. Then he shrugged his richly mantled shoulders. "It is no secret. Airgialla lies south-west of the Ulaid. South-west again is Connacht, and once linked with us, Sunspear may offer support to which of the Connacht factions he pleases, making his man the new king there—and, he supposes, his client. I think that would work. Now, Connacht is not over-rich in goods or gear or cattle, but if wealth be counted in tough-handed fighting men, Connacht is wealthy."

"Does the dawn break?" Caragh asked gently.

The dawn broke indeed. Felimid pictured a widening band of territory, unbroken from the Ulaid across and down to Connacht, territory dominated by Ruarc—and held together by agreements he obtained through the enchanted collar. A band of territory like a wedge between the northern and southern Uí Néill, splitting their power. To Sunspear's gain. Nor would he stop with that, no, not he!

It was obvious now it was pointed out, and Felimid had never perceived it. Gods of earth, sea, and sky! He was still underestimating Ruarc, it appeared. Bombastic he might be, but he understood power and its uses better than Felimid, and surely was more in practice there. For that matter so were Tadg and Caragh.

Connacht was the most obdurately pagan province, too. With Connacht on his side, Ruarc would be that much closer to his goal of war on the monasteries. Indeed, and truly, he must be stopped, and to that end, the golden torc must be destroyed.

Hum. With all my dislike of the monasteries, I am a curious person to be saving them, but it seems I must. Nor I've not forgotten your promise to destroy my own mother's foundation of the White Isle, Sunspear, and her with it. You should not have said that.

You should not, indeed.

Chapter Twenty-Three

... and Cuchulain struck off their heads ...
—The War For the Bull of Cuailgne

The morning came grey and heavy, leaden clouds covering the sky. It turned out to be an omen. Sunspear had planned a hunt, and Felimid had been prepared for an attempt on his life if he took part, but his enemy called it off for the way the weather was shaping.

"I'd full intent of staying close to you with arrows ready, if we did go hunting," said Tuathal.

"And I of throwing a javelin into Sunspear if any bad thing befell," agreed Eichra.

"Much do I appreciate the thought, my boys. But then you would both die at once. It's in my mind that we must avoid such extreme circumstances if we can. Do not forget, either, to stay away from Sunspear while he has the collar of compulsion on his neck. I do not think he'd command you to murder me, for he wishes that pleasure himself, but he might do. You must keep a distance from myself, then, if I'm close in converse with him. We're in a net here and it's not yet the time to cut ourselves out of it."

"I'll chase women, then," Eichra said with a grin. 'There are enough here in Emain Macha."

Then all three turned their heads as a watcher on the rath bawled, astonishingly, "Monks, monks bearing a cross, approach!"

"Monks?" Tuathal echoed, goggle-eyed. "They are forbidden to come here! Sunspear proscribed it, and the bishop forbade his folk to defy Sunspear's word!"

"Someone," Felimid said thoughtfully, keeping his look calm though his blood raced, "thinks he has cause to ignore the command."

They were indeed monks who came to the great royal rath, two of them, walking. One was aged, the other the tattooed redhead of Cruithni blood who belonged to a royal *fine*. He carried a carved wooden rood a yard high, holding it proudly.

Ruarc Sunspear received the knowledge with a curse and a snarling grin. Watching him, Felimid was sure of one thing; this did not come as a surprise. He knew why they were here.

Cuanach mac Rudgal, the spokesman, the messenger, confronted them for his king, cloak and hat of office resplendent under the clouds.

"Why have you come here, except to die?"

The elder monk looked back at Cuanach unflinchingly. "We come to hold your king accountable, and all flesh must die. Let Ruarc mac Amalgaid face us."

Cuanach sneered. "Often it is the king's will to speak directly, but with tonsured curs like you he communicates through his spokesman, and I am his spokesman, so. Waste no breath. You have not much left and you know it. What complaint do you make?"

"You are his chief spy!" the elder monk thundered. "You know our complaint! I, Brother Miluch, say it aloud, that our holy bishop, Ailill, was abducted in the night while he kept sacred vigil, and it is Ruarc, proudly called Sunspear, who knows why. Let Ailill be freed and sent back, or let Ruarc suffer cursing."

They stood with their cowls thrown back and their pates bare to the wind, listening to Cuanach laugh at them.

"Ruarc Sunspear? Care a straw in the wind for your curse? As for your bishop, who knows where he may be? Concern yourself with the king's promise, which he has made known far and wide, to have the heads of any Cross-worshipping monks who dare come to Emain Macha! Do you pretend you are ignorant of it?"

"We know," the tattooed monk said. "And Sunspear invites hell thereby. None but he would command Bishop Ailill's abduction. Let him come forth and answer if he dares. As for taking our heads, I, Brother Floclaid, have royal kin, and I am not the lone such brother. It would mean war."

"Sunspear carried the battle of Druim Derg and slew Failge Berraide." Cuanach smiled. "Surely, he'll tremble when I repeat your threat—but no, it may have effect, he may do himself a mischief laughing! It's not you who will be caring, for this is your last day." He gestured to the woman Sirega, who stood nearby wearing doeskin breeches and a short cape, fondling her great barbed spear. "Finish these two. They are not worth the king's trouble."

Felimid sighed resignedly and parted his lips to speak. The Fir Dicuil fighter, who did not care to be ordered like a bond-woman, forestalled him. Her voice dripped scorn.

"They are not worth my trouble either. I'm a warrior, not a rat-catcher. You command their deaths? *You* kill them."

Brother Floclaid spat on the grass.

"Indeed, manikin. You do it. I was a warrior before I was a monk; to my shame I spilled blood unjustly. Take a spear and give me one, and we'll see. Maybe with my point at your gullet you'll tell where the bishop is."

Ruarc Sunspear's resonant voice interrupted the yammer. "What? Will you argue like women at a market-fair? You, you, you and *you*, force these monks down to their knees, since they so like the pose! They knew the price of coming here! Give me an axe."

Felimid raised his voice. "No."

"No?"

"I might have killed two of your Fir Dicuil, great king. I let them live. I ask these two lives of you in payment for the lives I spared. It's an honourable request, so."

Ruarc curled his lip in splendid scorn. His long golden moustaches spread. A wan sunbeam touched them.

"It's an honourable request and I refuse it. The axe!"

"Then fight me," Felimid said, "for whether they live or die."

Sunspear glared. "You yap too loud. Fight you? Listen to my command, assassin of Dicuil. I'll kill these two here and now. On pain of death, no word more, stand still, and watch it with your eyes. I say again, this I command."

He was wearing the torc.

Felimid felt the thing's compulsion descend on him like a heavy, increasing weight. More subtly, like water seeping into a ship, he felt the temptation to invent reasons for obeying, say to himself that the monks were doomed, he was in Ruarc's seat of power, there was nothing he could do, that he only played into the other's hands by opposing him now.

He ground his teeth. Fighting the collar's duress, he reached for his hilt, willing himself to cry a loud challenge, call insults to which Ruarc must respond. Sweat spilled from his face and back; his muscles writhed. But the words locked in his throat and his fingers would not close on the sword.

In fury inexpressible he realised his struggle must look like craven fear. Sirega, standing not far off, Sirega who had refused to do this thing—from pride, not mercy, but still refused—looked at the bard with contempt and then looked away.

Felimid yearned to howl like a wolf and hurl himself at Ruarc, blade seeking his vitals. This was insufferable, fit to drive a man mad, to have one's own private will overridden, and then, heaped atop that, made a spectacle of degradation before a noble company. Finally, worst of all, to see the monks, Floclaid and the older man, murdered before him.

No!

Lips drawn back from snarling teeth, detachment and courtesy gone, Felimid made his clawed fingers close on Kincaid's staghorn grips and pulled half his length, glittering, from the sheath. His arm muscles almost tore with the effort. His legs quivered. Then, wholly against his will, his fingers slackened. Kincaid slid back into the sheath. Felimid's arms hung loosely at his sides.

Two men forced each struggling monk to his knees in the wet green grass. Ruarc Sunspear received the axe that was offered to him. His big shapely hands hefted it, trying the balance. The older monk said levelly, "What you do now ensures your damnation," and Ruarc smiled as scornfully as had Cuanach.

His shoulders bunched. The axe swung down. The older monk's tonsured head fell to the grass. Gore sprayed five yards from what remained of his neck. Ruarc swung the reddened axe again, and Floclaid's headless body dropped twitching, a second fountain of blood arching intense and over-bright. Ruarc glanced at his royal garments for stains, and finding none, threw the axe aside.

"Put the heads on stakes where the avenue begins," he said hoarsely. The rasp in his voice gave the only sign that he was moved at all. "They knew the penalty when they came here. Let all others know."

He stepped over the fallen oak rood.

Felimid's voice halted him.

"For this you will fight me, Sunspear. On horseback or foot as you like. I'll satirise you else. I'll mark you a coward across Erin. You will fight me."

"I'm afraid of your satires as I'm afraid of your swordhand. That is to say, not in the least. All here heard me bid you stand and watch the monks killed; all here saw you stand and watch with a face like whey. You are still my guest, I'll not revoke that—but go if you wish."

Felimid could not reply. The monks were dead and he was shamed. None approached him but Eichra and Tuathal. His foster-brother said without moving his lips, "The torc?"

Throat constricted, Felimid gave a slight sharp nod.

Eichra had a mere two words also. "What now?"

"Ask me later."

Wearily, he forced his brain to work. The monks had come to Emain Macha to demand the return of their chief, Ailill. They said—what was it they said? That he'd been abducted in the night. They had been sure Ruarc Sunspear knew why. So, now he considered it, thought Felimid. Who but Sunspear would have ordered it?

To what end?

Felimid's brain felt thick and slow. He made himself use it anyhow. His rare crimson anger burned the sluggishness away. Bishop Ailill was the chief of Padraigh's own foundation, which Ruarc had sworn to destroy. Ruarc was devoted to the old ways, and to the sun god Lugh, his ancestor. Lugnasadh, the festival of the sun, one of the four great feasts of the year, was only a month away now. Men had been sacrificed to the sun in old time. To Sunspear, the bishop would seem a very suitable offering.

All that felt right. It fitted, like a well-made shoe. It followed that Ailill was alive—until Lugnasadh.

Where?

Felimid had never been in Airgialla until now, but he did know there was a great and very holy Druid grove on the Lake of Eachad's southern shore, the lake whither he had sent Brandon and Muadnait. It was the most likely place to sacrifice a man to the old gods.

"The Druid grove," Felimid said low-voiced to his comrades. "That's where they will sacrifice him, for a wager, at the Sun's feast. And that's where they, most like, have him a prisoner now. None dares go there. So if the dreadful bad luck of getting killed should befall me, and you yet alive, it's for you brave fellows to go rescue the cranky bishop from his fate. I will not be asking you to kill Sunspear too."

Chapter Twenty-Four

... and there were three birds that flew by themselves, and they all went before the chariots, to the far end of the country, until the fall of night, and then there was no more seen of them.
—Birth of Cuchulain

The four comrades of Ruarc had their heads together over honey-mead, a strong brew in Emain Macha, and their topic of talk was Felimid. For once the bitter Mathgadro was in a high humour. He smiled broadly, showing his indigo gums, though he kept his tongue behind his teeth as usual.

"He's not sociable now," Mathgadro chuckled. "Down-hearted and solitary. Ruarc exposed him as a coward and he's brooding."

"He'll not have to be gloomy long," said Dub Dothar, he of the broad face and bull-like muscles. His fingers, though thick, were skilled upon the harp, and he touched the strings of his a little as he spoke, the notes eerie and foreboding. "Only until the king is ready to slay him."

"It's in my mind he has waited too long now." Tachdan the Sudden said that. Tachdan, who had received his by-name for being an impulsive hothead. "Once

Felimid mac Fal is dead, Ruarc can take the harp of Cairbre. What hinders him?"

"He plays with our smooth-faced friend," said Mathgadro. "I reckon just now Ruarc is savouring the way he made him climb down over the decapitation of those two monks. He has a way of command about him, eh? Stand still and watch, he said, and stand still and watch Felimid did, for all his brave talk. It burns him."

"He's dangerous," said Niall, last of the four; Niall of the Uí Dunchada. "Sunspear should get the harp of Cairbre away from him, and then have the fire elemental burn him in truth. Does he forget, do you forget, that this Felimid brought about Dicuil's death? Safe to play with he is not."

Mathgadro continued smiling, aware, with the acuteness of malice, that Tachdan remembered how Felimid had sung him half into the earth to teach him manners. As for Niall, Felimid had replaced him as the rider in a horse race, and done better than Niall could, quite aside from the matter of Dicuil the Fiery's demise.

Tachdan and Niall, also, as Bluetongue had noted with amusement months since, were disgruntled by the changes in Ruarc since he rose to kingship. They had been a quintet of swaggering hellions in the old days, making trouble as they pleased and settling it their way, Ruarc Sunspear their leader, but essentially comrades, equals. Now, more and more, Sunspear viewed them as minions, mere members of his court, and not the most important ones.

Mathgadro did not mind that so long as he profited. Sunspear requited him well for satirising his enemies, and he had little real pride. He could certainly swallow it so long as it meant basking in the glories of Emain Macha. As for Dub Dothar, stolid and—for the most part—more patient than the others, he simply accepted that Sunspear was now a king, and kings must govern. Loyal and a powerful fighter, he was among those who followed, not led.

Tachdan and Niall, though—much more of Sunspear's haughtiness and he might have trouble with them, a little. Only a little, and only briefly. Mathgadro had been watching them.

Content yourselves, lads, he thought. *Be discreet. The brash do not live long.*

Perhaps right about his companions, he had yet misjudged Felimid. The bard was not brooding on his humiliation, though it suited him if others believed it. He stood on the outer of the ramparts that cinctured Emain Macha, harp in the crook of his arm, and looked towards the two severed heads, their tonsures now clotted with black gore, that decorated stakes at the head of the avenue. He turned his gaze away, towards the big mound of ash in which the fire spirit lay quiescent—for now—pent by Ruarc's magic and Taladh Teisne's. It would rise in coruscating fury soon enough if they were to unleash it again.

Sunspear

The ghosts of Emain Macha were restless—and, it might be, offended. Felimid sensed it. They were powerful ghosts, spectres of legend—the treacherously slain sons of Usnech, jealous Conchubor their slayer, grief-stricken Deirdre, most beautiful and unlucky of women, and most cruelly wronged of all, the supernatural woman Macha, for whose twins this place was named. The story of Ruarc Sunspear, with his raw posturing, was tinsel to their stories. Time stretched thin here. The strings of Golden Singer could call strange things out of time. Sunspear did not know as much as he supposed.

The moment for that was not yet. Felimid had a lesser purpose at present, though an important one enough. Important to the captive bishop Ailill, surely.

He looked to the blue sky. There, in the restless moving air, sylphs were endlessly born, and as often passed from existence within hours, though they might grow to gales and storms first. Nothing save fire was more mutable. Except for fire, too, they were the swiftest of elementals, and they carried speech, which delighted them. As for poetry, it made them wildly drunk as liquor did men, and to get it they would blow far, oblige a poet in many ways, untamed as they were.

Felimid saw them with his bardic vision. He called to them on Golden Singer's strings. The notes flew high. Beings diaphanous as gauze, shifting their form like fire spirits (though not as swiftly), swooped down and circled

Felimid, stirring his hair, fluttering his cloak. He smiled. A successful beginning.

Now . . .

"Air sprites hear of those before you
Who loved and bled ere the welkin bore you;
Here grazed cattle in crimson herds,
Women hid in the form of birds,
And the fairest in Erin warred with words.
Much can be told to the sweet harp's strain,
Much to your pleasure and more to your gain;
All I would ask in return of you
Is reconnaissance sharp and tidings true
From an ancient oak grove Druids knew -
For which I can offer (no idle boast)
The single thing you desire the most."

The air sprites need no finer elucidation. They all knew the thing they desired the most. They asked in urgent whispers where to find the Druid grove, and he told them, in a different language so that no eavesdropping wizard such as Taladh Teisne might understand. Sylphs of the air comprehended all tongues. They flew on their errand, a half-dozen of them, in the shape of birds, of thistledown, of humans with wings instead of arms.

You did not use your nine times accursed collar to forbid me to do that, Ruarc, Felimid thought with satisfaction.

He waited on the rampart, hunched over his harp, coaxing a lament from her, a careful image of despondency. Nobody approached him. Presently, in a mere hour or two, for wind goes swiftly, three of the sylphs returned. They told him what he desired to know, and he could have laughed exultantly aloud, but he continued his pretence of gloom.

With evening coming down, thick with clouds and rain, he trudged into the feasting hall again, and suffered Mathgadro Bluetongue's gibes. His foster-brother saw through his assumed manner, and came to his side, ignoring Bluetongue. Eichra came too, and the look he gave Bluetongue was optimistic, yearning for trouble, but the satirist did not oblige him. Eichra composed himself to wait.

Before this is over, my charmer, he thought, *if anyone takes iron in the throat, it'll be you.*

Felimid's lips never moved as he said to the pair, "It's good news. The bishop is alive, in a cage in the Druids' grove, and I have sent word to Muadnait."

"How can that be good?" Tuathal asked. "And what can Muadnait do?"

"She's with Brandon and the monks, on the Lake of Eachad, and Odhran is with her besides. They can take word to Armagh, where, no doubt at all, by now the monks of that foundation know that two of them lost their heads by Sunspear's order. They'll tell the tale to their proud and high-born kindred, who will reach for their spears. But you may wager gold that . . . the captive . . . will be kept alive till Lugnasadh, and one way or another, this matter will be settled by then."

"By the monks?" Eichra said with a sneer.

"I fancy, by *us*," Felimid answered.

Tuathal frowned, thinking. "You have air sprites now who can bring you word from far, you say, but they do not have the power of Sunspear's fire monster. What is that single thing they desire most that you offered them? Or must it be secret?"

"Hardly secret. They crave a name, brother, a name. A poet has the power to give them one. Having that, they are no longer a mere eft of the air that comes out of nothing and returns thereto. Having a name, they have a particular self, and a stronger grip on being. Thus they crave one. When I had merely attained third rank I could not grant names to elementals, but now I have advanced to that level, the fourth."

"Ruarc," Eichra said. "You suppose he has granted the fire spirit a name? Is that why it obeys him?"

"Ruarc is still merely a third rank bard, and even the skills that go with third rank he has neglected as he strives for power." *And gains it, by all the gods!* "Maybe he has promised it a name—Taladh Teisne could surely bestow one—but it hasn't received one as yet. I would know.

Surely the last thing I would desire is that. I want the thing extinct!"

Tuathal fervently agreed.

Felimid, considering, felt somewhat content with what he had been able to achieve. Muadnait, who was trained in magic, and Odhran, who was a creature of magic, having seen and heard the message of the sylph, would tell Brother Brandon. He and his monks would be quick to tell the congregation of Armagh where their bishop had gone.

Two things achieved, the bard thought. Bishop Ailill's monks knew where he was held captive, or would in a short time, and King Muirchertach in Aileach knew the secret of Ruarc's irresistible persuasiveness. It was all well enough, but that source, the collar, had to be destroyed, a task of peril. And Felimid knew it was all his.

Despite its power the torc was made of gold, soft gold. The sword Kincaid would cut it like cheese. The difficult part of that would be getting Kincaid's edge past Sunspear's guard, with Felimid's head still on his own intact neck. So, then. He was committed; he had vowed that Sunspear should fight him or be the subject of a satire that should tarnish his name with cowardice throughout Erin, and now he was obliged, imperatively, to make that good. Even more than other men were bards compelled to abide by their spoken undertakings, with dire supernatural penalties if they should renege.

Ruarc Sunspear would surely fight when the time came, and not from fear of a satire. He would fight from pride. He endured neither insult nor defiance. And being in some ways predictable, he would wear the collar of compulsion in the duel, and use its power.

Probably he would not even see it as underhanded or knavish. He would be certain, sure as the next day's sunrise, of winning, with or without the collar. He would reckon a slight additional guarantee could do no harm, and blaming Felimid for his mentor's death, he would reckon it justified. Felimid was ready to wager he would also relish the thought of using Dicuil's creation against the man who had killed Dicuil.

Praemonitus, praemunitus, Felimid said to himself, having picked up a Latin tag or two in his travels.

Chapter Twenty-Five

. . . and they came through the green waves, and the seals, and the sword-fishes rising about them . . . —Battle of Rosnaree

Mile upon mile the Lake of Eachad stretched, calm and still on this day, reflecting the sky's pure blue and a few clouds. It reflected the reedy shore of a low island, too, where a curragh lay and an ancient standing stone pointed skyward, in fine pristine detail, better than unflawed glass. Brandon and his monks sat around the curragh. Their mouths watered at the scent of the lake's famed eels cooking in butter, and their stomachs growled impatiently, caring not at all for concepts like denial.

They wore tunics and trews this day, their robes discarded in the summer heat, and Muadnait had doffed hers for the same reason. She sat unconcerned in her shift, arms and thighs bare. The monks would not molest her, she knew, nor would they disapprove of her skin. Some monkish groups would, but Brandon's band was not prissy. As for Muadnait, it showed greater trust on her part that she showed her face and game foot to the daylight, than her calves.

She found this mighty lake, the greatest in Erin and all sweet fresh water, a calming place to be. There was no blazing, ever-changing fire elemental here, and it would hardly dare approach the place, nor were there any partly-human spawn of Dicuil the Archdruid, fiercely proud and combative. Instead, there were fisher-folk, rough but decent, and a tribe of selchies—not Odhran's tribe, who ranged the open sea, yet closely akin. Both fisher-folk and selchies acknowledged the aloof, mysterious Lake Lord, making offerings to him, though it was not at all certain he wanted the offerings—even noticed them.

Muadnait thought of the bard, her lover, her first in some time. He had wanted her and the monks to come here, to the Lake of Eachad and a measure of safety. He had urged it with a vehemence and authority he did not use as a rule. It mortified Muadnait to recall the eagerness with which she had complied. Her utter horror of fire had caused her to scurry like a mouse from Sunspear and his fire spirit, sail to this lake with Brandon and his monks and Odhran the selchie, and hide here. A shameful word, *hide*.

She should not have gone. She could ask herself what use it would have been to stay, and reckon all the sensible, sound arguments for going, and still they seemed shoddy and light. Felimid was in Sunspear's fortress, in his power, a power which would surely be fatal to the bard even if Sunspear did not have that accursed collar. And . . . he did have it.

Yes, and by Angus the Young, God of Love whose kisses became birds, she missed the kisses and the touch of Felimid, missed the swing and sway of her body beneath his, missed the sweet intense knowledge that the moment was near and nothing would stop either of them.

Don't be a fool, she told herself, *stopping Ruarc the Golden is a thing of more import and none but Felimid has a chance to do that, Felimid with his harp and sword and his heritage from Ogma of old, and Felimid has surely reckoned the odds and has some strategy in mind . . .*

Hasn't he?

Her fretting was interrupted, for the best, perhaps. Water rippled and sleek shapes, three, thrust pointed playful heads above the surface. Muadnait recognised them, even in seal-shape, though two were of recent acquaintance. As they scrambled ashore, they squirmed out of their skins, standing up as men, throwing their sealskins over their shoulders. Their human hides were white as cream, and one was Odhran, while the other two were selchies of the lake, named Tuirbe and Boch. Their tribe, when they were men, or herd, when they wore the skin, was peculiar to the lake and did not fare outside it. They were gentle, too, except at mating time, and that was a full month away yet, but like Odhran they bore the scars of former fights to gather a harem.

"Welcome, the sight of you gladdens," she said. "What news upon the lake?"

"Little, *banfili*, the lake is placid," Boch told her. "Not even fowlers disturb it this day."

"The spirits are quiet," Tuirbe agreed. Bigger and more corpulent than the other two, with heavy, steel-like muscle under the fat, he was the leader insofar as the selchies of Eachad had one. "We know when they are restive. We hear them wail, though most men do not, and the water roughens at such times, wind or none. It's soft the day."

Odhran, the selchie of the open sea, who had fared more widely and was even friendly with certain monks, raised his brown head and shook it.

"The lake is calm," he conceded. "The spirits are quiet. But there is a word from Armagh, a word fishermen heard from monks and carried here."

Muadnait looked at him and waited.

"The bishop of Armagh has vanished, gone from his church and monastery. His monks believe he was abducted. They accuse Ruarc Sunspear."

The *banfili* felt her skin turn cold. It must be Sunspear; who else? But why do this thing *now*?

"What have his monks done?"

Odhran looked troubled. "It is ill. Two of them travelled to Sunspear's dun and accused him of commanding the thing. They called upon him to free the bishop." Odhran paused, then said it, on a hasty, impelled breath. "Sunspear had their heads taken off."

Muadnait lived, had lived from birth, in a world where such things happened, often on sudden impulse. She was not astounded. She believed at once, and wasted no time gasping. Her mind sprang to what this meant. It meant war, of course.

"What said Felimid mac Fal to that?"

"He was there. He spoke in protest, but as I hear, he *did* nothing."

The accursed collar, the collar of command!

Muadnait leaped to her feet, stumbling on the lame one, and gazed across the mirror-smooth water. A puff of wind stippled it as she looked, then veered in zigzags, coming closer each time it shifted. Her trained gaze showed her this was no mere vagrant gust. It had a shape that changed as readily as fire, though less swiftly—a cluster of thistledown, a bird with boneless gossamer wings, wide as sails, and briefly a dancer with whirling many-layered skirts. This she saw with her trained *fili*'s vision so closely akin to the bardic sight. It was a sylph of the air and it moved her way.

Shaped again like a bird, it flirted its insubstantial plumage before her. It refracted the light passing through it to a warm pale yellow, and spoke in the archaic language of bards and sorcerers, one of many in which it was fluent. Mudnait had no difficulty with it; that too had been part of her training.

"Muadnait of Aran, I give you fair greeting," it fluted, "and bring word from the bard Felimid, a word of portent. Does it please you to hear?"

"It pleases me, spirit of air, master of tongues. It pleases me. What is Felimid's word?"

The elemental told her, in rhythm and cadence—all of it, the truth of Bishop Ailell's abduction, where he now was, and who guarded him. Muadnait grasped swiftly what it implied. If Ailill was being held captive, alive, in the ancient sacrificial grove, and had not been killed, then Sunspear had a purpose for him. Not a good one. Sacrifice was the most likely, and in ancient times—the times to which Sunspear looked back—kings had performed the sacrifice. Druids only presided.

When?

Lugnasadh, surely, the festival of the Sun.

Muadnait's own wits told her this before the sylph had spoken so far, and then the being confirmed it. Odhran and the lake selchies saw and heard the sylph as well as Muadnait did, but they were not much interested, as she saw when she scanned their faces. They would take some persuasion before they acted.

"Oh, bide here if you will, just for a time!" she called to the elemental. "Bide a short while! I will have a word for you to take back to the bard!"

A cool disdainful breath emanated from the sylph.

"The bard paid me with a poem to bring a word to you, *banfili*. Nothing was said of going errands back and forth. My obligation is done! I go."

With that it departed, now in the form of a dragonfly a yard long, shimmering in the day. It flitted at random, and the lake's surface rippled under it. Muadnait swore hotly concerning the capricious nature of such beings—but there was small time available for that.

The selchies, just as she had expected, were loath to meddle in the business.

"What happens to the Bishop of Armagh, as so he is called, is nothing to us," Boch snorted. "He preaches that we lack souls, are demons. Someday he would come here with curses to exorcise us from the lake, and with spears if his curses did not suffice."

Muadnait drew a breath and summoned her powers of persuasion, for she knew they would be required.

Chapter Twenty-Six

When Cathbad heard that, he agreed, believing him, and he went to the end of his arts and his knowledge to hinder the sons of Usnach, and he worked enchantment on them, so that he put the likeness of a dark sea about them, with hindering waves.
—The Fate of the Sons of Usnach

"Red beasts! Satan's own spawn!" Ailill of Armagh raved. "By the sword of Saint Michael, I shall be avenged a hundred thousand times! The pit gapes wide for you! *Aaaaarh!*"

His tirade ended in a frenzied yell. He gnashed his teeth. Foam whitened his lips. The seemingly endless days and nights in this accursed cage had fretted his ardent, furious nature until he felt close to madness. Futile struggles to undo or gnaw the lashings which held the wooden bars of his cage had proved precisely that—futile.

Because the cage stood on blocks a cubit off the ground, and the floor was also of crossed bars, stewing in his own filth had not formed part of his discomfort. The ground under the cage was even raked daily by an aged bondman with bent back and straggly beard. He never spoke to Ailill, presumably because he had been commanded not to, and six guards with the brindled red hair of the Fir Dicuil watched the captive in relays, night and day.

The bishop knew who it was they served—aside, he thought grimly, from the Devil. Their master on earth was that inveterate heathen, Ruarc, king of Airgialla, the declared enemy of holy Armagh. Ailill also knew where he was, and the meaning of the ancient grove. He should have had it hewn down and the stumps burned, years ago. He was conscious, besides, of Ruarc's boast that he descended from Lugh, the Sun Lord, and the imminence of the high-summer sacred day. (As if anything pagan was sacred!) He could form a deduction from that as swiftly as Muadnait could. Swifter, perhaps. He was the one in the cage.

Bishop Ailill lacked neither faith nor courage. He hoped for paradise and believed that martyrs received a shining crown there. He sprang from royal kindred and had fought battles as a younger man. But the horror of what these demons intended struck his heart and filled him with a desire to shake his bars, howling.

He ground his teeth and fought it. Rage and loathing came to his rescue when panic threatened. Dwelling on the torments of hell that awaited his captors was more pleasurable than contemplating his own fate, and he eased his distress by preaching that sermon to them, vehemently. At Armagh, he had preached it before.

"Oh, monsters! Fir Dicuil! Creatures bred of a demon-begotten sorcerer! Even as he was dispatched to hell again, so shall you be! Sorrow and torment and a struggle in burning swamps shall be yours while hawks with sharp red-hot beaks attack you, swooping, for all time and then for eternity! Yea, and yea, and yea! Mallets and flails shall smash your bones, and endlessly renewed shall they be so that the mallets and flails can shatter them again! In fetid stinking swamps where great maggots with sharp, rasping jaws gnaw your flesh forever! This unless you repent and release me and turn from serving the tyrant Ruarc who ranks for wickedness with Herod!"

Senan and Cathal, who had fought the bard and lost, were among his guards, and they looked at each other, amused.

Senan asked, "Who is Herod?"

His cousin shrugged. "Someone none too pleasant, I'd guess. What matter? This Cross-worshipping bishop has a flow of speech to admire."

"Nothing to how loud and fluent he will be in his last moments, when his entrails are ripped and his heart held up in the sun for augury by Taladh Teisne."

Senan did not trouble to lower his voice. Ailill, whose hearing was sharp, caught the gist of that from twenty yards off, and gripped the bars of his cage until his fingers bled. Then he began cursing his guards, and Ruarc Sunspear, with every malison, plague and woe recorded in scripture. His memory was comprehensive, his fury intense, and his voice loud. Senan and Cathal laughed at him again.

Ailill invited them to laugh when they duly arrived in the pit. But as his fury ebbed and his defiant spirit sank low, he stared through the bars at the mighty, sinister trees around him, trees that had been centuries old when Conchubor reigned at Emain, drunk sacrificial blood through their twisted roots, and been wreathed in the smoke of votive fires. To Ailill, his guts twisting as though they already felt a knife, it seemed the trees were thirsty, long deprived of blood and in their fashion, eager. It seemed to him they *knew*.

* * *

Less than a league distant, yet as though in another world, the sun shone brightly on the Lake of Eachad. Swans flew over its wide expanse and a small, shallow-draught boat made ripples. Brother Brandon pulled on the oars, his brawny seaman's arms tireless, and Muadnait, blue-cloaked, stood upright in the bow. Her friend Odhran and several of the lake selchies swam and dove about the wherry.

The *banfili* gazed intently into the depths. Here, well out from the shallow margins, they reached five or six fathoms. Eachad was not the open sea, with its waves, storms, and ineluctable power, but it was water in a huge expanse nevertheless, with faerie inhabitants and an inchoate lord who could be inimical . . . or friendly . . . it was enough.

Muadnait threw off her loose robe and sought balance on the prow for a moment. Bare as dawn, she made a somewhat lopsided dive into the lake, which welcomed her with a cool, silken embrace. Then all clumsiness was gone. She kicked out strongly, one foot as good as another in the kindly water, and angled downward through the greenish sweet chill.

Were I only a selchie myself, she thought.

A half-dozen of the seal folk swooped and circled about her, one of them a water-wizard of his kind. They made strange spiral patterns, with Muadnait at the centre. Her *fili*'s senses reached out through the water, attuning her to its power. Bubbles streamed from her nostrils like a trail of pearls. Eerie sounds came to her ears, carried by the liquid, that she would never have heard in the open air, and told her secrets few folk of flesh and blood imagined.

She swam back to the surface so powerfully that she rose into the sunlight a full foot clear of the lake, arching like a merrow, gleaming and shedding bright drops. She drew a full, needful breath before cleaving the water again, with but the trace of a splash, and went deep. The selchies kept pace with her.

Through her skin, through her ears, through her open eyes, Mudnait drew in the lake's magic. In a wonder like love she comprehended it. The wet dance of the lake selchies, with her at its heart, made it more intense, more transforming. Words in themselves could never have conveyed what was happening. Something was imparted—or she gathered something into herself by being open to it—speech did not describe.

Her companions flashed and turned in a wilder, swifter dance. Muadnait stayed with them, deep in weedy water for longer than she had ever been before without drawing breath. Her lungs should have been agonised and bursting, but she felt no discomfort and saw rare visions. They were burning in her brain still, when she broke the surface again and hauled herself deftly into the boat, gripping its wale and rolling sidewise.

"It's sufficient, the lake's power," she said with relief, "and I know that the fishermen and selchies are sufficient of fighters, though not men of war. What of your monks, Brandon? I know about half come of noble fighting kin."

"Yea," he agreed, "and a few became monks to atone for deeds done in battle or feud that had been better not done. Taking arms again to rescue the bishop, even if a sin, cannot be too heinous. And the fishermen—"

"Share a trade with some of your lord's disciples," Muadnait finished for him. "Two brothers were called Sons of Thunder, as I have been told. Let us bring those who took the bishop a taste of thunder, and give thanks that Taladh Teisne is not there. If he were he might be too much for us." She wrung out her hair before drawing on her robe. The droplets of water on her turned the garment damp and made it cling. "Let us speak to them, Brandon. Time's growing short, eh?"

* * *

Time *was* growing short. The days to pass until the sunset that would mark the beginning of Lugnasadh—and the dawn to follow that would mark the traditional, ancient hour of sacrifice—were few and growing fewer. The Druid grove with its sacred trees waited for the hour, and the rustling of its leaves in each passing breeze sounded like whispers of anticipation.

Bishop Ailill heard it as such, and cold sweat chilled his back, for all his faith and fortitude. He tried not to wonder if he would be burnt in a wicker basket, as men supposedly had been long ago, or if he would be gutted on the ground, as these red-headed demons had so glibly discussed. He tried not to consider how much, whichever end he met, it would *hurt*.

Less than a mile north, shallow-draught boats of leather came to the lake's edge. A dozen brawny fishermen with spears and clubs paddled a few of them, monks no less muscular a few more, their weapons iron-tipped staves. Some fifteen selchies flopped ashore through the reeds as grey seals, standing up as men when they gained the solid earth, to be handed their own sort of weapons from the hands of the monks—cords weighted at each end with round stones, and oak paddles from the boats. By the information they had, carried on the wind, sent by Felimid, they outnumbered the Fir Dicuil in the grove by six to one.

The Fir Dicuil could have reckoned those odds as greatly favouring *them*. Their battle skill and experience matched their savagery, they had better fighting gear than those coming against them, and they had prevailed against tenfold odds in the past, to litter red grass with decapitated bodies.

But let us see, said Muadnait to herself, as she walked ahead of her companions with as steady a step as her lame gait allowed, knowing this day might be her last. *Let us just see.*

The trees of the dense oak grove were in sight now.

She began to chant.

Grandsons and great-grandsons of a demon, or whatever that being had been, the Fir Dicuil scented magic as Aegean snakes and dogs sense a coming earthquake. Well ashore though they were, an uncanny reek of weed and mud, faint but sure sounds of fish jumping, the call of water-birds, and a sensation on the skin of wet coolness, came to them through the Druid trees. The shade was deep there, even in mid-morning, but now its grey-green leafiness was permeating by a kind of rippling blue gloaming, shot with silver. And the blue twilight deepened.

"Magic!" someone shouted. "Have a care!"

His warning voice was muffled as though by water—but there was no water, and breathing remained easy, though there was pressure on chest and limb, as there might have been at the bottom of a lake. Men lifted their weapons. Their arms met resistance, like that of some aqueous medium, and the more swiftly they tried to move, the more their feet slithered. The lightish cyan tint in the air deepened swiftly to ultramarine, and the floating silver eddies in it confused their eyes.

"We're attacked!" Senan bawled. "*Hahhhh*! Someone yearns to die!"

Through the deep-blue artificial twilight he saw shapes coming on, shapes of men, and even with limited vision he could perceive how poorly they were armed. He laughed. His fellows echoed it. Then, as they sought to meet the interlopers and carve them, the laughter died in their mouths. Their limbs moved as though against the resistance of water, slowly, robbed of force, denied the nearly inhuman celerity that was theirs in the usual way. Efforts to run or leap only made them flounder worse.

And they realised soon enough that their opponents, tyros though they might be at battle, were not subject to the same impediment. Nor were they weaklings. They flung weighted cords to tangle the Fir Dicuil's bodies and legs, drove barbed fish-spears into them, struck them down with bludgeons. The red-haired demi-demons saw quickly that their best tactic was to drop their weapons and grapple the foe hand-to-hand, strangling them or breaking their bones. Their opponents, though, could also wrestle, and they did not scruple to fight four or five to one, or to hit a man from behind while he was so occupied. The edge of an oaken boat-paddle could be fatal as a sword.

In the end all Bishop Ailill's guards lay incapacitated or bound. One appeared to be dead. Two monks, a fisherman and a selchie most certainly were.

The survivors chopped the lashings on the bars of Ailill's cage and hauled him out, cramped and wincing. They supported him while Brandon and a couple of his brother monks secured the Fir Dicuil's horses.

"These we can ride back to Armagh, noble bishop," Brandon said, "and it's in my mind we had better be quick as we may, for Sunspear will soon know what has happened here. He will have convulsions of rage."

"It's about four leagues as the crow flies," Muadnait said. "If we cannot do that by midday, on good horses like these, we deserve to be taken, even though some of us are not skilled riders. Bishop Ailill, are you fit for the saddle?"

"I'll ride bareback on the Gilla Deacar's contrary horse before I will bide here," Ailill croaked—hoarsely, but with feeling.

Muadnait laughed, and chose a steed for herself.

Chapter Twenty-Seven

"If the king's hospitality is gone from him," she said, "and if it is the way with him not to have room in his house for one lone woman to be fed and lodged, I will go and get food and lodging from some better man." —The High King of Ireland

Deep twilight lay upon Emain Macha, the rath of Ruarc Sunspear. Mist crept across the ramparts and outbuildings, the *Craobh Derg* where the king's trophies and spoils were stored, the *Teite Brecc* or Speckled Hall, the repository for weapons and battle gear, and the prosaic barns, byres, and stables. Tonight, the Speckled Hall contained even the swords of the proud warriors and guests who feasted in the chief hall, the greatest hall, for prevention of deadly quarrels, with Sunspear's command to strengthen the ban further.

Faint golden radiance glittered about the roof and balconies. This was a common effect when Sunspear was in residence, at certain times—if the king's humour was cheery and expansive—brighter than at others. Tonight, that radiance was defiled by surges of sullen, angry scarlet. Nor was Ruarc feasting among his folk. He conferred in his own inner chamber, the most magnificent of all, with his most secret confidantes.

He was not wearing the cabled golden torc that compelled obedience and agreement. He never did when he wanted the full, unforced yield of his underlings' wit. He wanted it now.

"It's beyond doubt, lord," the handsome Cuanach told him, to his face, boldly, as few would have dared confirm the news he was giving. Adroit spokesman and messenger, he was generally seen as little more, a court ornament, gambler, and woman-chaser. It was easy to forget Cuanach's qualifications in law, manifest though they were. Almost none but Sunspear knew him for the king's master spy.

"Yes. It is." Taladh Teisne seldom agreed with Cuanach on any matter at all equivocal, for Cuanach was no magician, less of a Druid, and in Taladh's view a self-assured pup, crafty but callow. "Ailill was taken from his cage and restored to his folk. Fishermen and selchies were in it as well as monks—and that *banfili* called Muadnait. She worked the magic that defeated Ailill's guards, for they all say it's as if they strove and fought under water, and crimson angry are they, and put to shame. One is dead."

"Felimid's doing."

Mathgadro Bluetongue's voice was the one that named Felimid. With him, Taladh Teisne the Druid, Cuanach and Ruarc Sunspear himself, there were five souls in Ruarc's splendid central apartment, the fifth being

Sunspear's favoured leman Aivene. She lolled in peacock silk on Ruarc's broad couch, holding up the gemmed necklace that was his latest gift. She appeared aware of nothing else, least of all the fraught discussion mere feet away.

Sunspear for his part seemed unaware of her. She might have been one of the spiral-carved red yew pillars with their circlets of bronze. Taladh Teisne had given her one disparaging glance when he entered, but had not thought her significant enough to suggest that Sunspear send her away. Cuanach and Mathgadro both looked at her with hankering, not for the first time, and maybe hoped for her favours when the king tired of her, but felt no concern if she overheard their talk. They reckoned her as vague and self-centered as she was luscious. Even if the matter of their conclave gained her attention at all, and she still remembered it an hour later, Aivene knew who supplied her comforts and luxuries.

"Who but Felimid?" Ruarc's studied grace and dignity did not desert him, but his voice vibrated. "The woman was with him at Aileach."

"If you can call her a woman and not an eyesore," Mathgadro interjected, and laughed. "Had she anything to do with this, indeed, I'll put a satire upon her that will make both sides of her face, yea, and both her feet, equal matches."

"A petty consideration," Ruarc snapped. "Keep to the purpose, my friend. They came from Aran together. They were at Aileach together. She did this thing for him. I doubt he'll even deny it when challenged."

"It had been better he died ere this," Cuanach said, "and away from Emain."

Dark humour touched Ruarc's mouth. "Senan and Cathal both tried hard to persuade him to die. They failed. That means there are few who could do it but I—and it may well be that I shall."

"He's your guest, lord," Taladh reminded him. "You did so proclaim him. There is a curse on breaking that law, and on killing a bard."

"He murdered a bard when he murdered Dicuil, and a far greater one. He has broken the law binding guest and host in honour, by meddling with my intentions towards that cantankerous bishop. It frees me from my obligation as his host. I am free to do as I wish in that respect, now. The question is what will best suit my purposes. It will *look* nobler if I finish him in personal combat, after I loudly remind all that he drew the dark mantle of death around my great mentor. And . . . insolent and presumptuous as he is, he may just give me fresh provocation this night."

"That can be contrived," Cuanach agreed, but there was perturbation on his smooth face. "Yet is it ill that the bishop escaped."

"The bishop will wait until I am ready to raze his offensive commune of monks to the foundations and drive them into destitute wandering, those I leave alive," the king said levelly. "My fire spirit cannot approach Armagh, but a war-host and natural flame in warriors' hands will destroy the foul place just as well."

"It's not that which exercises me, lord." Cuanach watched his king's face and spoke carefully. "The wise Taladh Teisne was to have read the future in auguries from the blood and heart. It's murky otherwise. Without that, do you move in a deadly way against Felimid mac Fal, the Druid cannot—none of us can—predict the outcome."

"I can." There was sure confidence in Sunspear's eyes and voice. "Oh, I can. Do he and I meet sword to sword I am very sure what the outcome will be."

Taladh Teisne smiled in his patriarchal beard. Cuanach did not know the golden collar's properties, and nor did the others, but Taladh knew them completely. He had helped Dicuil fashion it over seven demanding years.

Aivene sat gracefully up, reached across the couch with her back to the men, and poured herself a cup of foreign wine.

Others were drinking at that same moment, in their case a brew of fermented grain, not wine, and conferring on much the same issue as Sunspear, but in one of the guest-booths of the feasting hall, not a sumptuous princely chamber. They were Felimid, Tuathal and Eichra. There was little to talk about, for them, that Eichra's cynical wit had not surmised already, and this time Tuathal *an Saighdeoir* was not far behind him. He had watched the situation simmer for as long as Eichra. He was as certain as the Eel that it was ready to seethe over.

"If the bishop is now free—" Eichra said.

"I think he will be." Felimid broke a piece of honeycomb so deftly that his fingers stayed clean, and let the golden fluid ooze over bread. "I trust Muadnait and Brandon. We'll know if that confidence is sound soon enough, for if the bishop is now free, my Eichra, our host will be too vexed for dissembling. That perfect, gracious self-command of his comes from long practice, you know, with a deal of hot impulse under it."

"I would not be pleased by that thought in your place," Eichra told him. "His hot impulse may be to have your head off. By my own head, Felimid! I'm fond of honey too, but isn't so much of the stuff cloying you?"

"My nature is sweet and I need to maintain it," the bard answered gravely. He popped a fragment of comb into his mouth and crushed the waxen cells with his tongue, pressing his lips neatly together so that his chin stayed immaculate. Eichra vented a minute snort, half amused, half irritated.

"I reckon Sunspear knows," Tuathal said. "He's not with us. Usually he is here, to bask in homage. Taladh

Teisne, Bluetongue, they are not here either. You'd summon that pair any time you planned treachery."

"Add in Cuanach mac Rudgal." Eichra's crooked lip curled. "You would call him too."

"True. He's nowhere in sight. Now Ruarc's great pride will impel him to challenge me in person. Any wise gambler would lay to that, fellows. He needs a pretext, though, best an immediate one."

"No difficulty in taking or making it."

"And we haven't our weapons." Tuathal's fingers moved restlessly, yearning to feel his beloved bow. Eichra longed equally for a sword. Felimid missed the familiar weight of Kincaid at his side, also, but he, like his comrades, had taken sharp notice of precisely where his blade was placed in the Speckled Hall.

He might lack the sword of Ogma, first weapon to be forged of steel in Erin, but he had the harp Golden Singer, and while Ruarc had enjoined him, by the power of his torc, not to invoke the harp's better-known powers, he had not been comprehensive enough.

"Ahhh," Eichra breathed. "There come the magician and Cuanach. But not Sunspear."

"And not Bluetongue," Felimid said. "At any time those two have their heads together I'd anticipate an ill result."

Eichra felt the hilt of his knife and nodded.

Aivene came into the feasting hall shortly after, now wearing a long yellow over-tunic, bordered in purple, above her clinging peacock silk. She began bringing potations to the booths where men of most consequence sat, the smiths, lawyers, champions—and bards. Felimid saw her at once, and his linden-leaf gaze sharpened. His impression until then had been that languid Aivene did such service only on rare occasions.

As she drew nearer his place, he observed another thing out of the ordinary. Always, when he had seen her before, she had been impeccable, in her garments, her grooming, and the way her hair was arranged. Tonight, a lock of hair dangled wild, and her purple waist-band was turned to the side. Considering her face, he saw it less indolently composed than usual. Of another person he would have said she was hiding, trying hard to hide, offence or anger.

She filled one aged poet's cup with the last liquor in a flagon, beckoned a servitor to refill it, and then came to Felimid and his comrades.

"Surely you deserve, and would appreciate, better draughts than you have," she said.

She lifted the flagon, a little clumsily for her, right before Felimid's face. The wide sleeve dropped back from her wrist. He saw—could hardly have avoided seeing—bluish finger-marks on that white wrist, which would darken soon. Raising his glance to Aivene's face, he also saw, as she tilted the freshly filled vessel, a grimace of pain. It came and went swiftly, but there was no mistaking it. The weight of the flagon hurt her to raise. Someone had wrenched her wrist with savage force, done so in the last half-hour, and who would dare that but Sunspear?

Bending close to his ear, she said softly, "Sunspear will challenge you. Do not take it."

Then she gracefully poured drink in fresh cups for Tuathal and Eichra. Her wrist remained exposed. Eichra for one, like Felimid, had watched this woman and knew she was not clumsy. She had shown them her bruises on purpose. As she moved away, she let her sleeve fall back to cover the marks, a fair indication that she had meant these three men, and only them, to see.

"Light of the Sun!"

That voice, rich even when wrathful, and alive with force, belonged to one man only. Ruarc Sunspear strode magnificently from the entrance to his grand chamber, awarding Felimid a glower of equal magnificence. He wore his enchanted collar now. Felimid's blood ran cold for a moment. If he wore it tonight, he meant to use it.

"I'd not believe you had such daring if I had not seen! Handling my woman, holding her by force when she protests, and you my guest! Felimid mac Fal, were you a god, I'd not stomach this! And you are no god."

He infused the last five words with memorable scorn.

"Indeed no," the bard conceded. "Not entirely. And neither am I one who mishandles women. I think you are mistaken in what you suppose you saw."

"Suppose? I saw you. No supposition is in it. Aivene, did he handle you impertinently and then seize you overhard by the wrist, or didn't he?"

And here's the test, Felimid thought. *If she supports him it looks like blood on the rushes. Or the elemental outside spreading its flagrant wings. If she supports him.*

And why not? Her warning may not mean much.

"Indeed, my mighty lord . . ." Aivene said, and let a pause draw out for effect, before she continued, ". . . you must have perceived amiss. He did not. Felimid mac Fal and his friends have behaved agreeably."

Ruarc Sunspear flamed scarlet from throat to brow. He mastered his facial expression, but his eyes glared murder at his mistress for a heartbeat. Within the enchanted torc, his neck bulged with choler.

He drew a couple of breaths and spoke again. At what labour only he knew, his voice was gracious and indulgent. The big body that had grown taut as twisted cable now unclenched.

"Ah? I apprehend the matter. You are loath to cause upset over this slight fellow's affront, think him paltry, not worth it. Nor is he. But an affront to you I shall never let pass."

Almost, Felimid could have admired that. Sunspear was the one who had wrenched Aivene's wrist so hurtfully, no doubt at all, and done it when she balked at accusing Felimid falsely.

Eichra hooted a laugh, for his manners were sometimes raw. Tuathal shook his head in contempt. Only Felimid seemed oblivious to how thick with danger the air had become, idly rubbing his earlobe with one hand and clasping Golden Singer with the other. As for Sunspear, the king turned to Sirega, the Fir Dicuil spear-woman who had performed so lethally at Druim Derg.

"He has forfeited the rights of a guest. He was responsible for your cousin's death in the sacred grove. His pernicious scheming brought it about. Lead your kinsmen and cut him to pieces, here! He wearies me, and should offend you by breathing."

"There's a simpler way to resolve this," Felimid said, "and more elegant than bluster." He continued, maybe from tension, to finger his ear. "We be both bards. Merely let us speak the truth on our oath as bards, which if one of us lie will cost him his bard's powers."

"You hardly soothe me to remind me of that," Ruarc said terribly. "That was done, years ago, before a council of bards, after you murdered Dicuil—your grandsire, Sirega!—and the council protected you. Nothing shall protect you now."

Felimid had thought Ruarc would make a point of fighting him personally. He supposed he had let Ruarc's facade of the glorious, honourable hero deceive even him to a degree. That and Ruarc's great pride, which was real. Maybe that had even been Ruarc's plan, too, until tonight, and he was altering it from caprice or opportunism, if Aivene's failure to back his lie had disconcerted him.

"Eichra, Tuathal," the bard said softly, "run for the Speckled Hall when chaos surges, as it is about to. Get your weapons, and mine, then run back here even faster. You will know the time. And in the name of all gods, on your way out, tell Aivene to run from Emain Macha and hide!"

Ruarc cried like thunder, "Slay him!"

Chapter Twenty-Eight

"He will give you a right judgement, but it is only a brave man will ask it from him, for he is wise in all sorts of enchantments, and can do things no other man can do."

—The Championship of Ulster

The Fir Dicuil, like other warriors in the hall this night, had neither spears nor swords handy. They did not need them. They had knives at their belts, and one and all, they could kill with bare hands. They had all done so.

Felimid saw Ruarc's face as he cried, "Slay him!" and knew the Fir Dicuil were about to gladly comply. Heart beating hard but face composed, he said into the violent aura, "I supposed your brag was that you would slay me your own self. Take your sword and let me send for mine, and we shall see if you can—or have you changed your mind?"

He infused the last six words with prodigious scorn. Sunspear flushed carmine again. His composure was wearing thin. Amid something of an uproar, he said "Great Dicuil was my mentor. It would be my joy. But the right of the Fir Dicuil to retribution is the right of blood, and I will defer to it if they wish."

None could deny the truth of that. Felimid cursed mentally. Ruarc might be near to losing control, but he had not yet done so, and he still had his gift for manipulating a situation. Nor would any person there believe he was afraid to meet Felimid in combat. With reason, for he wasn't.

"We wish!" Sirega cried fiercely. "We will fight him one by one until one of us kills him. And I'll be first! Are we agreed on that, kinsmen? I am first."

There was some disagreement, the fiercest of her kin crying out against her claim, but as she told them scathingly, they should have spoken first if they desired it enough.

Felimid saw how the matter was going. Sirega was likely to get her way. He did not wish to fight her, or any more of her partly alien clan. He wanted Ruarc in combat. More accurately, he wanted to meet him sword to sword while he wore the enchanted torc. There would be no other chance to destroy it. Far preferable it would have been to search the king's private apartments for it, but none was allowed there while Ruarc was absent, or without his own express invitation, on pain of death, and Felimid of all men was least likely to get that opportunity.

Above all, the torc must be destroyed. Fighting the Fir Dicuil one by one was no way to that objective. Even if Felimid should defeat three or four in succession, starting with Sirega, and Ruarc then challenged him, impelled by pride or shame, the bard would be weary, and wounded in all likelihood, while Ruarc would be fresh. Getting the better of Senan and Cathal on the same day had been taxing enough.

"Go to the *Teite Brecc* and get his blade for him!" Sirega shrilled.

"I'll do it," Eichra said quickly.

"Yes," Felimid agreed, tone low and urgent. "Get your blade too, and Tuathal's bow, and by the womb of Earth Mother Danu, tell Aivene to flee."

"I'll tell her if I can, but then, by the womb of Earth Mother Danu, she can take her own chances! We'll be fully engaged, all three, so we will."

He left at a brisk pace. He would have done as Felimid bade him—aside from sparing any moments to warn Aivene—in any case, and needed no instruction. He wanted their swords and Tuathal's bow. They might all three die this night, but if they did, they would take as many as possible with them on the road to hell. Eichra hoped Ruarc Sunspear would be among them.

Felimid knew Ruarc intended to have him killed by the Fir Dicuil, but he was not about to play Ruarc's game, and in his hands he held a weapon more potent than even Kincaid. He took Golden Singer on his knee for what he knew might be the last time. With a strange fey smile on his lips he plucked her strings, loosing surges of enchanted sound. She was far older than Sunspear's collar of compulsion, and could do far stranger things. Sunspear had forbidden him, by the power of the torc, to play the sleep strain, the grief strain, or the mirth strain, or to summon the seasons out of their natural round, but those were the harp's only powers he knew about. His interdict was too narrow, his faith in the enchanted collar too wide.

Each hour Felimid had been in the reconstructed Emain Macha, he had steeped himself further in the magic of the place, breathing in its history, its heady distillation of love, treachery, courage, fact, sorcery, and legend. It was in the earth and air. The past was a shallow breath away. And Golden Singer was one of the keys thereto.

"Take your hands from the harp," Ruarc ordered him sharply. "I laid the command on you before, that you work no enchantment with her! You may not forget, and you may not disobey. Lay her down *now*."

Felimid continued to play, unperturbed.

You underrate folk, Sunspear. I reckon you always did. Were you supposing I would not perceive the power of your royal torc when you used it on me the first time? Once was sufficient. Tonight I am prepared.

The chords and strains rippled out. They rolled through the Red Branch Hall, rooting even the Fir Dicuil to the spot where they stood. They raised echoes of legend that could transcend even time. Perhaps the mighty ghosts of Macha, fleeter than horses, mother of twins, of Conchubar, of Naoise and his brothers, bravest men of their time, fated to die by treachery, and Deirdre, fated to cause the deaths of many warriors against her desire, and of Cuchulain and Emer, heard the echoes. All these and others were summoned by the music of Golden Singer. All Ruarc Sunspear's shouted commands to stint had no effect on Felimid, to Sunspear's baffled vexation.

It cannot be, Sunspear thought, amazed. *It isn't possible. No man can resist the torc's compulsion when I wear it and speak—no man or woman!*

But however that might be, the compulsion was now with the harp of Cairbre, and possible or not, Felimid was ignoring Ruarc's words.

It's a grave mistake you made when you in your pride built your royal dun on this site, Sunspear.

Glitters of faint radiance, not born of Sunspear's presence, appeared in the hall, like minuscule stars at twilight. Blue shadows in human form, and subtly other than human, walked among the long, splendid booths that stretched outward from the central chamber. The feasters stared and exclaimed, some in unaccustomed fear, as a phantom seeming of the Red Branch Hall—the true, the ancient Red Branch Hall—overlaid Sunspear's latter-day imitation, growing like ivy on a shoddy wall. A ghostly glitter of plated bronze covered the *Craobh Ruadh*'s oak panels. Phantasms—or true visions of a splendid past—brought lanterns of green *findrina*, the magic metal now almost unknown in Erin, to hang like glittering fruit from the rafters and shed soft light on the dumbfounded feasters, held immobile by Felimid's harping. Even the Fir Dicuil, those who yet tried to move their feet and hands in obedience to Ruarc's command to slay, found they were helpless to move. Sunspear, even Sunspear, stood fixed and thunderstruck.

The blue, anthropomorphic shadows thickened. Their features gained detail, though still ghostly and translucent. The colours of life came into them also. First to appear in that way was a tall, graceful woman, huge with pregnancy. She gestured in appeal to a man of kingly aspect, though with harshness and greed in his face, and he shook his head grimly to her appeal. Those who saw, even the Fir Dicuil, shivered, for that story was infamous, and that woman—that goddess's—curse on the kingdom a byword.

Detail and living hue came then to four shadowy figures of whom three proved to be tall men, comely, so alike they could only be brothers. The tallest had his arm protectively about the waist of a golden-haired woman beautiful as sunrise. The king who had refused the pregnant woman's appeal looked on them with a jealous scowl.

Spectres or memories of ancient times, or mere illusion, they stalked through Ruarc Sunspear's hall and daunted nearly all who beheld them. After the brothers and the woman strode a big stout man with reddish hair, his head sitting awry on a crooked neck and a severed head at his belt. Following him came a fair-skinned warrior, wavy-haired, his step bold and forthright, a shining many-coloured mantle around him, a spear in his hand.

After him appeared a third, at a glance the least of them, a slim young black-haired boy with sad eyes, but he carried a magnificent gold-hilted sword and crimson shield, and bore himself like a hero. But sudden fearful spasms went through his body. His eyes bulged, his limbs convulsed, and the muscles showed in stark outline through his skin, as he sprang from a standing start as high as the tallest man, whirling his sword irresistibly around him.

Ruarc outright ground his teeth, seeing these apparitions, and struggled to move his feet, but the power of Golden Singer and Felimid's skill held him fast.

There was one who could move. Felimid, watching Ruarc closely, did not see Taladh Teisne as he came out of the hall's deeper shadows, a spear in his lean corded hands. Fury twisted the mouth within his grey beard.

His eyes blazed as he resisted the harp's music with all his magical arts, placing one foot in front of the other, then again . . . lifting the javelin . . . summoning the power of his arm and body to the purpose of hurling the spear into Felimid.

Tuathal and Eichra were held where they stood, as much as the others. But they, having run to the Speckled Hall and seized their own weapons with the bard's, had not heard his music until they returned, and even then had been just within the doors. Tuathal strung his thick elm bow as he sprinted back. Now, sweating with effort, mazed by the phantoms he saw, he still observed Taladh Teisne, solid and opaque, and saw the glinting spear he raised. He drew and shot.

His arrow slammed into the Druid's chest with a harsh, fatal impact. Taladh arched backwards, dropping his spear, and kicked frantically until he perished. Felimid saw his comrades, saw the bow in Tuathal's hands, turned his head and saw the dying magician. He understood. More blood would follow this, and no melodies of Golden Singer's would delay it. The time for the harp had passed; it was time for steel.

Eichra held Felimid's sword, the blade that had once been Ogma's, with its slim blade and silver pommel, safely sheathed. With a wild laugh he dashed into the hall, under the glittering phantom lamps, dodging among the legendary figures out of the past, wondering if he had gone mad but never caring or pausing for that. He held the scabbard of Kincaid by its throat and hooked two fingers over the cross-hilt.

"Ha, Felimid, catch your glaive and do not fumble!" he yelled.

He threw it nearly as high as the roof-beams. It turned end over end as it came down. Felimid sprang on the table, leaped high from there, and caught the falling weapon.

After that he did three things; thrust Golden Singer into her worn leather case for protection, drew Kincaid from the sheath with a rasp and flash, and stepped from table to floor.

"Ruarc Sunspear!" he shouted over the tumult. "Come and fight me! Will you send your Fir Dicuil and be named a coward forever, or can you do your own work?"

"No, lord, he's mine!" cried Tachdan the Sudden. "Why lower yourself? Would great Dicuil the Fiery wish it? Give me your sword and let me carve him! I'll be honoured."

Sunspear glared at Felimid and said, "By the spear of Lugh, but you're kind, Tachdan. No. I shall let him have what he's asked for. Give him a shield, and I'll take mine."

He extended his left arm, and Cuanach the messenger hurried to fasten the royal shield on that member. Old beyond memory, it was said to have been King Conchubor's own battle-ward, the fabled Ochaine.

It began to vibrate and emit a low moaning noise.

"Danger!" yelled Niall of the Uí Dúnchada. "Danger! The Ochaine never wails but when he who bears it is in peril, and what peril to the king from this wretch, but by treachery? No, enough, even if his anger descends upon us! Dub Dothar?"

Dub Dothar roared assent, seized a set of hostage-chains from the wall behind the king's seat, and charged at Felimid, whirling the heavy links like a flail. Niall for his part laid hands on a long iron spit from a fire. They raced at the bard from different sides. Accustomed to fighting together, they agreed without words that Dub Dothar should whirl the chains about Felimid's sword-arm while Niall either stabbed or brained him with the cooking-spit.

They reckoned without Tuathal. Either they had not seen Taladh Teisne go down or they had not seen Tuathal loose his arrow. Now he shot two more, swiftly as he could bend the bow. They whistled across the Red Branch Hall, one splitting Dub Dothar's shoulder-blade and piercing a lung, one, aimed at Niall's chest, missing that mark and skewering his thigh instead.

The phantoms called from the past did not depart now the harping had ceased. They lingered, as though watching for the outcome. The dark-haired youth's terrible warp-spasm had passed, and now he stood as though weary, a black crow perching on his shoulder, an omen of death. The three brothers and the golden-haired beauty with them looked on as intently. The goddess heavy with child, for whom this place was named, whose curse had lain on the men of Ulster for nine generations because of their cruelty, stood and fixed her gaze on Ruarc Sunspear. He gazed back with a sneer on his mouth, as who should say, "Stare all you will, you will not cause me a twinge of fear."

He spun his long sword in a flashing figure eight, high and low, and grinned in Felimid's eyes.

"I said give him a shield, Tachdan, and I will have you do my bidding," he said, above the low keening of the Ochaine.

Women were tending the wounds of Dub Dothar and Niall, but Dub Dothar was choking out his life with an arrowhead in his lung. Niall's future was unsure. The spear-woman Sirega stood close to Tuathal and said to him softly, "Bend that bow again and you are a dead man."

Ruarc ignored the plight of both Niall and Dub Dothar. To Tachdan he said again, "Give him a shield."

Tachdan complied, but with gritted teeth and a look at Felimid that beggared description.

"Sunder him in pieces."

"I will. Oh, indeed I will."

Under those eyes spectral and corporeal, the pair moved to their fated encounter.

Chapter Twenty-Nine

"Go back now," he said, "for you have had a warning."

"I will not go back until I have fought with you."

Then Cuchulain gave another stroke with the edge of his sword that cut the hair close off his head, but drew no blood.

"You may go back now, at least," he said.

"I will not go," said Etarcomal, "until I have made an end of you, or you have made an end of me."

—The War for the Bull of Cuailgne

Despite the soft wailing of the Ochaine, and the goddess's condemning regard, Ruarc smiled in utter confidence.

"Presumptuous child," he purred, "I am going to cut off one of your arms, and then, in my good time, at my pleasure, the other. I'll let you guess which arm will be first. And last, your head!"

Felimid did not answer. He needed no telling that Sunspear was sure he would win; the reason gleamed around his mighty neck. Had the king *forgotten*? When he ordered Felimid to cease harping, to lay Golden Singer down, it had no effect. Perhaps—no, surely—he was certain of victory, of his own invincibility, with or without the collar of command. But a little thinking ought to have shown him why Felimid might be proof against the torc's compulsion tonight.

"Kneel and offer your neck to my blade, fool," Sunspear jeered. "It will save you trouble and dread."

Felimid did nothing of the sort, and a slight baffled frown touched Ruarc Sunspear's forehead. None who heard his bidding while he wore Dicuil's collar could resist, even if they made excuses afterwards for having obeyed, rationalised it down with the setting sun and up with the rising moon. As, generally, they did. Ruarc's own presence and force of character could serve as excuse enough.

With an impatient curse, he did what Felimid would not have done. He gave over the puzzle and moved to attack. Striking at Felimid's shoulder, he found the cut parried against the upper third of Kincaid's bluish steel, the strongest part, upon which the bard struck hard with his shield-rim at the outside of Ruarc's knee. Ruarc straightened that knee, thrusting himself to the side, and the blow missed. From the back guard position, Ruarc shifted at once to high, and swept his shining blade in a great overhand stroke at the bard's other shoulder.

Felimid lifted his shield straight up before his face. It impaired his vision for a heartbeat, but there was no other way; lifting the shield around in an arc to protect his head and shoulders while still leaving his sight clear would have been too slow a response. Ruarc's powerful swing knocked the bard a step backward. He did not leave his foe the initiative, though. He instantly advanced one foot, then the other, and drove his thin, bladed tip at Sunspear's thigh. The king deflected it with his shield's lower edge.

"Stars of the night!" Eichra hissed. "Lure him in, bard! He boasted he would cut of your arms one at a time! He's vainglorious, he will try to keep his word! Did you not hear him? Give him an apparent chance at your arm! He'll try to take it and you'll get past his guard."

"Stint it," Tuathal said past clenched teeth. "You talk too much."

He rather agreed with Eichra's strategic advice, but his nerves were raw because of his foster-brother's danger. The eerie presence of those ghostly figures from the past worked on his emotions, withal. The presence of the spear-woman Sirega at his side, alert and deadly, formed a third factor in his unease. If she even imagined he was about to bend his bow, her weapon's barbed head would plunge through his entrails. That would do Felimid little good . . .

Eichra did shut his mouth, not in obedience to Tuathal, but because he perceived it was the better course. This was no time for edgy chatter. The fighters seemed a fair match, the victor hard to pick. Although the bigger man, and powerful, Sunspear was marginally less quick. He had drunk more that night, but he had a strong head for it. Despite the bard's assiduous practice with sword and spear of late, Sunspear was the more in training.

Altogether, the Eel would have wagered on Felimid. He was left-handed, irksome and confusing to a right-handed man. His hands were remarkably precise, his sword-work imaginative and filled with surprises.

Yes. But he was still sorely out of practice over the past three years compared with Ruarc.

Eichra did not know what was in Felimid's mind. If he did it would scarcely have eased his own. The bard's overriding purpose was to reach that shining collar on Ruarc's neck and shear through it at a stroke. That should destroy its power, especially if cut through by Kincaid, the sword of Ogma. No matter how magical, it was gold, and must yield like butter to Kincaid's edge. Felimid meant to accomplish that even if he perished in the doing. Sunspear's winged rise to great power would end then, as swiftly as it had begun, in the usual way of over-kingdoms in Erin.

There would be one chance, though, one only. If Felimid tried, and failed, Ruarc would know at once what his enemy was about, and why. At present he did not seem aware that Felimid knew the collar's power. It seemed to the bard he should have guessed. A curious oversight.

One that must be taken advantage of.

Felimid set about convincing his foe that his lower body was in more danger than the upper. When Ruarc advanced, Feli mid aimed a cut or stab at his forward knee or hip. Once, he attempted to skewer the forward foot. That met with no success; the foot was a small target and could be suddenly moved. Ruarc grinned savagely and kept his shield high. When he had to block Felimid's sword, he did it with his blade, for as the bard was left-handed, sword opposed sword and shield opposed shield. Just as Eichra had supposed, he tried to find a way past Felimid's guard and sever an arm, either one, to fulfil his boast.

Felimid soon saw what his foe was trying to do. His guard remained strong. Himself, he concentrated on Sunspear's forward leg, whether that happened to be the left or right, trying to incapacitate it. Unless he made Sunspear stumble, he had small chance of reaching his neck with a sweeping cut, and nothing less would sever the intricately twisted cable of his enchanted torc. It might be soft gold, but it was thick.

Ruarc saw nothing out of the way in Felimid's concentrating his attacks below the waist. That was natural enough. Ruarc was taller. Fiercely he pressed that advantage, and his advantage of strength, seeking to drive Felimid back. Then he tried a quick false attack, whirling his blade from left to right across the top of his shield, and followed it with the true attack, stepping out with an overarm cut. It almost split Felimid's head.

Sunspear

The bard raised his shield. Ruarc's edge bit through the iron rim and stuck in the wood, whereupon Felimid turned his shield like a wheel, meaning to twist Ruarc's hilt from his hand. Ruarc wrenched his sword free with amazing strength, and followed on the instant with a diagonal cut at Felimid's shoulder.

This time he cut too fast, with his feet less than perfectly placed, and for a tiny moment his neck was a possible target. Felimid struck from his back guard, picking momentum almost from the ground in a sweeping arc that culminated at the side of the big golden king's neck. From the start he knew that if he had never timed a blow to perfection and given it all his force before, he had done it now.

The edge of Kincaid, forged by Goibniu from a fallen star, met the thick rope of intricately twisted gold threads and sheared through, destroying its magical pattern and wounding the muscle at the back of Sunspear's great neck. The rigid, complex cable had absorbed most of the impact; Felimid's edge neither reached the bone nor cut the great arteries near the larynx. Blood welled copiously, but did not burst forth in jets.

Ruarc's diagonal cut also went home, in nearly the same instant as Felimid's. His balance was imperfect when he launched it, his leading foot a trifle ill placed, or he would have cloven Felimid to the heart. As it was, he cut a wedge of shoulder muscle loose and severed the collarbone. Felimid was driven to one knee.

The collar about Ruarc's neck sprang wide open and fell to the floor, dripping bright blood. Golden flame seemed to blaze through it, and then dissipate. Felimid ever after was convinced he had seen that, though in the moment he had little time to ponder. Ruarc, staring aghast at the ruined collar, gave one cry of transcendent fury, and returned to the attack with reckless abandon.

Felimid's wound weakened his arm more than Ruarc's. He retreated. It occurred to him that he was probably about to die.

A roar, a bellow, a thunderclap from outside made Sunspear's yell seem like a squeak, and all eyes turned from the combatants. Ruarc himself was distracted for a heartbeat—long enough for the bard to lock his shield behind Ruarc's, lever the latter aside, and essay to drive his point under Ruarc's chin with a shortened grip. That purpose failed, due to his weakened weapon-arm, and Ruarc knocked the blade aside with ease, almost absently.

The irreplaceable carven doors of the Red Branch House burst open and blazed to their destruction. An intolerably bright white orb wreathed in streamers of yellow flame whirled in over the doorkeeper's corpse, charred to ashes. It was the fire spirit, captive and restricted so long, now free, wild with incendiary delight, free perhaps because the torc was destroyed, or Ruarc wounded and distracted, or for some other reason—but *free*.

Felimid shouted to his companions, "Out of here, now!"

They scarcely needed telling.

The elemental whirled up among the roof-beams, and massive as they were, they blazed like straws before its living incandescence.

Felimid seized the harp Golden Singer, his first concern even now, and ran for the burning doorway, bleeding profusely but paying no attention to that. Better if he bled to death than burned living.

A crowd of fleeing folk blocked his path. He cast a glance upward, for that was where the danger lay, from the great ornate beams burning through and falling. A couple were about to, and the Red Branch Hall felt like an oven already. The elemental's fire was unnaturally fierce and sudden.

Ruarc Sunspear faced the being he had summoned, and dared to treat as a horse he might bridle and spur, shouting incantations from lungs already searing. The being hurled forth tendrils of flame that wreathed about him. Sunspear staggered back, most likely blind, his words reduced to gagging incoherence. A massive roof-beam crashed down upon him. Felimid, gaining back some presence of mind, ceased to stare and struggled to reach the doorway.

He gained it. Twice he was knocked down, once trampled, but then, bleeding, agonised, he became aware of Tuathal and Eichra lifting him, frog-marching him into the open air, out to the ramparts, taking turns to support him, while the blazing Red Branch House behind them gouted fire and smoke halfway to the clouds.

He croaked, "Aivene?"

"Aivene?" Eichra mocked. "Gods and demons! What about us?"

"We rushed her safely out, as you bade us, before you and Sunspear crossed steel," Tuathal said. "She did not question. Last I saw, she was running like a deer with her skirts lifted high."

"That last no new experience for her, I'll take oath," Eichra laughed. "Now clamp your mouth and let us tend that wound."

"Best advice you will get this year," Tuathal agreed.

They crouched beneath a bush together while everything burned, the central hall, the treasure store, and the Speckled Hall where the weapons were kept. The ravening fire spirit did not spare the cattle byres or the stables, either, and men risked their lives—some lost them—getting the fear-maddened horses out.

Tuathal and Eichra did not offer assistance there. They were sufficiently occupied in seeing that Felimid did not die. By good fortune, or the old and new gods' favour, a heavy, drenching rain began, the one thing a fire spirit dreaded. It departed with the proverbial swiftness of fire, retreating above the clouds, and being also as fickle and instantaneous as fire, it seemed to forget both Ruarc and Emain Macha once it had satisfied its anger. It did not return.

Aivene, surprisingly, did. Creeping back through the grass, she arrived with her finery torn and stained, carried out a quiet, surreptitious search until she discovered the bard and his comrades, and then made herself useful tending him. Eichra, when she offered, expressed caustic doubt that she would know anything about it. More forcefully than her wont, Aivene snapped that she had been raised in a cattle-chief's dun and tended the hurts of more brawling fools than she liked to remember, before catching Ruarc Sunspear's eye. Nor had broken bones or sword-cuts been rare during her time at Emain Macha.

The last was true enough, and her other claims turned out to be justified.

Chapter Thirty

But what he saw was the whole of the palace as if on fire before him, and the heads of the people of it lying on the ground, and then he thought he saw an army going into the Hill of Cruachan, and he followed after the army. "There is a man on our track," the last man said. "The track is the heavier," said the next to him, and each said that word to the other from the last to the first. —Cruachan

"How did you disobey him? *How?* He was wearing that accursed collar and he commanded you to kneel and offer your neck!"

Eichra the Eel, for once, sounded awed. Or almost.

Felimid, lying on his back and hurting sorely from his shoulder wound, said past set teeth, "I cannot hear you."

"Cannot hear me? I know he cut you, but did he clout your head too? I am here beside you, man, and I am not whispering!"

He was not whispering, and his voice made the bard's head ache. Eichra and Tuathal, who had experience with sword wounds, had cleaned his with honey and potent wine, stanched the bleeding, and set his collar bone, which Ruarc Sunspear had cut cleanly in two. That last bit of business had caused Felimid to hiss, "*Maaaaaaacha!*" and lose his senses for a time.

"You told us yourself," Tuathal contributed. "No man who heard his words when he wore that torc could refuse him."

No woman, either, I can attest, Aivene thought, but she kept still and silent, wanting to hear Felimid's answer.

His foster-brother stared at him, puzzled and then worried.

"You cannot hear us, can you? What is it, a curse?"

Felimid apprehended the gist of what Tuathal was saying. He even grinned a little. Then, with some effort, he explained, in a feeble voice.

"I cannot hear you because I made sure I would not hear Ruarc either. It's simple as that. I blocked my ears before I confronted him."

"With what?"

That question was also easy to apprehend, even with blocked ears.

"Oh, my dears. Remember the honeycomb? I sucked the honey out and pressed the wax into plugs. I was not fondling my ears like that because they itched. You didn't notice?"

"Indeed," Aivene said to Eichra and Tuathal, "and we should get the wax out before we ask him to explain any more. My cosmetics box would be best for that, but it has gone with the Red Branch House." She looked through the fading rain to the hissing ashes of Ruarc's hall. She whispered, "It's all *gone*."

Her hands shook and tears spilled down her face.

"Yea, it's gone," Tuathal said harshly, "and best gone. A sorry imitation of the ancient Red Branch! We had better remove ourselves from here as soon as we can, if we don't wish the Fir Dicuil—"

"What is left of them," Eichra cut in.

"—to regain their wits and be cutting our throats. Can you stand and walk, foster brother?"

"He cannot hear you," Aivene reminded the bowman. "I'll mend that."

She took the cloak-pin from her shoulder and wrapped a little of her fine, costly scarf around the tip. Eichra dropped a warning hand on her shoulder and pulled out his knife. The woman stared at him.

"What is this?"

"I do not trust you near Felimid's ear with that long sharp pin. Take care how you use it, for I don't forget that you were Sunspear's leman, and as you said, all that you had with him—is gone now. I shouldn't wonder if there was ill-will and vengefulness in you."

"Much good that would do me! Listen, Eichra the Eel, I always did know I would never be Ruarc Sunspear's queen, and that one day he would discard me—unless he died in battle first. See, my hands no longer shake. Keep that knife handy by all means. You will have no use for it against me."

She began picking the wax out of Felimid's left ear as meticulously as if he had been her brother. Little fragments of the pale yellow-white stuff came out, and then a bigger clot. She unwound the torn bit of her scarf from its point, and twined another about it. Her garments were suffering this night. She had already crawled through wet grass in them, and shredded fine linen to bandage Felimid's shoulder.

Much more of this, she thought, *and I'll be bare as an egg.*

"There is all I can do that is safe. Now the other one. Later, when we can, we will pour warm water into both ears to sluice out the rest. You can hear now?"

"I can hear now. Thanks, Lady Aivene."

"Lady?" she echoed from a wry mouth.

"You have proven you are that by me! Tell me. Why did you give me a warning?"

"I fear the bad luck that comes to those who are accomplices in killing a bard. Sunspear was planning it with Taladh Teisne and the others, while I was present. So little they heeded me. He did not intend to give you an honest chance, either. A warning was the least I could do. And the most, perhaps. I think you guessed what he meant to do with no prompts from me?"

"An inkling," Felimid confessed.

"Now answer me a question. Is it true what the bowman was saying? When Sunspear wore that torc around his throat there was no-one could deny his bidding?"

"None who heard him. And I knew it. Thus I made sure I could *not* hear him."

Tuathal had been adding more fuel to a small fire they had going. Flames rose higher and gave Aivene better light to work on the bard's second ear. They illumined an odd tableau, there under the makeshift shelter of boughs and cord, covered with a couple of leather cloaks against the rain. They also revealed, or seemed to, an angry scarlet blush rising on Aivene's face. Felimid and Eichra both thought they saw it, and guessed what its cause might be; memories of nights when Ruarc had worn the collar while abed with her. Maybe he had used it to make her his concubine in the first place. A mortifying thing to reflect upon, no doubt, even for a pragmatical woman like her.

Tuathal, grasping his bow and sheaf of arrows, alert for the approach of foes, kept back and gave Aivene room. He evidently had not noticed her possible red mantling, or thought about it. Eichra gave it no further thought himself, and stayed near her, knife in hand, his cynical visage watchful. Aivene made an incongruous sight, her finery bedraggled and stained, her damp hair lying close to her head, picking the wax out of Felimid's ear with dainty precision.

The firelight dancing across Felimid's face revealed his pallor, and the bloodstained bandage padding his shoulder. He breathed slowly, with care. It hurt. Not in the finest fettle for thinking, he nevertheless had to think, and first of all about safety.

"We are needing refuge," he said. "Ruarc's four under-kings have most power now. Which of them is most likely to grant us protection, now that he's gone? Without him holding them together, they will be rivals for the pieces of Airgialla."

"Which of them survived the night's burning?" Tuathal asked. "Maybe all, maybe not. I saw little Irgal's bodyguard clearing a path to the doorway for him."

"I'll find that out, if you will trust me," Aivene said. "None will slay *me* on sight. Ask refuge for me too! I fear the Fir Dicuil. Even more I fear the King of Ulaid and his daughter, if they should learn I gave you that warning; all their hopes of power were built around Sunspear."

"Best you bide here," Eichra said, suspicion in his tone.

"No. I'll trust you," Felimid said. "The sooner we are under the wing of—one of these kings—the better. And one at least will be pleased that Ruarc is gone. Remind him, lady, that King Muirchertach is friendly towards me and will take it kindly if we are protected."

"I shall," Aivene assured him. "I'll mention the Bishop of Armagh too. Let your mind be at ease. I have not lived among the intrigues of Emain Macha without learning something." She looked towards the smouldering ruin of a great rich dun, in whose ashes were buried such beauty and craftsmanship, and whispered again, as though unable to credit the fact, "*It's all gone.*"

"You will be gone, also, if you walk around in the wet like that," Felimid warned her. "Take one of the cloaks off this shelter. The rain may start anew."

"*I* am not the one wounded," Aivene said with some asperity. "If the rain starts anew those boughs will leak. Let the cloaks stay where they are." A smile, female and rather wicked, touched her lips. "It may even help, so, if I look wet and forlorn."

She departed, Eichra reluctant to let her go, but owning that her best chance was now with them—and with any king they could persuade to shelter them—and expressing the sour hope that she was clever enough to know it.

"Instead of coming back with half a dozen Fir Dicuil," he added.

Felimid, his head swimming again, ignored that consideration. There was nothing he could do about it if it happened. The Fir Dicuil had their own troubles now, with Ruarc dead.

"Yea, that's it," Tuathal urged him. "Stop talking and rest. You have done what you must, destroyed the cursed torc. And Sunspear is slain. That was not altogether needful, was it, with the torc cut in two, but perhaps it's as well."

"By the gods, it's as well," Felimid said. The words were forceful if his voice was subdued. "He had promised to destroy the White Isle and all who dwell thereon, my mother first among them. He could—"

Coughing brought sudden agony to his shoulder, and he did stop talking, then, perforce.

"—could have gone there with three shiploads of stark fighting men and turned the White Isle red," Eichra finished for him. "True for you. He'd have done it out of spite, too, once he lost the torc. Erin's well rid of the bastard. Here. Drink, don't talk. We didn't use all the wine to wash your hurts. Drown your discomfort; the world will get by without you as its shepherd for a while."

Felimid grinned slightly, gave the Eel thanks, and sucked deeply on the strong vintage. It was like Eichra to have seized the main chance and a flagon of Ruarc's wine, even with the hall blazing around him. The jug in one hand and a sword in the other, beating his way out.

"The wax was clever," Eichra admitted. "I'm astonished, though, that Sunspear never guessed you had stopped your ears."

"He might have. I spoke as little as I could before we crossed blades. And Sunspear made an error in scorning foreign things—bar wine, women, and sumptuous fabrics! He never heeded foreign stories, either Christian or what the Christians call pagan. He should have. There's a tale of the voyager Odysseus, who stopped his rowers' ears with wax that they should not hear the sirens' fatal singing. My own self I borrowed the idea from that. Wilful ignorance—it is a mistake."

"One Sunspear won't repeat," Tuathal agreed.

Felimid drank the strong Gaulish wine until his head swam. He needed less intake than usual for that effect, what of his wound and his recent extreme efforts. Sleep became possible, if fitful. Sunspear strode boldly, haughtily in and out of his dreams, whirling his long, gold-hilted sword, with the blazing fire spirit in attendance. Muadnait and Odhran appeared there, too, plunging through translucent green water, swimming in spirals, and in other moments he dreamed of Tuathal and Eichra, helping him from the blazing royal hall. Once the wine's effect wore off, pain awoke him and he could not sleep at all except in brief snatches. Once he found Eichra crouched beside him, cleaning a red sword.

"Mathgadro Bluetongue," the Eel said laconically. "He was skulking about, trying to find us, no doubt, and betray us to the Fir Dicuil. He wasn't as surreptitious as he reckoned. I caught him. And I settled him."

"His head is off his shoulders," Tuathal confirmed. "He'll extort from honest folk with his satires no more."

"That is good to hear," Felimid said.

The time until sunrise was long. It came at last. Aivene returned, bedraggled as before, but accompanied by four weapon-men who bore an empty litter, and a smile of triumph lit her visage. She sat, indifferent to the wet ground beneath her nates.

"How is it with you, Felimid mac Fal?"

"Might be worse. I shall live, thank you." *Unless this wound takes infection*, he added in his mind. "How with you?"

"It's good," she said. "I think, for us all. Of Ruarc's under-kings, Bithrich died in the blaze and Irgal, the weakest in land and men, is seeking to align with the strongest. That is Ninedo. I foretell that Ninedo will accept him as a client erelong, and he's ready to give you shelter. The other two present no menace to you, I think."

"You are King Ninedo's men?" Felimid asked of the four.

"We are that," was the proud answer. "His hearth companions and battle brothers. We'll bear you to his camp if that pleases you."

"It pleases me well."

And surely I do not have so many choices available to me this morn as to confuse me.

"What are the Fir Dicuil doing?" Tuathal asked.

"The ones who survived the conflagration are banded together in a camp," Aivene said. "As always, they look with mistrust at those who are not of their own weird kindred. Factions are forming, but—they have not taken sides with any as yet."

"The spear-woman Sirega has taken charge, for the present," said the man of Ninedo's who had spoken before. "In short order they will be robbing and looting. That is sure."

"And I'd liefer be far away when they begin," declared another.

Felimid felt himself in full agreement with that.

As the sun lifted higher, it shone on the remains of Emain Macha, rebuilt by one man's prideful ambition, splendid for less than three years, and now reduced by fire once again. The drifts of ash among its blackened timbers still had crimson embers within, for all the rain than had descended upon them. Despite that scorching calescence, men were digging and raking in the rubble, some seeking the bodies of kin or friends, some scavenging for the many objects of value to be found—silver cups and lamps, gold pins, brooches or buckles in the Red Branch Hall itself, many searchers hoping to find Ruarc Sunspear's sword and sundered collar, or the moaning shield, the Ochaine. Many were combing the wreck of the treasure room, where pickings were richest, and coming to blows over what they discovered. The weapons in the Speckled Hall were gradually being found, too, and though their wooden parts had been consumed, the spear-heads, sword-blades and axe-heads all had high value, being the work of master artificers.

The spectacle was sad. There was something squalid and pitiful in this aftermath of Ruarc Sunspear's vaunted splendour. As for Felimid, hurting and weary, he felt relief more than jubilation. The collar whose damnable properties Dicuil the Fiery had unleashed in Erin—and left on his death in the hands of maybe the island's most vainglorious wishful hero—was a tainted memory now, and nothing more. There was none, assuredly not with Taladh Teisne also dead, who could make another.

Cairbre and Ogma! I hope not!

King Ninedo's men helped Felimid onto the litter, and carried him to their master's camp. The king proved to be a rheumy-eyed man of middle years, with a waist too broad for any figure out of the hero-tales. He appeared none too grieved by Ruarc Sunspear's passing, and was freely ready to offer the bard, Tuathal and Eichra shelter, along with Aivene, whom he favoured with goatish regard in spite of her unkempt state. She recognised it; he was by no means the first to ogle her in that fashion.

Felimid observed it too, and found that this kingly lust nettled him.

Let be, silly fellow, he advised himself. *No doubt Aivene can turn aside his advances. If she wants to.*

Chapter Thirty-One

"What is that?" said Conaire. "It is easy to know that," said his people. "The king's law has broken down, and the country is on fire." "What way had we best go?" said Conaire. "To the northwest," said his people. —The High King of Ireland

With the hall and outbuildings of Emain Macha gutted ruins, those who lived through the disaster made the best shelter they could, and fed themselves as they could. Although the cattle that had been trapped in burning byres were still there, dead, their meat spoiled, those that escaped were soon found and butchered. Midsummer was hardly butchering season, but neither was this a normal midsummer. Tuathal might have gone hunting for a stag, even brought one down, but that proved unnecessary and he did not wish to spend his remaining arrows when he might need them yet for two-legged marks.

Some survivors guested at farmsteads in the country round. King Ninedo and his following—joined by Irgal and his folk—occupied a large *fulacht fiadh*, a cooking-place in the open, such as even kings used while travelling or hunting. It boasted long wooden troughs in which water could be heated, and pits lined with stone where whole carcasses could meet a sizzling apotheosis. Linden trees provided this one with a dense leafy roof. Felimid was there, given a welcome by Ninedo, lying on a makeshift bed.

Greatly to his relief, the Fir Dicuil had not made themselves a nuisance. Not even they, perhaps, were indifferent to the curse that went with slaying a bard. Besides, they had been shocked to their heels by the death of Ruarc and the destruction of the royal fortress.

He said something of the sort to Eichra.

"Others may give us trouble," the Eel answered. "Look. Here they come. Tuathal and I best spit on our hands. No, let you not move, you are not fit."

Caragh of the Ulaid was approaching, she to whom Ruarc had dangled the bait of marriage. She rode a dappled mare, behind her father Tadg, on a restive brown stallion. Both looked like thunderclouds—for Caragh something of a feat. The number of armed men with them made Felimid glad that Ninedo had more, and of rather better quality. None belonged to the Fir Dicuil. That weird kindred seemed to be holding aloof yet.

The king glowered, and gave no polite greeting.

"Pity 'tis you are not dead," he growled. "We hope you may be soon. The law against killing bards protects you. For now. You slew Sunspear, and he was a bard. Your foster brother here arrowed a bard to death and wounded another, who may perish too. You will face lawsuits at the least for that! With luck you will go into exile. Do not make the mistake of setting foot in the Ulaid, whatever. Not at any time. Mark me well on that. Bard or no, you would not leave but on a bier."

"And my father would not have to give the command," Caragh said viciously. "A hundred warriors in the Ulaid, all men of their hands, would kill you, now, given any chance, on their own initiative!"

"Talk less wildly," Ninedo said. "If any man of your father's lifts hand against the bard, my guest, none of them will leave this spot alive."

"Oh, indeed." Caragh did not look even moderately comely now. She looked ugly, and her voice sounded it. "You are pleased enough that the great Sunspear has died, Ninedo! You cannot wait to pick the bones of his kingdom, can you?"

"He was destroyed by the firedrake he conjured himself, lady," Tuathal reminded her. "That, and because he carried away and would have slain the Bishop of Armagh, and made a quarrel with the wrong man in my foster-brother here. He overreached. In more ways than one."

King Tadg was more than twice his daughter's age, and used to hopes proving empty. He knew it was useless to rail, but could not wholly contain his bitterness. He glared at the recumbent bard.

"Too cowardly to speak?" he snarled. "You spoke freely enough to Ruarc."

"And I was not too cowardly to fight him. I'm saying little now—but it's loss of blood, not loss of heart. Maybe Sunspear did not cut as deeply as he wished—but deeply enough."

"May it save me the trouble of doing more about you!" Caragh spat. "We had hoped to find you dying! Had Ruarc lived, I might have been queen of a restored Ulaid, greater than Maeve of old, and queen of all Erin, eventually."

"No more, daughter," King Tadg said. "We've wasted time enough. We will take our leave."

Felimid watched them depart.

"The real Caragh revealed, is she?" he murmured. "She based great hopes on Sunspear's plans. You were right about their desires, Aivene."

"I reckon she will not forget," opined Eichra. "Watch your back, when you are recovered, and take care what you eat and drink. It's for the best that I finished Mathgadro Bluetongue. If I hadn't, he would be making a satire of cursing now, to turn your wound putrid."

Tuathal expressed agreement. "Best that I shot the fine Taladh Teisne, also. He'd be bent on doing you harm with his magic, while you were laid low, and his magic was not a trifle."

All this was true. Felimid thought that there were others alive and at large who wished him ill. Cuanach mac Rudgal, go-between and cunning spy, was one such, no doubt, but he did not feel equal to making a catalogue of the others now, or inclined to worry. Ruarc Sunspear was gone. The menace he presented to Erin's peace (such peace as there had ever been) was lost in the mist and twilight of all dreams of power. What mattered more, the threat he had presented of establishing utter, unquestioned kingly power in a land that had never known it, was gone, with luck for centuries, and the torc of command was gone, destroyed. No other could use it.

Felimid meant to ask his host, at the right moment, to send messengers after Muadnait and Odhran, to inform them they might approach Emain Macha in safety. But there turned out to be no need. They appeared just after midday. Brother Brandon and several other monks carried the *banfili* in a makeshift litter, to spare her a long walk on her lame foot, and Odhran the selchie walked beside it. They surveyed the devastated royal site with awe and some consternation. After searching awhile, they found the bard.

"I wonder that you are alive," Muadnait said. "Oh, thanks be!"

"Yea, thanks to God," Brandon seconded. "Is't true, what we hear? You fought Sunspear, and he is dead?"

"He's dead." Felimid told them, tersely, how it had befallen. "And the enchanted torc is destroyed."

"The fire spirit?" Muadnait asked, fear in her voice. "Where is that, do you know? Now that it's free, it might go anywhere, on the instant, at will."

"So it might. Even into the Otherworlds. I'm thinking it would have no reason to linger in Erin. Its preference would be for somewhere less rainy."

"I confess," said Brandon, "I hope it has opted for hell, and remains there."

"And what about the fine Bishop Ailill?"

"Oh! Less than grateful or gracious for his rescue! To the wise Muadnait he was outright insulting. To us he was peremptory. I had heard he sees himself as master of every holy foundation in Erin, and now I have met him I avouch it is true! Probably he will give credit to his own malisons, and curses, and execrations, for what happened here."

None of them had expected much else from Ailill.

"Let him believe and say what he chooses." Felimid would have shrugged if his shoulder had not hurt too much. "What you did at the grove of sacrifice was a wonder, nothing less. Except that you rescued the bishop, Ruarc might not have been angry enough to fight me, and do so wearing the collar. I'd never, otherwise, have come close enough to the thing to cut it apart."

"We did nothing as perilous as what you did," Muadnait said with a touch of impatience. "Now rest, for the love of all gods! I'll tie you down if I must."

"I'll not put you to that much trouble, *mo chridh*, no. Rest is an excellent prospect to me this day."

He closed his eyes.

"I can scarcely believe it's done," Tuathal said, looking around again at the devastation. "Ruarc Sunspear gone? What always fretted my mind was the prophecy that he couldn't die but by a threefold death. I never quite saw what that meant. It seems to have been a bad foretelling, though."

"No!" Muadnait clapped her hands to her cheeks. "Lir of the wide green sea! No, I think it came true. Felimid cut the golden torc from his neck and wounded him. That, I suppose, freed the fire elemental from his control, and it set the Red Branch House ablaze. Then a burning roof beam toppled upon him. I've heard a few say this. He died in three ways! Wounding, burning, and crushing. The foretelling was true."

That prophecy anent Sunspear had troubled Felimid, a little, though he had never granted it overwhelming weight. He knew how men embroidered stories, and how they grow. Even better, he knew how prophecies which came true were remembered, and those which did not were quickly forgotten—or still given credence no matter how erroneous they proved. Were all good stories discarded when they turned out to be false, men and women of the bardic profession would go very hungry.

This one, though, did seem to have proved true. Sunspear's death had three distinct causes. Failing any one of them, he might have survived.

Another score for Felimid's doubts that any prophecy, true or false, did any person a rag of good or helped them avoid disaster!

He rested, and slept when he could, though his wound kept him awake a good deal. Vaguely he was aware of King Ninedo sending his nominated heir and his spokesman back to his royal dun to arrange matters there, and bring an armed muster to defend it if needful. Ninedo himself, with his retinue, set out for the Grianan of Aileach, to arrange a pact of clientship with the Uí Néill before someone else anticipated him. King Muirchertach would be pleased to know Sunspear was gone, and pleased that Ninedo had succoured the bard. Felimid in a litter, Muadnait on a pony, most others tramping afoot, they made their way northwest.

Felimid's litter bearers stumbled at times, or had to traverse rough ground. That hurt. He became febrile and light-headed, before they arrived at Aileach and for some time afterwards. Muadnait tended him with gentle, meticulous care and stayed beside him. Perhaps it was that, and the chimerical state of mind that came and went, that caused him inquietude about her—even in his sleep.

They had been lovers only briefly. With his shoulder wound he would not be anybody's lover for a while. She was strong. She was a woman of power, a *banfili*.

She was also a girl who had been hurt and disfigured. What if they parted? What if she thought it was due to her face? Aivene, who travelled with them, whose face was her fortune, avoided looking at Muadnait, as Felimid observed in his lucid hours. *You could never have rescued Bishop Ailill, girl,* he thought with some anger. He did not wish to be ranked with Aivene, or that oaf of a ship's captain who had discarded Muadnait so roughly. Maybe losing proportion in his illness, he fretted lest Muadnait be left brokenhearted.

Be relieved, he told himself, *that you've only this to trouble you now, and not the prospect of flame and blood across Erin. Come. Did Muadnait say, did she hint at all, that she wanted a lifelong troth?*

No, but she would not have done. Not while Sunspear's ambitions threatened that reign of fire and blood and, in the end, absolute kingship in a land that had never known it. She had been as aware of that menace as he was.

Then his wound became infected, and for a score of days while his body fought the infection, he was delirious. In dreams and while waking, he saw Sunspear stride across Erin, brandishing his long naked sword, the fire elemental blazing above him in the sky, the torc of command dazzling about his throat. He sweated with relief when he came back to full awareness and remembered that Ruarc was dead, the collar sundered.

They reached Aileach, and King Muirchertach was no less relieved to hear those tidings. His physician Brona tended Felimid with skill that undoubtedly preserved his life, Muadnait and Brandon and Odhran the selchie never far away. Queen Duinseach followed his progress closely herself.

"It's a fine thing to see you out of danger," she told him. "Na, let you not speak! After high fever like yours the weakness is too great for anything but rest, however strong you are. And by the greatest powers, strong you must be, to have the best of Sunspear!"

Felimid managed a smile. The actual fight's outcome had been equal. He had wounded Sunspear and been wounded in return. The fire elemental had finished the business. He scarcely cared if his reputation was enhanced or impaired so long as his wound mended well.

Muadnait came to his bedside daily.

News arrived from Airgialla. King Ninedo asked to become a client of the mighty Uí Néill, and they obliged him. He received a herd of cattle commensurate with his rank, and the legal standing of *aithech*—debtor—to seal the bargain.

The Fir Dicuil, banded together against the world, as usual, were riding far and wide to pillage. That had been expected by all who knew them. Many complained loudly that something must be done, but none seemed eager to take the initiative against them.

One of Ruarc's former subordinate kings, so the gossiped word went, had become a client to Tadg of the Ulaid. He being the least of them, it made little difference to Tadg's power. No doubt he and his daughter Caragh nursed grudges. Cuanach, lawyer, messenger—and spy—was said to have sought refuge at their court, but that too had no great import beside Ruarc's death and the destruction of Emain Macha.

The day came when Felimid could walk again without reeling. He began doing so daily, eager to be active. Tuathal generally walked with him, his bow ready and a long knife at his belt, lest his foster-brother's enemies try to reach him even in Aileach.

Some days afterwards, perhaps too soon, he mounted the steps to the ramparts and descended again, precarious though that footing could be. His injured arm bound securely across his chest, and a stick to steady him, he made the climb with care, and the descent even more gingerly. As his strength returned, he performed that exercise twice, and then three times. His shoulder ceased to be outright painful, but the healing flesh itched to a maddening extent. He prowled restlessly at odd hours to alleviate it.

Aileach lacked the magnificence of Sunspear's dun, but it had lofts and alcoves. It had underground storerooms dug deep. Felimid, in favour with the rulers, used that indulgence to explore, not only from restlessness, but in case he needed to evade an assassin. It was possible, and he preferred to be ready. Ruarc Sunspear's minions had lurked in Aileach before.

Sunspear

It was no skulking murderer he heard one mid-morning. Plainly, and discernibly at once, it was the reverse. From behind a leather curtain came a sound very like a seal's sudden bark, repeated, then smothered to a yip, and a woman's voice gasping, "Odhran!" Another might have mistaken it, but not a bard with his hearing trained from boyhood. He had not misheard the name Odhran, and he would merely have shrugged, been pleased that the seal-man had found a girl, and passed on his way—but he recognised the woman's voice.

He recognised other sounds, too, as he approached the curtain, a sweet slippery bouncing that grew swifter, and mingled shaking breaths. By the Young God! Odhran, and—Muadnait?

Startled, for a rare once bemused, Felimid moved away. But why not? It was scarcely as though Muadnait had made *him* promises. Or implied any. Yet the bard felt a jealous pang.

Balor's destroying eye! She embraces Odhran almost as soon as I'm on my back, wounded! No. When did that begin? Just after they rescued the bishop, maybe? I was not wounded then . . .

But why not? And what does the time matter?

He walked further away, out of Muirchertach's hall, into the open air. This was one thing he had not expected! He began remembering the way he had fretted over Muadnait's possible heartbreak if *he* went away, treated their brief passion as no great matter. Her imagined heartbreak. The conceit of that, given what he had just seen, did verge on the fatuous. Bard, master of the harp, man skilled in magic, all of that, he wasn't, he had to own, above fatuity yet. Was any man?

The humour of it tickled him, then, and he choked back a surge of laughter.

END

Afterword

This novel opens with the battle of Druim Derg, at the beginning of 516 A.D. The Annals of Ulster record it, and the victory of Fiachu. (No surviving records describe the part Ruarc Sunspear and his war-band played in the battle.)

The rest of the story, from the meeting of Felimid and his mother with Brandon on the White Isle in May or June of 516, takes place about three years after the end of *Bard V: Felimid's Homecoming*. Felimid had spent most, though not all, of that time at his bardic studies and training. A couple of adventures during that time were *On Skellig Michael*, which appeared in Andrew J. Offutt's anthology *Swords Against Darkness II* (1977) and "*Night of the Burning Ghost*" in the Hallowe'en anthology *Samhain Sorceries* edited by Dave Ritzlin (2022).

The general political situation in Erin, as regards the growing power of the clan Uí Néill in its northern and southern branches, is as depicted. Airgialla, composed of nine tuatha, or minor tribal kingdoms, existed at the time, but its territory was encroached upon throughout the sixth century, by both the northern and southern Uí Néill—presumably after the reign of Ruarc Sunspear.

Some of the other characters are known to history, their names at least. The seafaring monk Brandon, young in this novel, later traveled widely, founded monasteries, becoming both an abbot and a saint. He was the subject of a famous medieval narrative, the *Navigatio Sancti Brendani*.

King Muirchertach mac Muiredaig is mentioned in the Annals of Ulster as victor at the Battle of Ocha in 483 (at which Felimid's father and grandfather were present). Since Muirchertach is also recorded as having died in 534, about fifty years later, the dates are probably not quite correct. In any case he seems to have reigned in the first half of the sixth century, as lord of the Cenél nEógain, a powerful clan of the Uí Néill, whose royal site was the Grianan of Aileach near the upper end of Lough Swilly (in this novel the Lake of Eyes). The massive stone ramparts of Aileach still stand, an imposing sight. In legend it was said to have been built by the Dagda himself, a mighty chief of the semi-divine Tuatha De Danann.

Bishop Ailill of Armagh (traditionally the see of Saint Patrick) held that position from 513 to 526 A.D. He may not have been as fiery and intolerant as he's here depicted. On the other hand, he may have been more so. Patrick's monastic foundations followed the customs and usages of Rome, deferring to the supreme authority of the Pope, while other native Celtic churches took a stubbornly independent stance. It's fair to assume that Ailill would not only have clashed with a king like Sunspear, but also with any monastic community that denied an outside authority's right to dictate matters of doctrine.

Clashes, often violent and sometimes amounting to war, did take place between different religious foundations in Ireland down the centuries. Until the first real towns were established by Vikings in later centuries, the monasteries were the largest communities in the country. As Felimid tried to tell Ruarc, though, he had not the power to drive the Cross-worshippers out of Erin, nor would he have been able to gain it, enchanted collar or none, and even if he had, in the teeth of Irish individualism and pugnacity, he could not have prevented more missionaries and saints coming from over the sea.

As Eichra also observed, Ruarc was not immortal, either. Even had he lived a long life he would eventually have died and been forgotten except in legends.

He might, though, if Felimid and his comrades had not stopped him, have left one lasting achievement. Not a good one. He might have turned Irish kingship into a more autocratic institution than it had been from time immemorial, backed by standing military forces—to the extent that Irish society and economy could support them.

In the event, that did not begin to happen until after Erin's long bloody struggle with the Danes ended at Clontarf, when King Henry II of England prevailed on the Pope to grant him the sovereignty of Ireland by papal bull in 1155—and tax the Irish for the privilege of being ruled by him.

They did not take it any better than they would have taken it from Ruarc Sunspear, and proved it generation after generation, to the Plantagenets, Tudors, and Stuarts.

Coming Soon!

KEITH TAYLOR'S

DAMNED FROM BIRTH

England, March of 1911, Robert Brandon Quinn of Boston, under suspicion of murder. Wilfred Tussmann, a rival scholar with whom Quinn had a bitter controversy, has been violently killed in his own mansion while Quinn was there. The killer was not human, but the monster-god of a strange ancient temple in Honduras which Tussmann had damaged and defiled while searching for gold. Quinn knows this but doesn't say so, well aware that he would never be believed…

**For more information
visit: SpeakingVolumes.us**

Now Available!

KEITH TAYLOR

BARD
BOOKS 1 – 5

**For more information
visit: SpeakingVolumes.us**

Now Available!

P.M. GRIFFIN

STAR COMMANDOS
BOOKS 1 - 8

**For more information
visit: SpeakingVolumes.us**

Now Available!

KEVIN D. RANDLE

SCIENCE FICTION / FANTASY

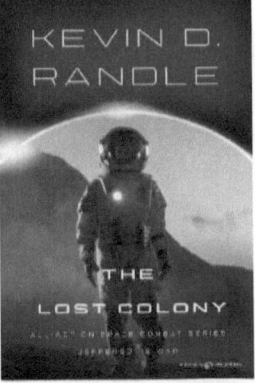

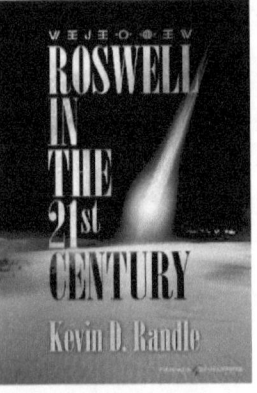

**For more information
visit: SpeakingVolumes.us**

www.ingramcontent.com/pod-product-compliance
Lightning Source LLC
LaVergne TN
LVHW091619070526
838199LV00044B/860